Chris,
Live free!
Enjoy the read ♡

Sea Of Treason

Pirate's Bluff, Volume 1

Stacey Trombley

Published by Stacey Trombley, 2019.

Visit the author's website at **www.StaceyTrombley.com**[1].

First Edition

Cover Design by Kelley York of Sleepy Fox Studio

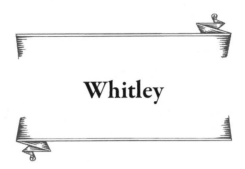

Whitley

The first thing I notice about the south is the water. It's bright blue, like crystal. Excruciatingly beautiful.

I wiggle my toes in my tight boots and bury the desire to rip them off and feel the water. The tingle of cold on my sore feet would feel glorious, I'm sure of it. But my father would kill me. The wind ruffles my skirt as I watch sailors heaving boxes and trunks and bags as they unload the ship—our escape vessel. Sweat pours from their faces, red under the high noon sun.

Though it's only a few hundred miles away from the city we fled, this place, with its sticky heat and beautiful water, is nothing like New York.

A man limps past me, grunting with each step. I resist the urge to wrinkle my nose in disgust. The smell is like New York, at least.

Working men smell. That's a universal truth.

My father marches up the dock, buttoned up in his most dapper suit, freshly shaven and beaming with pride. He doesn't look at all like he's just completed a three-day journey. Not to mention the rushed nature of our departure—chased from our home in the middle of the night. While my father seems to have let that terror slip off of him

1

like dust from his shoulders, it's not a moment I'll soon forget.

Then again, he's always been a good actor.

I put a pleasantly fake smile on my face as he approaches. "Father," I say in greeting.

"Beautiful place, this."

I nod. "Very."

"Infinitely better than New York, I think."

"Perhaps."

This is polite conversation. It's about as transparent as New York City water—murky brown. Thick with what I wish I could say aloud.

What I'm not saying is: *sure, it's pretty, but that doesn't make up for you tearing me away from my life and forcing me to follow you on your stupid quest for wealth, prestige, and power.* He probably thinks I'm mad about Jeb.

Jeb has been my best friend since childhood and was planning to propose.

He was my way out. My escape plan from whatever ridiculous marriage my father would have set for me. Now, not only have I lost my only friend, I have no excuse not to marry whichever cruel rich suitor my father will inevitably choose.

I'm stuck, more so now than I have ever been before.

My life would have been just fine in New York. My father's, however, had been heading in the direction of the gutter. He owed a lot of debts he couldn't pay.

Here, my father can play the part of a wealthy businessman. In reality, it's stolen money that bought him his stone castle atop the hill, looking out at the beautiful water.

Here, in some little town on the North Carolina coast, he is far away from the men he owes.

I, of course, must play the part of the doting daughter, never having a choice in anything.

"Come, child," he says, turning from the ship that brought us here. He walks up a small hill paved in newly laid cobblestone. It's rather steep, and I struggle to remain graceful in my heeled boots. My ankle wobbles and twists. Though I manage to stifle a cry of pain, my expression must expose me. My father notices.

"Walk slowly if you must," he says under his breath.

I sigh. I don't understand why it matters, why he cares so much. We were humble farmers in Wales before we came to America. I barely remember it, but once my mother died and the drought took all the crops, my father came up with a new scheme. He "borrowed" enough money from his brother to take us to the shiny new United States of America, where he was convinced we'd live like royalty. Anyone can be *someone*, he says. *This is the land of freedom.*

Yet all I've found are chains. Like this breath stealing corset, my laced boots, and all of society's ridiculous expectations. Marriage will be another, more permanent, prison.

The problem with my father's obsessive notion is you can't make yourself wealthy just by believing it.

Stealing money, then pretending to be an up-and-coming businessman... well, it's a clever scheme, but it doesn't make us part of high society. You can't hide awkward feet no matter how expensive the boots you wear.

BY THE TIME WE MAKE it to the top of the hill, my brow is slick with sweat. Not exactly ladylike. There is a stone building with beautiful flowers all around. Colors of purple and orange and pink and scarlet scattered everywhere. The shapes and sizes are unfamiliar to me. Flowers do not grow so diversely in New York. There's something wild about it—what the world should be.

I look off into the distance and wonder what lies beyond those hills. Farms and open land, most likely. There are several newly established towns speckled across this part of the new nation.

Perhaps, here, I could learn from my father. I could run off to some new place and pretend to be someone else. Anyone else.

My fingers curl into my palm as I work to hide my frustration and fear. I want anything other than *this*. And yet I know I'm too much of a coward to reach out and take the freedom I crave. This world is not kind to young women when they are alone. My father has ensured I know this fact well and good.

We finally reach level ground as we enter what I assume is the town square. Fresh brick paves the street as far as I can see. Lanterns and potted flowers stand outside every building. It's small compared to what I'm used to, but the entire town has a charming air to it. It's very obviously newly established, with at least the attempt at being posh. A horse-pulled coach awaits a fancily clad couple exiting a small shop. Several servants pile bags and boxes into the back of the coach. The girl wears a gold and white embroidered dress. Her skirt is bigger than any I've ever seen actually worn. She holds a dainty white umbrella used to keep the sun off of her. I can't help but think she's like a child playing dress up.

The man who holds her arm turns in our direction just before climbing into his carriage. A smile bright and large spreads across his face. "Mr. Klein! How wonderful to see you've finally arrived."

Klein? I've never heard that name in my life. We've always kept our original family name from Wales: Davies. But it doesn't seem to bother my father. I suppose it shouldn't surprise me that we'd need a new name. A new disguise.

"Yes, a long journey to be sure."

The woman with the umbrella turns towards us, her cheeks still full of adolescent pudginess. She's hardly a woman, I realize—younger than me, I think. Maybe fifteen? Her nose is turned up, as if my father and I carry a bad odor.

"My daughter. Whitley." My father motions to me and I force a smile.

"Whit-leigh, did you say?" the girl says in mock surprise. "What a unique name."

This is polite speak for: *You poor thing, what was your father thinking?*

I smile. "Indeed."

"Well, it's very nice to meet you, Whitley," the man says. "I am Mr. Collin Washerby, and my new wife Mrs. Collin Washerby."

I hold back a chuckle. Can she really comment on my name with a name like that?

Despite his kind and warm expression, Mr. Washerby is old, with gray speckles in his hair and lines across his forehead and under his eyes. This poor girl will be a widow before her children are grown. This will be my fate, too, I realize. The most I can hope is that it's a kind man my father forces me to marry. I find that unlikely, based on the company he most chooses to keep.

My stomach twists thinking of Jeb. We hardly had what any would call a sweeping romance. In fact, he seemed to avoid intimacy at all costs. But he was kind. He was a friend. He would have allowed me to be who I am, or at least some subtle version of it.

"You can call me Mary."

I raise my eyebrows, focusing back on the young woman in front of me. Talk about a unique name. I knew about two dozen Marys in New York.

She holds out her lace-gloved hand, which my father takes gently with a nod, then releases. She gives me a subtle curtsy. Dainty. All the while shooting her eyes all the way down my body as if sizing me up. "You are not married, are you, Miss Whitley?"

"No. No, I am not." I send a glare at my father, who smiles awkwardly.

"Perhaps I can help with that. There are several eligible bachelors in town, and I'm sure they'd all love some fresh blood. We're having a small gathering tomorrow evening. You simply must come."

I force a smile. *I'd rather kill myself.* "I would be delighted."

"Of course, you're welcome as well, Mr. Klein," Mr. Washerby says with a bow. "We'll send up a card immediately." Then the odd couple turns and enters their awaiting coach. Dust billows behind as they retreat.

Without another word, my father turns on his heels and marches down a worn stone path which leads back towards the water, though on high ground.

"Where are we going, Father?"

"The fort."

"The fort? What business would you have there?"

I struggle to keep up with him as he flies down the path.

"Many men around here have business at the fort. It's in all our best interest to keep this place pirate free."

"Pirates? Here? Now?"

"Unfortunately, they are still bothersome in this area. We are not far from some of the most legendary pirate ports in this part of the world. And away from the largest cities we have little protection."

"I thought there were no more pirates after the war?"

"The war is precisely the reason for the pirates, my dear. Nations are eager to use them for their violence, then discard them when their use is no longer necessary. The smart ones took what they could, under the guise of *privateer*, then hid with their new wealth. Others lost everything or didn't know when to stop. We must snuff it out now, before it grows like the plague as it has in the past."

"I still don't understand what that has to do with you."

"Don't worry about that, dear."

A brush off. He doesn't want me to know or expects I wouldn't understand if I did.

Past a few market stands, with merchants selling fresh fish, tackle, or trinkets, we continue down a flat path toward the open sea. We finally make it to a stone building right beside the edge of the cliff.

"This is the fort?" I ask and Father nods.

Though most of the fortress isn't visible from this perspective, it was impossible to miss as we docked in Tar. It hangs over the water, surrounded by a wall of stone with cannons sticking out on all sides—a massive fortress.

My father flies through the door like he belongs here and immediately greets a man with an unkempt beard and rough clothing, clearly not from the same part of society as Mr. Washerby. They exchange a whispered conversation with occasional sidelong glances towards me. As the unmarried daughter, I am not trusted with anything important. A child. I spin away, hoping to distract myself with a little exploration. Something I don't get away with often, especially in as interesting a place as this.

Grey stone lines every wall, cold and dark, with weapons and parchment the only decoration.

There are several wooden doors, which I consider examining, but then I come to a stairwell that catches my attention. The stone is a similar color as the rest of the room, but the edges much more crude, giving it a cave-like appearance. The sign above the entrance reads: **Enter at your own risk.**

Excitement fills my limbs as I peer down the passageway.

Bluff

Every prisoner is on alert the second the door to the prison hall squeals. I rise from my uncomfortable spot on the cold concrete floor and press my cheek against the rusty bars in hopes of spying something interesting. There are very few reasons we get *visitors*. Guards don't come down here for anything other than bringing or taking prisoners. It's not near time for grub. That accounts for most our options.

I see naught but vague movement in the shadowed hall, but I can hear. The footsteps are light and slow. Only one person, not in any hurry.

I examine the men around me. Who will be taken today? No one is scheduled for a date with the gallows.

"Hey there, lovely," a gravelly voice calls, echoing through the chamber.

I blink at that. Is a prisoner calling a guard lovely? It could happen, but it would certainly require a bold soul and I'm unsure this lot has it in them.

A small gasp, the kind that could only come from a dainty thing, is the only sound in response.

That is not a guard.

I catch just the flash of a blue skirt from my vantage point at the end of the cell block. I stand on my tippy toes,

9

eager for the chance to see this princess that has decided to grace us with her presence, but it's very hard to see much of anything.

The light footsteps continue, my heart pounds in anticipation. She's coming closer.

As she nears, a head of prissily pinned blonde hair comes into view first, until finally, I get a full view. Her neck is bare of jewelry, which could mean she's of low status, but every other sign says otherwise: primly pressed dress with bright color, immaculate hair, clean nails, and hearty leather boots. She's recently been traveling, I suspect.

A pretty young lady, new to town, has come to visit the prisoners at The Fort? I raise my eyebrows as I watch her silently.

She stops right in front of my cell, eyes the stone wall dead end ahead of her. She has no choice but to turn back, and in order to do that... she turns to face my cell, crystal blue eyes staring straight at me. My heart beats faster.

She looks me in the eye and confusion crosses her face. "How—how old are you?" she stutters, then immediately blushes like she hadn't meant to utter a word.

I can't help but give her a smirk. Is she impressed to find a pirate as young as her? Or disgusted?

"Seventeen," I tell her.

Her head tilts slightly.

My eyebrows rise in amusement. *What a strange creature.*

"What— what are you doing here? Who are you?" she asks.

I listen closely to her words—the slight accent hidden behind years of practice— wondering what is going through her mind.

She jumps suddenly, as the stone door slams shut in the distance. Panic crosses her face, and the guard has his hand around her arm in a matter of moments. He doesn't speak a word, just pulls her away from my sight.

Another man must meet her at the entrance because it's not the guard who scolds her. "What in heavens name are you doing, Whitley?"

Whitley. The name echoes through my mind like a whisper. I swallow as a strange shift pushing through my gut.

"Wait," she calls. "There was a boy back there. A young man who shouldn't be there."

Again, my heart flutters uncomfortably. She's concerned for me? *How adorable.* I study my fingers gripping the bars, covered in dirt and scattered with scars. I'm not exactly on her level of society. The thought makes me chuckle.

"There is no boy here," a commanding voice tells her. "They're all men. All of them."

"No, he's... he's too young. He can't have done anything so bad that he would be here. Please, go see for yourself, in the last cell."

There is a pause of complete silence for a moment, followed by an annoyed huff and pounding footsteps. I adjust quickly, shifting to a less noticeable form. The guard stops in front of my cell, gives me a good once-over then turns back. I put my hands in my pockets and wait.

"Who are all those men?" Whitley's hushed voice is just loud enough to hear through the quiet chamber. "Why are they being kept like dogs? Worse than dogs."

"They're vermin. Thieves, betrayers, and pirates," the guard says, spitting on the ground for good measure. "That's what happens to men who pillage, act against the laws of God and man, on sea or on land, makes no difference to us. They will all hang for their crimes." He pauses. "After a fair trial, of course."

I let out a chuckle at that.

He leaves out that at least half of these men were privateers during the war. They're essentially soldiers... who didn't stop fighting fast enough.

"Hang? You mean you're going to kill them? Even the boy?" Her voice quivers endearingly. "Surely the new country wouldn't allow such a thing?"

"There is no boy," the guard's deep voice calls. "The man in the last stall was an old man. Silver hair, blue eyes. He's over fifty and well knows the choice he was making when he attempted to take over the *Marry Anna* two weeks ago. He killed two of my sailors in the process."

Well, that's a rather grand tale. Those two men died of the pox, though I did "attempt" to take over a ship. I was only caught because I wanted to be. I've been waiting for *her*.

I plop back down onto the concrete floor as their footsteps fade away, our excitement for the day done and gone.

"What was that about?" the man next to me asks, standing over me.

I pick at my fingernails and shrug, unsure if he noticed my shift in appearance or if he's simply asking about the girl and her reaction—as if I'd have any clue. Or perhaps I do, I just don't want to believe it.

All the signs are there, after all.

Is it possible she'd find me before I found her? I chuckle bitterly. Fate is such a strange thing. Clearly, I must work harder if I'm going to win this sick game.

To think, I've been watching her from afar since the moment her father made a deal with Captain Stede and now she's found *me*. My stomach knots as I consider the sea witch's prophecy.

I'd still rather believe all of it rubbish, but I can't take any chance. If this is the girl, the subject of the prophecy, and that prophecy happens to hold merit... I swallow.

I will not be controlled. Not now, not ever.

The conversations about our pretty visitor last for nearly an hour. I occupy my thoughts away from their disgusting fantasies by searching what little of the sea I can from my cell. There is only one small, uneven opening, but if I press my cheek flush against the cold stone and wait a few moments to allow my eyes to adjust to the sudden brightness, I'm able to get a decent view. Or at least, I can see some of the water. Maybe I could even spy a ship coming in to dock, if they passed in the perfect position.

It's time for my exit plan, I realize. But I'll have to wait until the most opportune moment. Dusk sounds ideal, perhaps even midnight. But those are the most expected moments. A better plan is one of sincere patience. I will act just before dawn, right before the morning guards begin their duty.

The squeal of the main door pulls the crowd's attention back to reality.

"*Did she come back?*" someone whispers.

"*Come here, princess,*" another hisses under his breath, causing more than a few snickers.

"Shut up!" a guard barks from the hall. "Unless you're eager to meet the gallows now."

Several jaws snap shut. The entire prison chamber is quiet for a long moment before the movement begins again. Several sets of footsteps pound down the hall, accompanied by the characteristic scrape of feet dragging along the concrete floor.

Appears we're gaining a new prison-mate.

"Welcome to your last home, mongrel." One of the three soldiers spits as they toss the thin, scraggly man into an empty cell three down from me. I can smell the sea on him.

Another pirate, perhaps? I stand on tiptoe to catch a glimpse of the new addition. Could it be someone I know?

The body remains on the ground until the soldier's chain the door closed and retreat.

"Oy! Mate," the prisoner next to him calls. "You alive, or dead?"

The pirate coughs and finally lifts his head. "Water?" he asks through dry lips.

His neighbor shakes his head. We get food and water once a day at best. Don't bother asking for a bathroom.

"What ship are yeh from? Where did they get yeh?"

"*The Freedom,*" he says through heavy breaths as he works to push his body upright. I jerk my head up. I know that ship. I know that crew. One of the few true pirate ships left in these waters.

This bloke doesn't seem familiar, however. He could be a new hire, a bloke that didn't last long on an easy ship. That, or he's lying. His long stringy hair falls over his face. "Bloody gripe over a game of dice got me tossed overboard. Damn bitch. I was *rescued* by the navy and tossed in here."

This loses the attention of several pirates, but it causes me to laugh. Based on his outburst of colorful language, I fully suspect Rosemera is to blame for his swim. But I'd wager it wasn't over a game of dice.

To the rest of this lot, a pirate tossed overboard isn't likely to be rescued by his crew, which means he's worthless to them.

"I have news, though," he says, eyes darting around like he's bothered by their quick dismissal. "I saw Stede."

A hush falls over the chamber. Now this is news they want to hear.

"Where?" one lone voice calls.

"South, at least a day away. But he's headed here, if the rumors are right."

Whispers echo through the chamber in earnest now, cell after cell, rough voices feeding off one another.

"He's coming."

Every man here is sentenced to die. Some still have a trial awaiting, but there's no doubt of the outcome. *Quick drop, sudden stop.* So to hear of a powerful pirate sailing towards us here and now—well, it's a possible way out of their current predicament.

It's *hope* to the hopeless.

To me, though, it's an annoyance. I am not eager to meet Captain Stede face to face yet again. He's not nearly as despicable as his reputation suggests, but he's worked hard to live up to his namesake—a legendary pirate of a century ago. He even named his ship after Stede Bonnet's of the golden age—*The Revenge*—and copied his old pirate flag.

The more folk (like me) doubt his misdeeds the more he feels the need to prove himself and do something worse than before.

And this time, I know what he's after. I just have to get there first.

Getting out of this prison has never been a problem. It's a temporary holding cell until the time is right. My goal is keeping this perceived *treasure* out of someone else's hand to save my own skin. It's keeping this grip over my illusive freedom from falling altogether. I can't lose.

If Stede is on his way—that means the time is now.

I must get to her before he does.

Whitley

"You're beautiful, miss."

I bite my lip, unsure I agree, staring at myself in our full-length mirror—a luxury I never had before. My handmaid is old, her back bent forward with age. Not exactly a good judge of beauty.

"Thank you," I say in a near whisper.

She approaches slowly, like I'm a wild animal she's concerned she'll spook, then pulls one small clip from my hair, letting a slim strand of blonde hair fall against my face. Oddly enough, that simple act makes me prettier. More natural.

"Thank you," I say again, but this time it's sincere. "What is your name again?" I ask. She's our servant here. I don't like the idea of servants, because honestly, I should probably be one myself. We're only pretending to be anything other than low class.

"You can call me Angela."

"That's a very pretty name."

She lowers her head as she backs out of the room, and I take one more look at myself in the mirror, wondering if there will ever come a day that I'll accept this as my life. Ever a day I'll be happy heading to a high society social function. Ever a day I stop looking to the horizon, imagining what may lie beyond, peering past every turn for an escape route. My fingers glide over the broach on my chest.

"Wait," I call to Angela just before she disappears down the hall.

She pops her head back in. "Yes, miss?"

"Have you seen my necklace? It's an emerald ring on chain. It should have been in the jewelry box." If I have the broach, it means my mother's ring should be nearby as well.

"No, Miss. Would you like me to search again?"

"Please. It was my mother's. I wanted to keep it with me on the journey here, but my father insisted we put it in the box for safe keeping."

"Of course, Miss."

"Are you ready, Whitley?" My father's call sounds through the house. I whip my head towards the hall, not at all ready to leave this room. I may never be ready. But I know father won't wait long.

"Just a moment!" I call back.

I turn back to Angela as she searches through my very small collection of jewelry. Two small pieces from Jeb, the rest humble relics from our former life in Wales. She shakes her head. "I'm sorry, Miss. I don't see any rings here."

"All right, thank you. I'm sure it'll turn up somewhere."

"*Whitley*!" my father calls again.

Angela nods, her concern not totally hidden. Perhaps she understands the meaning of such an item.

I sigh and leave my full-length mirror behind, the heavy skirt of this horrid dress swooshing as I turn the corner.

"Ah, there you are," my father says as I descend the marble staircase, eyeing the crystal chandelier all the while. I have no idea how he afforded this place. If he couldn't pay back his debts, but could buy this extravagant place... how much did he actually owe?

"Didn't I tell you she was beautiful?" Angela says, appraising me. Now I believe she means it. No matter how crooked her back is.

"Quite presentable," my father says with a grin.

I resist the urge to roll my eyes. By "*presentable*" he means "*it'll do.*"

Again, I feel ugly, frumpy. Stupid.

Still, I smile at Angela, thankful for her kind words. If only I didn't care what my father thought. I wish more than anything I didn't.

"Come," my father holds out his hand for me to take. "Don't want to be late."

I take it, knowing full well we do actually want to be late. Much better to make a grand entrance that way. The "gathering" will surely be full by the time we get there.

There is a grand coach, pulled by two horses waiting for us. One horse is solid black, and the other is white, speckled and splattered with black and gray. I wish I could forgo the coach and just ride him into town, wind blowing my hair back. Perhaps I can steal a ride tomorrow while my father is sleeping off the drink he'll surely overdo tonight.

Perhaps I can ride her over the hills and never come back. That's a thought that may just get me through the evening.

"Come," my father says from inside the carriage. There is a servant, a man, holding out a gloved hand to help me in. His expression catches my attention. It's not a polite servantish smile. It's more like *amusement*. I narrow my eyes at him, but I enter the carriage to appease my father.

The man hops onto the carriage with the step of a younger man and urges the horses forward, much faster than is appropriate.

The coach bumps and jumps as it coasts down the hill into town.

My father grunts and clears his throat, annoyed at the driver's urgency, but he says nothing. This sincerely surprises me. But the ride is so short, only a moment later people dressed in their high-society best are visible outside out coach's window. I assume he doesn't want to risk anyone from town hearing him scold a coach driver in public.

We stop in front of a brightly lit house, larger than the one we just moved into, but only just. Its walls are made of white stone that almost shines like marble.

The driver hops from his spot on the coach and opens the rickety door. "My lady," he says, his eyes twinkling, a crooked grin on his face. His expression is so strong, I almost suspect he's *flirting* with me.

The grimace my father gives the servant could kill, but he grips his hand and exits the coach behind me. Except his feet miss their place on the step, causing him to stumble onto his knees, and scuff his right pant leg.

Was it my imagination or did the servant purposefully put his foot there?

I stifle a laugh, and the driver winks in my direction. Something about his eyes draw me in. They're familiar. Grey eyes. Where have I seen such eyes before?

Was he one of the sailors from our journey here?

My father grabs my arm and pulls me towards the party. I follow hesitantly.

"Miss Whitley!" Mary calls to me. "My, you do dress up nicely." Her smile reaches from ear to ear. My blue silk dress is humble compared to hers, which is yellow, adorned with beads about the neck, cut lower than I'd be bold enough to wear, with a bustle, making her bum appear larger than is at all natural.

"Oh, well, thank you." I say, politely as I can manage.

"Come!" she says, wrapping her arm in mine. "There are so many people for you to meet."

She pulls me through the crowd, introducing me to several people in a whirlwind. I try my best to greet them appropriately and remember them after, but the girl's enthusiasm makes that difficult. The social "rules" here are certainly different than what I am used to, then again, Father was always stricter than others. He was always intent on me learning the "proper" way, even though many American's didn't bother with much of it.

As we shuffle through the crowd, Mary continues whispering various scores of gossip in my ear. This is her idea of a "little gathering." I should have known. This is nothing short of a ball.

The attendees' dress shows varying levels of wealth in the room, but that's unsurprising considering the size of this gathering in such a small town. They must have invited nearly everyone.

Eventually we make our way over to a table full of refreshments. A quiet servant woman keeps her eyes cast down as she pours liquor in crystal glasses. I force a smile as several forgettable people introduce themselves. They are all very polite. Which is polite speak for *boring*.

"Did you hear?" Mary says excitedly as soon as the last person is out of ear shot. I sip my champagne and raise my eyebrows as if I'm interested.

"A prisoner escaped."

"Prisoner?"

"Yes, from the fort. It's all very exciting."

Exciting. Yes, I'm sure. My mind jumps to the disgusting men and the comments they made as I passed their iron cages. The thought of those conditions still causes a tightness in my chest.

"Who was it?"

"Oh! No one's quite sure. Or at least they won't say. One of the pirates probably. I did hear one story that was simply fantastic."

"Oh?"

"Yes, you see—" Mary looks around as if nervous someone might overhear our conversation. I find it strange how different she is here from on the street. All of a sudden, the excited fifteen-year-old girl is bursting out. "When the guard went to check on the prisoners, well, he says there was a child in the cell. A boy, only about eight-years-old."

I suck in a breath. "That's terrible."

"I know!" she says giddily. I wonder if not much happens around here. This girl is enjoying this far too much. "So, of course the guard opens the door to get the boy out—and he changed!"

"Changed?"

"Yes! Into a great big man. He grew four feet and attacked the guard. That's how he got out."

"*Changed*," I say, no longer believing her story.

"Yes, like a shape-shifter or something. I heard my husband talking all about it."

My eyes drift away from Mary. She's a bit delusional to be sure.

That's when a surprisingly handsome man steps in front of me and holds out a hand, asking me to dance. He's closer to my age than any man I've seen yet. A set of dimples appears as he grins, his soft brown eyes shining.

"May I have the pleasure?" he asks.

I'm not sure this is appropriate, given I have no idea who is he, but I take his hand, because, well, I've never danced with someone this handsome before. Mary gasps, but she says nothing as I leave her behind.

The stranger swings me out onto the dance floor. I glance back once to see a Mary's mouth hanging open, but my attention is ripped away as I'm swept through the crowd in the stranger's arms and I fall into step with the waltz.

"I don't believe we've met," I say to him, noting his crooked grin. Does everyone smile like that in the south?

"Hmm," he says, not seeming very interested in telling me who is he. I raise my eyebrows. "And you are?" he asks, as if he told me his name and now it's my turn.

"Whitley." My eyes narrow. "Are you going to tell me yours?"

"Not right now."

I stop and begin to pull away from him. What kind of game is he playing? His grip tightens, and he pulls me in close.

"Would you rather I lie?" he whispers into my ear, his warm breath tickling.

Lie? Why would he lie? "You can't just tell me the truth?"

"I could, but then I'm not sure you'd continue to dance with me. And that would be a shame."

I pull back to meet his eye, our feet still moving mind-lessly to the beat. "Tell me, or I won't ever dance with you again."

His eyes glisten, and his smile broadens. "Bluff."

"What?"

"I told you."

But I don't let go. His hand feels good on my waist, and truth be told—I don't want to stop. My father may grow angry if he witnesses the gentleman's strange behavior, but that's all the more reason to continue. I take joy in every small rebellion.

But a crash of shattering glass whips my attention from my strange dancing partner.

The music stops abruptly, and all heads turn towards the entrance of Mary's home. Standing in the doorway is an odd-ly dressed man, with blood shot eyes, a large black beard and a black scar stretching temple to chin across his nose. His skin would likely be fair, if not for the layer of scum over every inch of his face. He makes the man at the fort look like the New York City mayor.

I rationally muse he could be a military man, but my heart is throbbing, stomach squirming. Images of the night the mob came for us flash through my mind. Every instinct inside me is screaming that whoever this man is, he is not friendly.

Several other men file in behind him, dressed in a similar fashion most with beards and tattoos all over. Though I don't recognize a single one, their general appearance is reminiscent of the pirate prisoners.

My heart leaps to my throat, and I no longer question the truth: these are definitely pirates. And it's not just one escapee—it's an entire crew.

The screaming starts before the first pirate even flinches. Both men and women are desperate to find an escape before it's too late. The bearded pirate pulls a large sword from his belt and holds it in the air, and his crew immediately charge into the crowd.

I don't move at first. I'm too shocked. Too confused. I search for my father, but he is nowhere to be found.

Someone grabs my arm and pulls me from the crowd, away from the rampaging pirates. Through a doorway to another room and into a shadowed corner. The touch is gentle. I do not feel threatened, so I don't turn to see who it is. Even once we're in the other room I crane my neck to see what's going on— much more interested in the violence in the next room than in my savior. People are running and crying, falling in panic. *Why do I feel so calm?*

I jump, though, when lips brush my ear. A light hand runs down my arm.

My attention is brought back to the current situation. Who has me held so close? And why don't I push him away?

"Tell me," the voice of the stranger I danced with whispers in my ear. The panic around me fizzles out and there is only me and this man's voice. *Bluff.*

"Are you worth saving?" he asks me, still whispering. I feel a strange shift in my chest, and then there is the strong urge to close my eyes and let his lips explore other places.

His rough hands grab my arms again and spin me to face him.

But it's not the same man. I blink rapidly, taking in the image before me. He's smaller. Younger. With grey eyes and silver hair.

My stomach sinks and flips all at once. "You," I say to the boy from prison.

He smirks. The same smile of the dancing man and the carriage driver.

"I don't understand," I say. "How did you escape?"

His body shimmers like a mirage and shifts, shrinking down until the young man in front of me is a child.

I swallow, hoping I don't lose the contents of my stomach, thinking of Mary's outlandish story.

An eight-year-old boy in a prison cell, turning into a large man in order to escape.

I retreat a step, my back hitting the pantry door. He shifts again, and again his amused expression is the same through each form—the coach driver, the handsome man who danced with me. The boy with silver hair.

It was all him. Why? How?

"You're... a pirate," I say stupidly. He nods but his eyes aren't on mine now. He's looking into the grand hall in which the screams are still flying.

"Are you with them?" I ask, my heart throbbing as I wonder how very impossible my survival is at this moment.

"No."

"Over here!" a creepy low voice yells from the hall. Bluff's eyes narrow. I realize now why he would have had to lie when I asked him his name. He told me the truth. Bluff is his pirate name.

He grabs my arms and pulls me into a pantry with him.

It's a tight fit. Our bodies touch one another in a way I've never touched a boy before. His lips are at my ear again. "Answer my question. Are you worth saving?"

"I—I don't know."

"Too honest," he whispers, but there's amusement in his voice. Footsteps echo just outside the pantry door. Bluff pulls the handle towards us, and it cracks as wood separates from metal.

No! I want to yell, but panic constricts my throat, stealing my breath.

He exits the pantry, no longer the boy with silver hair. Now he's a dark skinned, muscled man in ragged clothing. "No one in here," his deep voice says, and then the footsteps pass by, moving farther through the house.

The next several moments are silent, only our breaths audible. Outside the pantry there is no movement.

Everyone else must have escaped or been captured. How many of them are still alive? Whose blood is staining the marble floors?

"Keep searching!" a call resounds through the house, causing me to jump.

"*Where is the gracious Mr. Davies?*" The same voice, a room over, dips lower, sinister. My body goes cold. "*Or should is it Mr. Klein now? So hard to keep up.*" The pirate's voice echoes through the house, mocking but angry. So incredibly angry.

What did my father do? I shudder.

Bluff re-enters the pantry quickly, a finger at his lips.

"What's going on?" I ask in a whisper. "They're looking for my father?"

"He's questioning his few captives. But he's not really after your father. He's looking for you."

"What?" I say too loudly. Bluff presses his hand to my mouth, but the damage is done. His eyes are wide with horror. We're completely silent, listening for signs that we've been caught. The questioning continues in the main hall. Cries for help. Screams. Some are women and I can't help but wonder if one of them is Mary. She has been my friend for about five minutes, but I would feel horrible if she were hurt by the pirates. Especially if they are only here for me.

Bluff

I slowly open the pantry door, and peek out. Whitley's hand is wrapped around my arm as it grows larger. She gasps. I enjoy the shocked expression on her face as I change into Drake, a dark-skinned pirate from Stede's crew, right in front of her.

She pulls her hand away, and my face falls.

I open the door and turn to motion her forward. "Hurry," I whisper.

She follows me out, tiptoeing, but her heels click with each step. I suppress a groan and ignore it. She walks slowly, carefully, but still isn't as quiet as we require—which is completely silent. We reach a stair case, and I pull her into the shadow of the underside. Then I turn to her, my expression annoyed beyond all reason. "Take them off," I hiss.

"What?"

"Your shoes. You can't escape from a gang of pirates with clickity shoes on."

Her lip twitches in amusement, but I turn away while she pulls her shoes off, clenching my jaw and silently cursing Stede. He's the reason I must deal with this brat in the first place. Without his interference, his irrational interest in fates that do not belong to him, I could have silently pulled strings to ensure her safety and distance from the battles of the seas without ever actually having to utter a word to her.

I turn back to ensure she's ready and notice how she wiggles her toes, a quiet expression of joy on her face.

What a strange, strange girl.

I grab her hand and pull her through the dark house. We come to a stairwell that leads to a wine cellar, but I stop. A creak of wood echoes up at us. Someone is down there.

I sigh and retreat, back to the stairs leading up. These are our only option, apparently. "Where are you taking me?"

"They're blocking all the exits, and you can't stay here forever. They'll find you eventually." I pull her faster. "No matter how massive this damn place is," I say under my breath.

"There isn't a way out up there!" she whispers up at me as she stumbles, working to keep her feet under her as I pull her along.

"There are windows."

Her gasp is stifled by another sharp pull of my hand. It's stupid—if she falls, we'll be found out and we'll both be dead—but I can't help it.

We reach a room with white walls and lace hung around the windowsill. No furniture, but I suspect this will be a nursery. That poor child of a girl will have a child of her own soon.

My pity is fleeting, though. She chose this path. Every life has good and bad, some just more obvious than others. She'll be pretty and rich and more important than those around her, but she'll be trapped all the same.

Her prison just smells better than my mine did.

"They must suspect you'll still be inside. Many of Stede's crew are searching the town. The rest are guarding the exits. The only way out is the only way they won't be expecting."

"But how?"

My lips spread into a sly grin. *Well, this will certainly be fun.*

"Wait here."

I head back into the hall, rummage through a storage closet and come across way more than I was hoping for. The coast seems clear enough in this part of the house, so I allow my body to return to its usual form and I reenter the soon-to-be nursery carrying a bundle of ropes. It's not quite sailor's rope. It's thin, but I'm impressed I found even this.

"How... Where?"

"Mr. Weatherby has entertained a pirate or two in his day. It was either this or chains. I'm thinking the rope will be more silent, and much easier to hold." Okay, it's a bit of an embellishment, but I didn't get the name Bluff for my trustworthiness.

I lean out the window, enjoying the cool night air rush over my hot skin, and then search for something to use as a hold. A flag hook only a few feet above the window will do nicely. I stretch my arm up, but I'm unable to reach.

"Oh, be careful."

I bend back down and meet her eye. "Are you worried about me, lassie?"

She seems taken aback, and her eyes dart to the floor. "You personally? No." Her eyes narrow. "But my one and only savior at the present moment? Yes."

Ah, finally a little cheek.

I transform my body into Lennard, an old school friend who was taller than any of our adult teachers by several inches. "The giant," our classmates called him, despite the fact that he was thin enough to see his ribs. With Lennard's body, I am able to easily reach the hook and tie a nice loop around it which I tug tight.

I throw the line over the side of the house.

"Come along," I say as I easily swing myself down, my feet hitting the side of the house every few feet I drop, rope slipping through my well-worn hands with ease. I relish the expression on her face as I drop.

This was never part of the plan, but I do enjoy shocking a pretty princess.

"You expect me to do that?" she whisper-calls to me.

"It's not as hard as it seems."

She crosses her arms. I stop half way down the wall. "Don't make me climb back up there," I tell her. "That part is not easy. Besides, I'm sure those pirates will find you pretty soon."

She sends a glance over her shoulder. After a deep breath, she wraps the rope around her shaking hand, and stands on the sill, her bum facing out towards me.

"Nice view," I say without actually looking up.

She stands up straight and turns back to me, her jaw set.

"Aw, come on," I taunt.

"Nope," she says, crossing her arms again.

"Alright, alright," I say with a laugh. "I won't look."

"You expect me to trust you?"

"You're throwing yourself out of a second story window. Yes, I expect you to trust me."

She sighs.

"Besides, you must come down. Those pirates will do much worse than look at your undergarments."

The red in her cheeks deepens, and amusement bubbles up in my chest. After a quick deep breath, she hops back into the house and rummages around. *What in the world is she doing?*

"Close your eyes," she says with a shaking voice.

I laugh and close my eyes.

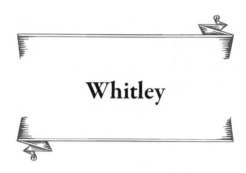

Whitley

My teeth chatter as I prepare to throw myself from a second story window with a pirate boy waiting below. My chemise is now securely tied between my legs—my only chance at modesty during this *endeavor*.

I try to take comfort in that and instead focus on the not-dying part.

Truth is, the old Whitley could do this. I miss that girl. Bold and adventurous. The girl with muddy feet could do this. Except that my father beat that girl out of me with a stick.

But I can still be her, right? She'd enjoy this, in fact. I try to remember the feeling I got when I first entered the pirate prison at the fort. The excitement. I loved it, even then.

I stand tall, wrap the rope around my hand tightly and practically leap. The rope constricts my hand as my weight pulls it tight. I hold back a yelp at the pain shooting up my arm and to my back as my shoulder hits the stone wall. I squeeze my eyes shut, vision flashing black.

Then I press myself against the wall, using my feet the way Bluff did, and unwrap the rope. I'll just have to trust my own hands.

Now I fall easily, palms burning as they slide down the rough cord. But within a moment I'm nearing the ground. Bluff is already there, brushing off his pants. I surprise him as I descend so quickly that I nearly land on him.

"Whoa!" he says, half word, half grunt. He grabs me just before I hit him, his arms wrapped around my legs, holding me. I let go of the rope. My thick skirt is bunched up around his face, his hands on my bare legs.

He blows out, practically spitting to get my skirts from his face. Then he slowly releases, my body sliding against his. He meets my eye as his hand glides higher up my legs until my feet land gently on the stone.

His gaze is intense. No longer is he the jokester. But then he clears his throat and breaks our eye contact, letting go of me so I can straighten out my skirts.

He turns away, pretending the moment didn't happened, which I suppose is best. Its dark out, and we're still very near to mortal danger.

"The brigades will be coming soon," he says. "The pirates will be heading back to *The Revenge* empty handed. They'll probably ransack your home first, though. Hopefully your father wouldn't be so stupid as to head back there."

"So what do we do?"

"This town won't be safe for you. Not for a long while."

"I don't understand. Why are they after me? My father...what's he done?"

"Your father is in big with those pirates. He owes them money. Borrowing from a pirate is a fool's affair. Not paying them back—that's worse. Then he tries to turn his back on them by siding with the navy, hoping if he can catch them, he won't have to pay his debts."

I suck in a breath.

He crosses his arms, glancing down towards the harbor. "Even fairly docile pirates, like Captain Taj, are eager to join in on the dismantling of a man that brazen."

"What a fool." It's the first I've spoken out against my father in years. It feels good—honest. "So what? The pirates will just keep coming back? Won't the army catch and kill them eventually? Besides what do they want with me? What will that accomplish?"

"Pirates are clever folk. Dirty drunks, obsessed with money and treasure, sure, but when you mess with them they will stop at nothing. They know people. They'll buy people if they must. If Stede and his crew want you—they'll get you. And as for what they want. Two things. One: a ransom. They'll use you as leverage to get the money they're owed. And two: to hurt him. They'll torture you. Make sure when you do go back to your scum of a father, you won't ever be the same."

My breath hitches. I can only imagine the things men like that would do to me. "I think they're overestimating my value," I whisper.

He peers past me, out towards the sea, ignoring my comment. "There is one place they won't expect you."

His eyes glisten more than I've ever seen them before.

Oh no. "No," I say, only half understanding his implication. He's a pirate, I can only guess he has a ship somewhere.

"You'd rather stay here and be pillaged? Did Captain Stede Bonnet capture your fancy? I hope so, for your sake."

"Ew." My stomach sinks thinking about it. "How long? How long will I have to be away before I can be safe again?"

"Depends on your father. Besides, I can take you some-place else. Another town. You're not exactly pirate material so..."

"New York?"

His eyebrows rise. "I suppose. Hope you know people there though. That's not an easy place to be a vagabond."

"Jeb will take care of me," I assure him.

He raises his eyebrows. "Husband?"

"Not yet."

Bluff purses his lips. "Alright, I'm sure we can catch you a ride there, so long as we catch *The Freedom* before they de-part."

BLUFF PULLS ME THROUGH the streets of town at a run, my bare feet stinging as the hard, jagged stone rips through my silk stockings and into fragile skin. I remember a time when my feet were well worn and prepared for rough streets.

I remember a time when my lungs could handle a run without growing weary. And now my lungs are burning, my corset constricting my breath further.

As a child, I loved to run around barefoot, but as I got older, I was no longer allowed. More and more my father in-sisted I behave "like a lady." At the time, I wanted to be one. I wanted to grow up and be beautiful, marry a rich, handsome man and live happily ever after.

I wanted to please my father.

Now I have trouble seeing the point. I find myself wanting to go backwards and become the girl who played ball in the muddy streets of New York again. Furious father or not.

I grit my jaw through the pain, forcing air through my lungs until my vision becomes spotted. I refuse to complain about the first bit of freedom I've been given in so long—as small a thing as it is.

I'm completely lost, but Bluff pulls me between houses, over fences. Then suddenly we come out into the open, and the only thing between us and the dock is the market—one long cobblestone street lined by brick and stone buildings, with shuttered windows. Everything is all closed up now. We're alone, which seems like a good thing, but we're completely in the open. Exposed.

We stop before the dark open road, knowing there is nowhere to hide.

Voices nearby make me squeeze Bluff's hand harder. He doesn't move. We wait and listen. Several sets of footsteps sound from the alley a street down. The voice is gravelly and jovial, "Would ya look at that!" I turn my head towards the voice only to realize he's inside the closed shop just feet from us. I take a step back, knowing if there are men here—pirates, I'm guessing, sacking whatever they can while they can. We can't be seen. But Bluff doesn't move. He stands firm.

"Shouldn't we hide?" I whisper.

"Not necessarily. Just wait."

A sudden crash makes me jump, and a man comes barreling out of a shop, smashing the wooden door to pieces. I leap away from Bluff now and press my body against the nearest building, heart hammering in my chest. I stare at the tattoos that line the pirate's arms, as he slams a sledge hammer into what's left of the wooden door... for good measure, I suppose?

"Carlos!" Bluff calls. I gasp.

The pirate freezes and looks up, a wary look covering his previously joyous expression. The light hits the tattooed man, casting shadows over his face. A piece of metal sticks out from his eyebrow.

The man squints as he takes a few steps towards us. Then recognition crosses his face and his eyes lighten. "Bluff?"

Bluff is smiling now too. "Am I ever glad to see you."

"The 'ell you doing 'ere? Thought you was locked up."

Bluff releases my arm and walks closer to the stranger. "You think that place could hold me? Besides, I heard Stede freed all those pirates."

"Aye. Didn't know you was one of them, though. Thought you was in some place up north."

Bluff shrugs. "This is north, you ask me. And Stede had nothing to do with my escape, that's for sure."

Carlos laughs, and I shift awkwardly, not willing to move any closer. I still don't know how much I can trust Bluff. Maybe I should take the opportunity and hide somewhere until morning. But the moment the man's eyes drift to me, my muscles tense. Too late for escape now.

"Got yourself a trophy?" His eyes travel all the way down my body, and I grit my teeth, resisting the urge to cover myself. Anything to get this man's eyes off of me.

Bluff smirks and then stomps over, wrapping his arm around my waist, and very quickly leans in to whisper in my ear, "Go with it." Then he turns a big smile to Carlos and says, "Pretty, ain't she?"

Carlos winks "'Bout time, boy."

Three more pirates appear at the end of the market street and my muscles begin to ache from the constant tension.

"Looks like she needs bit of a loosening." Carlos laughs.

I shiver. "All in good time." Bluff laughs naturally. So natural, in fact, I wonder if he's serious. If not, he's one damned good liar. I'm not sure which one scares me more.

Down at the docks, there are three new ships. Ships flying black flags.

Obviously, Bluff knows a few of these pirates, but how do I know who is "good" and who is bad? And how much will Bluff risk to save me? His life? He barely knows me.

"Where's Iron?" Bluff asks, keeping his voice calm. But he takes a step back, pulling me back with him as the new pirates approach.

"Ship's there, you comin'?" Carlos points out to a far dock.

"Didn't get much here," an old man with a missing arm says. "Not with Stede raidin' all them rich houses."

"Dissapointin'. We ain't got a chance to raid a place like this in a 'ell of a while."

"I did alright," Carlos says, holding up a bag that looks awful heavy. "Lots of rum." He smiles.

The old man slaps him on the back with his only arm.

The boom of a cannon makes us all jump. Before I even know what's happening, the pirates turn and run towards the ship. Bluff and I are left behind, his hand still around my waist. "This is our only chance," he whispers, "but they cannot know who you are, understand?"

I swallow. "Who are they? They're not after my father too?"

Bluff shakes his head. "No. They just came for the easy spoils of an already conquered town. Let Stede do the hard work, since he was so determined, and they'll sack whatever is left."

I nod. I suppose that makes sense.

"This is a crew I know well. I'll be welcomed. But if they know that Stede wants you, well, they certainly won't want to cross him, and the price will be well worth it to betray me."

I peer into Bluff's grey eyes and know that I shouldn't trust him. He's a pirate. His name basically means "Liar!" but if I turn back, I'll be faced with a much worse reality. If they're really after me and my father, I don't know when or if I'll ever be safe. My only chance is to get back to New York. To Jeb.

Right back to my old prison. It was the best possible future I could have imagined for the longest time. Better than whatever my father had planned for me in this Carolina town. So why does the thought cause my head to spin unpleasantly?

What other choice do I have? Where else could I go but back to the only person in the world I trust to actually care about *me*? Even if I'm unsure I actually want to marry him. Life, it seems, is rarely about want.

I allow Bluff to pull me down the dock at a quick pace. The ships are already bustling, with men scurrying and shouting things I don't even understand.

"Who is she?" The voice booms as soon as we reach the ship. The man's voice is so low, so quiet but strong, that it sends a shiver down my spine. He is so tall he towers over us. Though his muscles aren't as large as most of the pirates I've seen, there is still something menacing about him. Perhaps it's the loop piercing through the center of his nose.

They stare at one another for what feels like an hour, then a smirk spreads across Bluff's face. Still keeping his eyes focused on the huge bull-like pirate, he reaches over and grabs me by the waist, pulling me towards him. "She's with me, captain."

"Well come on, then!" the captain calls to us. "Can't waste time, not on a night like this."

Another cannon booms as my feet hit the ship's deck. This time I don't jump.

I take a deep breath and try to convince myself that this is okay. This is the best option available to me.

I guess whatever my future holds, it's going to start with a pirate ship.

Bluff

Seaweed and sweat, rotten fish and rat scat, all rolled into one horrible scent—that's the smell of a pirate ship. The damp wood beneath my feet creaks, and for a moment I forget the girl next to me. The ship itself is as much of a home as I've ever had.

But there is still a sense of unease. Every time I step onto a ship, dread fills me. Itching and crawling, it shoots up my spine and into my head. I love it and I hate it.

I try to ignore the yelling and grunting of the crew as they make ready. That's the part that scares me. Not the crew—the setting sail bit.

A ship should just stay docked. It might be pleasant, then.

A small gasp escapes the girl's lips, and my eyes dart to her. A particularly nasty pirate named Lucky Seven has wandered a bit too close, his dirt caked arm rubbing hers as he passes. I smile at her discomfort. She's a little princess on a pirate ship

This will be fun.

She seems to have forgotten me as well. As soon as the pirates are clear of her, she walks forward, leaving me behind. I follow quietly—out of curiosity, of course.

43

She just stares out at the sea in wonder or in deep thought as she watches the dark rippling waters.

Is it just me, or is it longing there?

Could this girl, who doesn't know the first thing about sailing, who spent her whole life in a city and corset, possibly love the sea?

That's a horrifying thought.

I hate the sea.

I hate the way it controls you. Pulls you.

Truth is, I couldn't stay away if I tried.

The sea is a part of me, as much as I try to deny it. It owns me.

And I'll never forgive it for that.

"Bluff!" someone calls. Whitley and I turn to the caller simultaneously. A dozen men are on deck, pulling up the anchor, dropping sails, tying rope, pushing us off. Standing in the middle of the main deck is a girl, dressed like the other scallywags around her, but with a white smile that only someone who takes care of themselves possess. She wears her signature black feather in her pinned black hair.

"Get your smimey arse over here and help me with the rig!" Rosemera calls to me.

I smile and jog to help her. Together we heave the main-stay far out to catch the north facing wind. It catches immediately, and the ship heaves in eagerness.

"Whoa there!" the captain yells, even though there's nothing we can do about the wind. It'll blow how it wants to. And right now, it wants us out to sea.

It wants *me* out to sea.

That's the real reason the captain's yelling. And the reason Rosemera turns to me and smiles. "That was easy," she says, her eyes shining.

They know the harsh winds blowing through the sails are my fault. They just see it as a blessing, the way the sea calls to me. Just another part of my power.

I see it as a curse.

But at least they don't have to worry about bad storms with me on board. We usually get fair—if a bit overzealous—winds and blue skies.

A gust of very deliberate wind blows over the ship. It feels like a hand wisping through my hair, but it continues past me and hits Whitley full in the back. She stumbles forward, catching herself on the damp railing. It blows her hair and dress forward, violent at first but then gentle. A caress.

The winds like her too.

That can't be good.

She turns to face me, hair half in her face. She doesn't look how I'd expect. I'd expect annoyed, inconvenienced, or even scared.

Instead, there's intensity. Fierce beauty.

I hate that it crosses my mind that it's the expression one lover gives to another, not that I've had much experience with lovers. At least not any I'd like to remember.

I swallow. Despite what the crew must think, I will not be learning any more about lovers tonight. Still, my stomach flips at the sight of her. Her eyes glisten, her cheeks blush. Her hair blows in the wind, wild and free. The way she was meant to be, only she'll never know that. She'll live her high society life far away from all of this. At least if there is anything I can do about it.

The ship presses into the waves ahead and rocks suddenly. Whitley stumbles and grips the rail to keep balance.

Let's see how much Miss Princess likes the high seas.

Perhaps my ocean friends will help me out here.

"Who is she?"

I turn to Rosemera, realizing I've probably been watching the girl for a lot longer than I should. Her big eyes study me. She's always been beautiful, Rosemera, but she's like a sister. She nudges my arm.

"No one important," I say in a flat voice, then I walk away. It's the biggest lie I've ever told her.

The ship is well on its way out of the bay, so my work is done. Just in time, too. Another cannon sounds, this one aimed at the docks. Stede will have to be off soon, empty-handed, most likely. He might have managed to get a hand on the bastard traitor, but serves him right if he did.

I just hope he doesn't catch sight of *the Freedom* before they give up their search or he very well may put two and two together and follow us.

I'm always a step of head of you, Stede.

Speaking of which, I need to speak to Captain Taj about heading up to New York. Won't be his favorite port, but he owes me a favor. Or ten.

I walk slowly towards the front of the ship where Whitley stands, watching the dark water as *The Freedom* carves through the small waves.

The ship bounces harshly. Even with just small waves, most landlubbers have trouble getting used to the rocking of a ship in the open sea. Whitley surprises me by standing with one leg hitched, comfortable.

Rosemera shoves in front of me and jumps up the steps two at time to reach the helm. She walks right up to Whitley with a big smile. I roll my eyes and follow.

"Welcome aboard, Missy!" Rosemera says, in an exuberant but kind voice.

Whitley smiles politely.

"Suppose I'm not the only lass on board for a few days." Whitley's smile doesn't falter, but she gives no other response. "What's a girl gatta do to get a catch like Bluff here?" Rosemera says, another tactic to get the girl to open up a little. She's on a pirate ship for damn sake. Does she really think she has to be prim and proper here? Or does she just know nothing else?

Whitley's eyes flash to me but then she smiles, turning back to Rosemera. "Pure luck, I think."

"She came to visit me in prison, unlike *someone*," I say, nudging her arm with my elbow.

"Oh yes, that woulda been a splendid idea. Me at the fort." Rosemera laughs, "Did ya help him escape?"

Whitley's eyes widen. "Oh! No. He managed that all on his own, then surprised me later." She laughs a small, polite sort of laugh. You can tell she's trained for propriety. She knows just what to say.

Makes me want to yawn. Or barf. Either would be an appropriate response.

"He's good at surprises," Rosemera says. I'm not sure what she thinks about this whole situation. Does she believe that the girl is a potential lover like the rest of the crew? Since they all just assumed and it seemed like as good a story as any, we just went with it, but Rosemera knows me better than the rest. I search her face and wonder if she suspects there is more going on here. But as much as I want to trust her, I don't trust anyone.

"Indeed," Whitley says.

Rosemera glances down, then shrieks. "Boy!" she says, with fire in her eyes. I actually take a step back, knowing that tone cannot be good. "Tell me you did not bring this girl on this ship without shoes!"

I look down and sure enough, Whitley's feet are bare. Well, almost. Ripped stockings are barely hanging onto her ragged feet. Her toes curls under, like they're hiding.

I blink and nod slowly. "Forgot about that."

Rosemera narrows her eyes, and I can't help but let out a quiet huff of a laugh.

"That isn't funny. A pirate ship is the last place a girl like this wants to be barefoot. No offense."

For the first time, a full smile spreads across Whitley's face. I find I like it, but I press the feeling away.

"It is a bit gross down there." She points to the main deck where water and who knows what else slosh around. She does have a point. "But it's fine here."

"Come on, I'll get you a pair of fresh shoes. Perhaps next time you'll find a boy that actually takes care of you!" She's yelling it now, and I might be embarrassed if it weren't so damn funny.

Rosemera pulls Whitley down the stairs and into the captain's quarters, where she lives as well, being the captain's daughter and all.

What I am sincerely surprised about, I realize, is that Whitley didn't say a thing. She walked through the main deck, in a full inch of nasty water and rat scat, and didn't so much as turn up her nose. Sure, she walked right up to the top deck for the high ground, I'm sure. But still, that's not exactly the behavior I'd expect out of a *princess*.

I walk down to the main deck to join the rest of the crew. They're breaking out the rum already. They expect easy sailing with me aboard, and they very well may be right about that. So long as Stede doesn't catch on to us too quickly.

Luster, a small man in cut-off tunic, holds out a bottle. I grab it without a word and take a nice long swig. He's not the most experienced sailor, but he's the only one on board with medical knowledge, making him one of the most well-respected men on this crew.

I wince as I force the burning liquid down my throat. The stuff is *nasty*. Pirate rum will never be the smoothest beverage but it gets the job done. I've gotten used to hiding the reaction, but I'll never get used to the taste.

"Spill!" Joke calls out.

"What?" I say as I sit on a small stool waiting for me.

"What's she like? Never had a broad like that before," his voice is already slurred.

"Couldn't say, haven't much had the opportunity to find out."

The men groan as one.

"Take the captain's quarters! He'll give it to ya, know he will!"

I'm sure he would. But that doesn't mean I'd want to take them.

"You could get away with murder here, boy."

The men laugh heartily. I know more than one of them has gotten away with murder, and I wonder if that's why they're laughing. But I get the point. Yes, everyone wants to do Bluff a solid. He'll return the favor.

But these men know I'd help them out, favors or not.

They're like family.

One hell of a barking mad family, but a family nonetheless.

I've spent my life jumping around, pirate ship to pirate ship. The only time I ever lived a near normal life was during the few years I went to a fancy school on the coast. I hated it. But it did help me to learn the behavior of non-pirates, which is very much needed in my line of work. Does no good to change your appearance if you can't act the part. So, *The Freedom* isn't the only ship I've spent a good amount of time on, but over the years since the war, the pirate population has been shrinking quickly. This is one of few free ships left in these waters.

"Speaking of which, where's the captain now?"

Carlos points back to the aft. Past the main mast. I stand. "Thanks for the drink, gentlemen. I'll be back soon."

They're laughing the second I leave, but I didn't hear the joke. I've always been the kid, so not many of the jokes are for my ears anyhow.

I'm the golden child—a living breathing treasure and one hell of a bargaining chip.

But I'm hardly one of the crew.

I head up to the captain, who smacks my back affectionately. "My boy!"

"Thanks for letting me aboard."

"Don't be silly, boy. You know I'd never turn the likes a you away. It was the girl I questioned. Girls like that cause trouble, ya know?"

"I know." I nod, also realizing that it's not like he resisted allowing her aboard very hard.

He nods and smiles. "Let me know if it's worth it." He says while staring out at the sea like it's his real lover, the real girl who he hopes to God is worth the trouble. It's not.

I just don't have the heart to tell him that.

"I do have a favor to ask."

He smiles. "Course ya do."

"The girl, she's a need to get to New York."

This grabs his attention. "That city?"

I nod. It's not the largest city in the country, but it's one of fastest growing and very well protected.

"Not an easy trip, that. I'd have to pull out the old privateer flag and hope they don't ask too many questions."

There's a flash in the captain's eyes. He doesn't talk much of his time as a privateer, but I'm aware of enough to know it's a sore subject. He gathered a massive fortune by sacking British cargo ships during the war. Legal pirates, they were. Unconventional soldiers allowed to keep their spoils.

Many say the war would have been lost were it not for privateers.

When the war was won, the most successful of the lot went on to be part of upper-class in the new country. No questions asked. Captain Taj would have been one of them, had his first mate not betrayed him.

Left with nothing, he gathered a new crew and new ship and never looked back. Doesn't matter how many spoils he wins, I don't suspect he'll ever seek out the life stolen from him again.

"I'll take care of it. That you know I'm good for."

He nods and turns back to the sea. "Aye, I'm sure I'll find a good reason to head to the big city. No piracy, a' course, but bargainin'? Yes, we could use a simple trade route. Good suggestion, Bluff. Go ahead and tell the crew our heading."

"Thank you," I say, sincerely, and head back to the crew.

"Oh, and Bluff, let me know if you want to draw out the trip. Ya might desire a little time to..." I wince when the captain winks but cover it with a smile.

"Thank you, Captain, but I'm sure I've got plenty of time as it is." God knows that's the truth. Get this girl off my hands as fast as possible. It'll be a three-day trip as it is.

"That's my boy."

I turn away and head to the crew.

"We've got a heading, boys."

"Where to?"

"Captain's got a bit of business in the big city a' New York. Simple bartering trip, I expect."

The crew stare at me without a word. I admit, it is a bit of a weird heading. Not too often do we head for a city like New York. It's much too big and too well protected to do any pirating. Even as sailors with a privateer flag, we could be discovered as pirates and round up. If the military takes too good a look at our cargo holds, there'd be no mistaking our true nature. It takes a bit of bribing to get by well-guarded areas most times—and that's if we're lucky.

Pirates only head to New York if they've got a damn good reason.

As far as I'm concerned, dropping this girl off and getting her out of my hair is a hell of a good reason. Away from Stede and away from me.

"New York?" Barns stands, chewing on a piece of straw I suspect he's been saving for months. He grew up on a farm and only became a pirate when a drought and scarlet fever struck his family at the same time. I'm not sure if he carries the straw as a reminder of what he lost or for the comfort of the familiar.

"If you got a problem with it, take it up with the captain," I say, even though I'm sure most of the crew already suspect the strange heading is my doing. And that's the exact reason they won't question it.

Barns grunts but turns away and tends to a fraying rope laying on the ground. No point. It's too far gone to fix. He knows it, I know it. Just gives him something to do with his hands.

I don't like inconveniencing the crew too much, but I'm fairly certain they'll live through one short trip to New York. No promises, though.

I take a walk around the ship to clear my mind. Just a few days. Then this bloody business can be done and over with.

"Hey."

Her voice is soft like cotton. I stop but don't turn.

"You don't have to talk to me if you don't want to," she says.

I turn to her now. "Well, we do have a bit of a ruse going that we're 'together'. Would be a bit odd if we never actual spoke."

She nods and turns to the open water. I join her by the edge of swaying ship. The wind is still on our side. We'll certainly make good time.

For a moment, the smallest of moments, I love the sea. Vast and open. So incredible for something so small to be so damn big.

"I just wanted to say thank you," she says.

I blink.

"For saving me, I mean. I still don't know why you did. I'm honestly not sure I want to."

"I had my reasons, plenty. Trust that. I might not be as much a scallywag as these boys, but I'm a pirate just the same, and pirates always have a motive."

"That's what I'm scared of," she says like a whisper.

I sigh, ignoring the dizzy feeling in my head. I shouldn't want her to trust me. She shouldn't trust me.

"I might not be as honorable as you're used to, but believe me when I say your safety is my priority. Just don't expect to ever know why."

She nods, and I hope it means she won't ask any more questions. I have no answers for her.

"As for the 'honorable' men I'm used to... you forget who my father is."

My eyebrows shoot up, surprised. "I suppose that's true."

"Can I ask you one more question?"

I take in a deep breath and close my eyes as salt water splashes my face.

"It's late. We should find a place to lay our heads or we'll end up sleeping here."

"Here's not too bad."

She's right about that. There's a nice little nook right by the bow where the breeze is gentle and the view pleasant. But that doesn't mean it's a good place to sleep. "More than one good sailor has rolled into the sea while he slept. Best to stick to the cabins."

She stands, accepting my words. Maybe she does trust me, after all.

Dumb broad.

Half the crew is below already. The other half is laughing and drinking by the mast.

Someone whistles to Whitley, and I'm surprised when she doesn't react. "If you've got a taste for older men, I'd welcome you in my bed, sweetheart. Ya know, if Bluff here doesn't quite do it for you."

A quiet anger fills my chest, and I have half a mind to start a fight. It would be convincing to our relationship, at least. Instead I pull Whitley in by the waist and wink. "I can be anything she wants me to be." Which gets a few proud laughs.

"It's not about what you look like, boy. It's about what you can do with the raw materials. It's about experience."

Whitley shudders in my arms, and I can tell his tone sickens her.

"Women you pay to tell you how good you are? Yes, I'm sure you're an expert," Rosemera calls out as she skips down the steps from the aft.

The men laugh, but I'm fairly certain they'd laugh at anything right now. Talking about women, their beauty and their flaws, always lightens the mood. Especially in a half-drunk crowd.

She walks right up to me and holds out a key.

"What's this?"

"Key to the captain's quarters."

"Seriously? I didn't ask for this."

"I know." She smiles at me. It's an understanding smile, but I can tell she's enjoying this.

"Your goal is to keep her safe right? I don't care who's watching—with this bunch, she won't be safe."

"And what about you?"

"I'm taking the crow's watch. Besides, I stabbed Wes six months ago when he tried groping me, and my father threw Fouad to the sharks the time he snuck into my bed. No one will mess with me now."

I hold back a laugh about Fouad, who I'm guessing was the pirate from prison a few days ago. Thrown over for a game of dice, eh?

Honestly, I care a hell of a lot more about Rosemera than I do about Whitley. But she's probably right. The crew knows better than to mess with the Captain's daughter by now.

I take the key with an embarrassed "thanks," knowing that tonight is not going to be near as fun as everyone else expects. In fact, I'm pretty well dreading it.

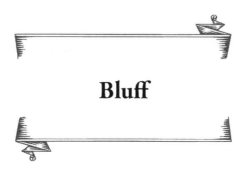

Bluff

The crew calls out to us as we unlock the thick wooden door to the captain's quarters. There's hooting and hollering and, of course, belly laughing galore. They're all certain it'll be the best night of my life. I'm certain it will be the most awkward.

I usher Whitley into the dark room, the wood groaning as we enter. Moonlight streams in through the window, but it's hardly enough to see by. I quickly light a few candles. The captain's quarters are the nicest place you'll find on a pirate ship but I realize it's probably pretty awful to a girl like her.

"Bluff," she whispers.

I close my eyes and shiver at the sound of my name on her lips, but I push back the feeling. "We're just gonna sleep. Don't worry about me."

I don't look to see if she acknowledges the statement. I don't want to know if she's relieved that I won't try to seduce her or whatever sick idea she has. And I certainly don't want to know if she's disappointed.

In fact, just the thought is like a kick in the gut.

God, I need to get rid of this girl.

She walks slowly across the room, wood creaking beneath her feet. With a sigh she sits on a bench by the window, moonlight shining on her face.

I tear my eyes from her and take the opportunity to get ready for bed. If I'm sleeping in the captain's bed, I'm not sleeping in my rotting tunic—the same tunic I wore in prison. I pull the shirt over my head and toss it to the corner, then rummage through a chest of clothing laying on the ground. These are Rosemera's, and I know she wouldn't mind me taking some. In fact, she's offered on more than one occasion. For a Moroccan girl, she certainly likes her English clothing.

I find a soft pair of trousers that will do for the night. I slip my old ones off. New ones on as fast as possible. Whitley doesn't even glance my way.

When I'm finished, I approach her.

I can't help it, I'm curious.

Standing over her shoulder, I look out the window and try to decide what she's looking for.

"You love the ocean," I say. It's not a question. I can see it in her eyes, the same way I saw it when she first boarded the ship. It's a fact that scares me more than she will ever understand.

She jumps but doesn't move. "I've never thought about it like that. It's just... beautiful out there."

I look down at her moonlit face and nod. "It is, isn't it?"

She looks up into my eyes, and I realize how close we're standing. My chest is inches from her shoulder.

My breathing slows. My heart pounds louder but not faster.

I'm calm, here, next to her.

Her watching the water, me watching her.

But I know it can't last.

I take a small step away, just enough to break the spell.

She blinks and smiles, glancing to the window and then looking at me like she can't decide which is more important.

"Can you change into anyone?" she asks, but then blushes like she can't believe she said it.

My eyebrows rise, and I wonder if there's someone in particular she wants to see.

"My shifting is pretty much limitless. I can change as much or as little about myself as I want, it just takes some concertation. So yes, I can become anyone."

"But how?"

I shrug. I don't mind questions, but that one is a bit loaded.

"Do the crew know?"

"What?"

"About your... ability?"

I cross my arms and smirk. "Yes, of course. It's gotten them out of more than one bind. Saved a few of their lives, even."

She nods.

"Do you always ask so many questions?"

She smiles. "Only when supernatural boys save me from savage pirates."

"Touché." It's quiet for a long moment, and I assume she's done with her questions. "We should try for some sleep. Dawn will come sooner than you think."

She peers down at the bed, furrowing her brow.

"Something wrong?"

She sighs. "This dress isn't exactly for sleeping."

Heat rushes to my face, and immediately I regret it. Not like she's gonna sleep naked.

"You need something to sleep in?"

Her eyes narrow a little and then she shakes her head. "It's not really the dress, but the stay beneath."

"Stay?"

"A corset of sorts."

"I see." I smirk and hope it's too dark for her to see my blush. "You want me to help you out of your dress?"

Her mouth and eyes open in surprise. "I... I mean."

I laugh. At least I can be amused by her discomfort instead of worried about the feeling in my chest. "Turn," I say. She pulls down the outer layer of her gown, exposing a small white chemise and corset.

She turns back, looking out the window again, and I tend to the string knotted at the top of her dress.

"It's tied very tightly."

The knot comes lose immediately. I start at the bottom of her back, losing the string all the way up. "I'm a pirate. I'm good with knots."

"Right," she says in a near whisper. Brushing the hair from the back of her neck, I let my fingers run over her shoulder, pushing the fabric down.

"I think I have it from here," she says more firmly now.

I smile, my heart pounding. But I won't let her know that.

I hate pulling my hand away, but I do.

Most of all I hate that I don't want to leave her. *I can't want her.*

This feeling is more dangerous than Captain Stede. Wanting her will lead to... well, I don't want to even think about that. If I were to see her as anything more than a pretty princess on her way back to her fiancé...

I take in a deep breath and think about the future. She'll be safe in New York with her rich future husband, and I'll be free of the curse. A prophecy that says I'll fall in love with her and she'll become my destruction.

I just need to survive two more days. Two more achingly long days pretending to be with a girl I *cannot* have feelings for.

I crawl into bed with my soft English pants and roll away, my back facing Whitley. Moments later, she enters silently but I can feel her heat.

"Thank you," she whispers.

I'm not sure what she's thanking me for—saving her, taking her to New York to be with her beloved Jeb, or not seducing her when I have ample opportunity?

Which makes me wonder what she would do...

No. I can't think like that. I must sleep and not dream about high society girls. Even if her blond hair and blue eyes shine, she looks at the sea a way I wish she'd look at me, and I can still feel her bare legs sliding down my hands as we escaped the pirate invasion.

I close my eyes and picture that moment, because, well, sometimes you need to indulge your fantasies. In my mind Whitley wraps her legs around me and lets my hands rest on her legs. I push her against the wall and press my lips—

No! God, what is wrong with me?

I shake my head, subtly enough that I hope Whitley doesn't notice. I recite the prophecy in my mind, over and over again, a reminder of what I stand to lose if I let myself become entangled in her spell.

> *Daughter of the scheming land-dweller*
> *A man so bold as to betray a pirate*
> *A beauty of golden hair and secret of low birth*
> *Will control the Son of the Sea, cause him to fall*
> *She alone holds the power to enslave him*
> *Control him, even to his death*

I clench my jaw. Just two more days.

Once she's married, the prophecy will be annulled. At least that's what the sea witch said. Until then she'll be safe inside a city too well guarded for either siren or pirate to take her. If we can get there in time.

Stede expects me to love her, they all do. Every prophecy has several possible meanings, but they all think I'll fall in love with the *beauty of golden hair and secret of low birth*. And when I do, she'll gain the ability to literally control my power. She'll be my destruction.

But I *won't* love her.

I won't even let myself get close.

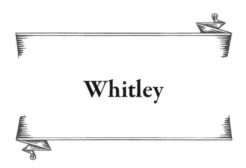

Whitley

I wake to an empty bed.

As an unmarried woman, anything else would be obscene, according to everything I've been taught. And yet, the space beside me feels unnaturally cold. Like Bluff *should* be there, next to me.

I roll out of bed and stretch my back, then brush my unruly hair with my fingers. I find a few remaining pins and carefully remove them, one by one.

The ground beneath me rocks and sways, the wood creaking. Water splashes and whooshes behind the paneled walls, while men grunt and holler obscenities just outside my door.

How in the world did I go from a ball—with a corset gown, lace boots, and hair pinned to perfection— to waking, half-naked in a pirate ship after sleeping beside a strange man, in a matter of twelve hours?

The whole night, I was aware of Bluff lying beside me, his warmth seeping over. We never touched, not once. And yet I could feel him.

I shake my head.

My feelings for Bluff are so strange, so contradictory, that I can't quite work them out. I want him near me, though

I shouldn't. I rely on him for salvation, to free me from my pursuers—and yet I know I can't trust him.

He didn't save me out of pure kindness—that much I know. And based on last night, it wasn't out of desire either. I know there must be more to this story.

Part of me longs for nothing more than to uncover the secret to his motives. What is he hiding? Why did he save me? The other just wants to get home and forget it ever happened.

Sunlight streams through the window, making the room bright and open. I decide to get up and redress before someone enters and sees me in my chemise. That would be embarrassing. The stay corset is difficult to lace up on my own, but I manage well enough.

Next, I explore the captain's room a bit more. I saw a little when Rosemera brought me in to get me new shoes, but now I'm alone and can rummage through some of the odd trinkets.

There are objects from all over the world, like the Jamaican coin on the table, or the piles of cloth in a crate labeled Mughal Empire.

There are chests and drawers filled with clothing and maps, and books, copper pieces, and devices I can't even figure out the purpose of, all from islands and nations I've scarcely even heard of.

I find no jewelry, no gold, just *things*. These are treasures, just not the kind my world would find valuable.

Maps cover a mahogany table in the corner. I peer over at them but can't comprehend what all the lines and circles mean.

The door to the cabin flies open, slamming against the wall with a bang. A bearded man limps in, grunting but paying no attention to me. I'm as still as can be, hoping he won't notice me at all.

He rummages through a box of papers on the floor, grabs a pistol off the table and a roll of parchment, and then huffs back through the door.

I release my breath.

These men are allies, I remind myself. Dangerous, but allies nonetheless. I peer out the partially open door, out onto the ship where ropes swing and strange, dirty men walk about. Men who said countless vulgar things to and about me last night. I shiver. Men who think I lost my virtue just hours ago.

I don't want to consider the images likely floating through their minds.

So what if they think I'm a floosy? I'll never see these men again, and if this strange new reputation is what saves me, it's worth it.

I grip the door's edge and take a few more breaths. I have to be the barefoot girl in New York. Unafraid. Bold.

This is an adventure. And probably the only one I'll ever have. I need to make the most of it.

With all my strength, I force the door open and a massive gust of salty air blasts me, tossing my already messy hair all about.

The ship is astir with sailors rushing around, pushing and pulling ropes, knotting them, climbing up the nets. I watch in awe. None of these men are particularly attractive, but some of them could be with a bit more hygiene and a good shave. Nevertheless, I notice the strength it takes to climb and adjust the sails. Their muscles bulge and contract, their faces taut with concentration. I'm impressed, to be honest. And for the first time I'm glad I'm on this pirate ship. Even if it's only for a few days' time.

Especially since it's only a few days' time.

This is something most people never get to experience. Never get to see. I know most of the women who will be in my company soon—women married to upper class men, won't have much interest in the reality of pirates still in our waters, but perhaps the men will. Perhaps Jeb will.

My stomach gives a surprising twist at that thought. Don't I want to go back to Jeb where I'll be provided for and safe for the rest of my life? I bite my lip.

"Enjoying this?"

I jump and spin quickly to face Rosemera with her beautiful brown eyes and braided hair. In my society we cherish fair skin, but her complexion is so beautiful. I find myself wishing I looked more like her.

"A little."

"Not what you expected from a pirate ship?"

"Not at all." My smile is sincere and relaxed. Rosemera may never know how much I appreciate her presence on this ship. Just to have another girl here, one that belongs as much as any man, makes me wonder if I too could belong here—in a different life.

But even more so than just what she is, every word from her mouth, every expression, is reassuring and sincere, and that is far more than I could have ever hoped for.

Dimples form on her cheeks when she smiles. "Pirates are sailors first, always. They don't become scallywags until it comes time to fight for what we need."

"Treasure?"

Her smile turns to amusement. "Gold is rarely on our minds. What we seek is much more valuable. Basic supplies. Survival. Comfort. Freedom. That's the name of our ship, you know? That's all we're really after."

I nod absently.

"We are in need of medicine, food, clothing, rum. Not much we can do with gold if no port will allow us in."

"Ports don't let you dock?"

"It depends. At some we can get away with using our privateer flags or forged merchant documents, but it's always a risk. Not many pirate ports left in these waters."

I walk a few steps to the starboard side of the ship and peer over at the waves below. Already the water has turned deeper blue. The breeze that rushes over my skin leaves goosebumps. I shiver at the coming cold.

"How long before we make port?" I ask, eager to change the subject.

Rosemera takes a few strides to meet me by the edge of the ship. "The day after tomorrow, most likely. We're making great time."

"That's good." I cast a glance at the water swirling behind the ship, frothing and splashing as we leave it behind, then settling and smoothing out farther behind, our ship already forgotten. The horizon is empty, and I realize Stede must be behind us, somewhere.

"Looking for something?" Rosemera asks.

I clench my jaw. "No. What would I be looking for?"

"Someone you left behind? Someone you're running from? I don't know your story, miss. But I know you have one."

I bite my lip as I continue staring at the horizon behind us, half expecting the mast of a new ship to appear in the distance. "Please don't call me miss."

Rosemera smiles and nods. I lean over the side of the ship as I notice the water fading into a lighter color, turning... green.

Rosemera follows my line of sight and puckers her lips. "Bluff comes with his own baggage, you know."

I nod, but find myself distracted by the green swirls. As it turns brighter, I see something glowing beneath the waves. Rosemera rips her head back, as if afraid of peering too long.

"BOYS!" she hollers out, making me jump. "COVER THOSE EARS." The ship rumbles, the planks beneath my feet vibrating.

The crew pauses for only an instant before jumping into action and shoving anything within reach into their ears. Mostly small bits of rope, laying here and there of cloth from their own tattered clothing.

"Should I be doing something?"

"Hide," she says, but I can't tell if she's joking or not. Then she leans in and whispers into my ear, "You're about to meet some of Bluff's baggage face to face. Be prepared."

Bluff

A chilly wind tickles at my neck, making me shiver. The breeze should be growing colder as we travel further north, but not in an instant. I know right away it's not a natural shift. This is more.

I grit my teeth and press my eyes shut, forcing out all the anxious thoughts that push forward. I don't want to see *them*, ever again. Especially not now, with her on board.

And yet, I knew it was inevitable. I can practically feel fate laughing at me, its rumble in the wind.

I suck in a long breath, preparing for the coming nightmare.

Rosemera's sharp voice sounds through the ship. I'm surprised and thankful she was able to catch the signs so quickly. I should have been the one to warn the crew. Today, I was distracted.

Every pirate pauses at her words: "COVER THOSE EARS." I can feel their terror—and excitement—as it twists through every man aboard.

The crew burst into action, preparing for the only type of deadly supernatural being a pirate is ever eager to meet. I slowly turn to find Whitley.

She meets my gaze. Caution crosses her expression, but every muscle in her body is relaxed. There are no stress lines on her face, no fear. Does she not know what she faces?

The depth and wonder in her eyes tells me she knows much more than she should.

The vibration under my feet escalates, and the ship slows, despite the wind that blows furiously through the sails. I slowly approach the bow to meet my unwanted fate.

A gust hits me in the face, blowing my hair back and making my eyes water. I stare out at the sea before me, and slowly, a form materializes. She's tall and thin, with green iridescent skin, bright silver hair, and a fish's tail where her legs should be, curled over the railing like she's sitting rather comfortably. She stares at me with her grey eyes and spreads her lips into an inhuman smile, exposing her nail-sharp teeth just inches from my face.

The siren hisses—a noise so high pitched and sharp it even makes me wince. The men behind me fall to their knees, feeling the magic, fighting the pull. But their faces don't show the agony that should be there. Instead, they are alight with bliss.

My face remains blank. I am much less excited about our meeting than she is.

"We meet again, my boy," she says in a slithering voice.

I suppress an eye roll. "Hi, Mom."

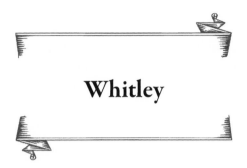

Whitley

I watch in awe as Bluff meets a siren face to face.

My heart thuds, and my hands begin to sweat. *A siren*. A creature both terrifying and beautiful, that should not exist. I've read stories about them. The sailors I met as a child on my way to America were quite taken with the idea. But for all intents and purposes, I'd believed them legend. Not real.

And yet, there she is, with haunting eyes and silver hair that matches Bluff's.

I half expect a song to come forth from her lips, instead it's a hiss. I know the stories—creatures of the sea who lure men to their deaths with their alluring beauty and magic filled song.

Then, the missing melody drifts forth from the waves, far off and undefined. It's not coming from the merwoman with Bluff. There must be more.

Rosemera takes slow steps back, staring at the two figures at the front of the ship. She removes a dagger from her belt, exposing a rusted blade. Her jaw is tight, her lips trembling. The men below clutch their ears at a new sound escaping the siren's lips—a call, high-pitched and creeping.

Across the ship, mouths hang open as several sets of shimmering hands clamp onto the railing. Followed by forearms, and soaking wet heads of shining hair.

I jump away from the edge of the ship, gasping as more slink aboard near me, some more human than others. A red haired, black-eyed siren creeps towards me with unnatural movement. Her bottom half is a slimy, scaly tail which drags behind her as she pulls herself forward with her arms.

Another more human looking than the rest is able to walk, using two leg-like appendages.

Rosemera gasps, cowering against the helm. I step back, away from the coming creatures, but I force my neck straight, keeping my head up as the beautiful sharp-toothed creature comes closer.

A shaky breath leaves me. I suck in another, mind racing, unsure what I'm supposed to do. Run? Hide? Stand my ground?

Her cheeks rise, lips spreading over her fangs in a strange smile. "I fooound her," she says in a hiss.

The hair on my arms rises.

"There she is," another says, slinking in my direction. Suddenly a dozen sets of unnatural eyes shift towards me.

In only moments, they surround me and my back is pressed against the ship's giant mast.

My gaze jumps to Rosemera, who doesn't try to hide her horror and inches herself away from the growing crowd of deadly sirens.

The ship has stopped dead in the water. I freeze where I stand.

One reaches a webbed, clawed hand out to me, and I wince. She strokes my blonde hair.

"Very pretty."

"Very pretty, indeed," another agrees.

"What do you want?" I ask with a shaking voice, eyes still closed. The less I see, the less I fear.

Somehow these creatures have something to do with Bluff.

A slimy hand slides down my forearm, then grips it tightly. "We have something to show you," she says in a whisper, and this time the voice doesn't sound so inhuman. It's smooth and calm.

Alluring.

"Come with us," she whispers again. Deep within my bones, a tiny thread of longing pulls me forward.

I open my eyes, and the sight makes me jump—fangs dripping with green slime. "No!" I say, suddenly. They all hiss.

"No, I don't want to," I say.

The red-haired creature's expression turns from soft and sweet to angry. I've spurned them. The hand on my arm tightens, squeezing so hard it hurts.

I pull back, though that makes it sting even worse. "Let GO!" I say with a voice so strong and loud it surprises even myself.

The pressure on my arm vanishes, and the creatures jump back, hissing and squealing. Several of them leap into the sea, but a few remain, standing their ground.

"Leave," I say firmly, wondering if that's all it takes—just a strong will against them.

The redhead's eyes narrow, and she says, "We'll find you again, little one." Then one by one, they leap back into the sea, leaving me breathless.

I search the deck and notice a pile of cowering men watching me in awe. Then I see Bluff, still at the bow of the ship. A siren twice the size of the others stands over him and smiles in a way that causes a shiver to run down my spine.

A salty sea breeze rushes through my hair as I hurry forward, unsure if Bluff is in trouble, or if he *is* the trouble.

Perhaps he called them. Maybe that was the plan to start. Perhaps I was intended to be some kind of siren sacrifice.

I stop a few feet short of the two, heart pounding, head nearly spinning. I try to channel the power I just felt when I forced the sirens to leave with only my words, to remember that I'm not powerless, at least not right now.

"Hello there," the large merwoman says.

I swallow and look to Bluff, whose face shows only intense fear. It is easily the strongest emotion I've seen from him.

I don't speak, and after several long moments, Bluff turns back to the siren. "I'm taking her away from the sea. Stede won't get his hands on her."

The siren smiles again. "You think that's all it will take to avoid fulfilling the prophecy?"

Bluff clenches his jaw.

"You're already falling. Can't you see it?"

"Leave, now," Bluff says firmly. She lets out a chuckle.

"I can already feel it—the shift happening inside of you. You may not be able to get her off this ship fast enough." She winks.

Every muscle in Bluff's body clenches, like her words cause him physical pain. I don't know what the prophecy is, or why it would have anything to do with me.

"She'd make a pretty siren, don't you think?" The giant merwoman's shoulders shift like she's going to approach me. I step back, all power I thought I had fading under a fresh wave of panic.

Bluff slams his hand down onto the ship's railing, blocking her path. The siren gives him an amused look. Then she leans in. "I'll see you soon, my boy," she whispers. Then she, too, leaps back into the ocean, and the green light fades away, leaving only a calm blue sea.

Bluff

Whitley stares at the water as the glowing bubbles disappear. Her dumfounded expression softens.

I don't blame her for her inability to comprehend what she just witnessed. There's too much she doesn't know, things she never will if I have anything to do with it.

The ship sways with the waves, quickly picking up speed once again. Finally, she snaps her gaze from the ocean and latches it onto me. I resist the urge to wince.

"What in the world was that?"

"Sirens," I say with a shrug.

"That's not what I mean." She swipes a strand of sticky hair from her forehead.

Her expression is hard to read. Panic, confusion, awe, determination, and others I can't name swirl in her eyes. I rock back on my heels, unsure how to respond. I act casual, as usual—shoulders relaxed, hands in my pockets, expression blank.

The less she knows the better, and she's already proved herself smarter than I gave her credit for.

"Who are they to you?" she asks, and I find myself having a hard time tearing my gaze from her crystal blue eyes.

I open my mouth but pause, unsure how to explain. I could go the ignorant route and tell her there is no connection, but there's no way she'd believe it. I could tell her the truth and hope she trusts me more, but then who in their right might would ever trust the son of the Siren Queen? No matter how much I tell her I hate sirens. My best bet is something in between, except I'm not really sure I've got a story for that just yet.

"That's hard to explain," I start. My eyes jump to the figure walking up behind Whitley, and my breath catches, my mind still on my monstrous family, but then I realize it's a stunned Rosemera and my shoulders relax.

"Hey," I say casually. "Everything okay?"

She nods, though her face is still a little pale. "Perhaps I should be asking you that?"

I give her a flat grin. "We're alive."

She nods. "Always a good thing when sirens are involved."

"Is it a... common occurrence?" Whitley asks, stepping forward, her arms crossed and her expression determined. She wants answers. Answers she will not get.

Rosemera, wisely, pauses and gives me a look.

"Happens on occasion," I say. "Supernaturals draw other supernaturals, unfortunately." That's about as good of an explanation as I can give.

"So they did come because of you." Her eyes search my face.

Her expression and body language tells me she's certainly suspicious of something, but what is going through her mind? Does she suspect my relationship with the sirens? Does she think I have some sort of... alliance with them?

"In a way."

Rosemera's eyebrows shoot up, and I frown. She might not be talking, but she's giving Whitley plenty to read into.

"Did you call them?"

"No!" I say too loudly. "Of every person on this ship, I hate coming face to face with a siren the most." I shiver.

"I might give you a run for your money on that one, mate," Rosemera says under her breath. I notice her hands still shaking insider her pants pockets.

"You might think so, but you're wrong," I say firmly. It's true. They might not harm me physically, but they know exactly how to hurt me without leaving marks.

Whitley watches Rosemera's shaking hands closely. "I thought sirens only affected men?"

I let out a breath I hadn't realized I was holding, relieved to have the attention off of me and my connection to those evil things. This topic is much safer. Some women are unaffected by sirens alluring nature, but not all.

Rosemera and I shake our heads together. "Women can also be seduced by sirens," I say.

"And we have another risk..." she says, and my eyes shoot to Rosemera, face full of panic.

"What?" Whitley asks quickly. "What other risk?"

Damn it, Rose. "They'll try to drown you," I say quickly.

"Yeah," Rose agrees. "Their magic can—"

"Sirens are violent and mysterious. Never trust one, okay?" I say pointedly, ignoring the glare from Rosemera. Whitley doesn't need to know all the lore. Not now.

"They tried that before?" Whitley asks. "Have they hurt you?" Her voice is suddenly low. I watch as her blue eyes turn lighter, her whole expression softer.

"Not today," Rose whispers. "Today, it was you I was concerned for. I honestly don't know how you made it out alive."

Whitley blinks rapidly, her face pale.

Wait... what happened? "What do you mean?"

"They had her surrounded." Rosemera's hands run through her hair. "At least a dozen of them. Then all of a sudden they leapt back into the ocean."

I swallow a lump in my throat. What in the world does this mean? Whitley stares at the damp wood planks below her new boots. "What happened?" I ask her this time.

She looks up, her eyes big, expression unreadable.

"I don't know. It happened just like she said. They were all around me. One of them grabbed my arm and tried to pull me towards the sea, but then..."

I hold a breath. Whitley stops, and I realize I'm leaning onto my toes. "Then what?"

Her eyes dart around as she clearly considers her words carefully. "I pulled back, then they left but said they'd see me again."

I rub my hand over my face.

"Why? Is that bad?"

"Yes," Rosemera whispers. Her eyes dart to me now—a silent question she knows better than to voice. *Why?*

Sirens enjoy messing with people in any way they can, but they rarely target one person in particular. They too know of the prophecy which makes me think...

Whitley searches my face, her fear now obvious. I turn to Rosemera. "She can't be left alone. Not until we reach port, which we need to do as quickly as possible. So long as she's at sea..."

Rosemera nods and hurries away to relay the message to her father. Getting to New York immediately has never been more important. I knew Whitley would be a sought-after commodity, but if sirens want her too, this game just got a whole lot bigger.

Whitley reaches out to grab my forearm. The touch of her fingertips on my skin sends sparks through every limb.

"What does it mean? They want me in particular? Why?"

I wrinkle my nose, pulling my arm back. "Hard to know for sure, but I don't intend to find out." I have plenty of ideas, but none I'm willing to voice aloud.

She pulls her hand away, her jaw clenched, her eyes leaving mine. My stomach churns with guilt. She knows I'm lying to her. Well, not lying, just withholding the full truth.

I hate that I care. I'm not supposed to.

I can already feel it—the shift happening inside of you.

I retreat back to the main deck to check on the crew. Whitley's footsteps tap behind me. At least she's smart enough to follow wherever I go. I don't have the strength to be a nanny, but this is also imperative. The sirens cannot get their hands on her, no matter what.

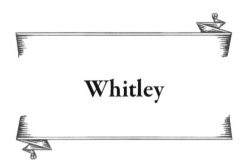

Whitley

I follow Bluff as he briskly crosses the ship and heads toward the main deck where most of the crew are gathered. They chatter excitedly, but I also detect a tremor in some of their voices.

"Did you see that one's eyes? Prettier than the English girl, I swear."

A man shorter than I am with a bald head hops onto his toes. "The redhead touched me! Left a mark too!" His voice is high pitched with excitement as he runs his dirty plump fingers over his arm where a portion of his skin is shiny red and bubbling like he'd been burned.

I shiver.

He liked seeing the sirens despite their touch *burning* him. The others are no different. Each man is enraptured by the encounter.

"Barns, you need go get that wrapped," Bluff announces, grabbing the short man's arm. "Chuck, you have ointment, aye?"

A man with curly hair, speckled with grey, and one pale eye steps forward. He grabs the short man and pulls him along. Barns looks back and gives the crew a cheesy smile. They whistle in response.

Strange, strange men.

"Look!" another pirate hollers, causing them all the jump. "There's a siren still aboard. There! There she is." I wince as the man points right into my face. His finger smells oddly of fish.

All the men chuckle, smacking each other on the back.

"Don't do that!" a large pirate with tattoos all over his whole body yells, his eyes wide with fear.

The crew chuckles heartily, and one holds out a glass bottle. He doesn't smile but accepts the beverage nonetheless. Across from him is a younger pirate with dark green eyes, and though he could certainly use a bath, he's probably the most attractive pirate I've seen yet.

Besides Bluff. But I have a hard time putting Bluff in the same category as these men. He's cleaner, his language is much better, and he's so much less crude.

But he *is* a pirate. I need to remember that.

Because even though he's standoffish around me —and is most certainly harboring immense secrets—sometimes the way he looks at me causes a stir deep in my chest.

I cannot trust him. No matter how he makes me feel.

"Back to work, boys!" Bluff shouts over the jubilation. "We have a heading, and we're getting behind."

A man with blond hair and a straw between his teeth pushes the bottle into Bluff's chest with a challenging glare.

"I'll drink, only if you hoist the main stay," Bluff responds, his lips spread into a mischievous grin that make my stomach flip.

"You drink first. Then we work."

Bluff narrows his eyes, but there's a hint of amusement there. I forget these men are like family. He tilts the bottle straight up and lets the brown liquid drain down his throat. He attempts to hide his reaction to the harsh rum, but I notice the awkward arch in his back as he swallows and the quick wrinkle of his nose as he finishes.

Several of the men grab ropes, and one climbs a ladder on a huge pole in the middle of the ship. I have no idea what they're actually doing, but I do find it fascinating to watch as they work.

One pirate with a scar across his chin takes a step toward me. "I'll work when she drinks."

I take a step back, fear swirling in my chest, but then I notice the twinkle in his eye as well and I set a determined gaze. I don't want to be the damsel in distress. I don't want to be just some prissy lass to these men.

It might be foolish to care what a bunch of pirates, whose paths I will certainly never cross again, think about me, but I do. I want to be the girl I once was. I want to make that barefoot, mud-caked tomboy proud. Show her that I haven't lost all of what I once was.

Bluff holds the bottle out to me, the smirk back on his face, his grey eyes glistening with amusement. I love that expression. I wish I could capture it in a painting or sear the image into my brain to retrieve whenever I need a kick in the pants.

The look in his eyes tells me he doesn't think I'll do it. And that's the exact reason I will.

I take the bottle and, without hesitation, lift it to my lips and let the cool liquid enter my mouth.

Bitter. Sour. Rotten. That's the taste of this rum. I grimace and swallow. *Blast* does it burn all the way down.

"Ack!" I can't help but shout and stick my tongue out to the salty air as soon as it's rum-free. I jump up and land on one foot like somehow that will help rid my body of the taste.

I'm impressed Bluff is able to hide his reaction as much as he does.

The crowd laughs heartily, even Bluff. And there is that look again—the shine in his eye that I can't help but feel like is only for me.

I hold the bottle back out to Bluff. "Keep it," he says with a smile. "Though we're making good time, we still have a whole day's sailing ahead. Might as well make the most of it."

BLUFF AND I SPEND ANOTHER awkward night sleeping beside one another but never touching. He shifts periodically, tense like he's afraid of even brushing against me. Does he think I carry the plague?

The rocking of the ship lulls me into a fitful sleep. I dream of New York and Jeb and ball gowns. It's the first nightmare I've had since I boarded this ship.

IN THE MORNING, BLUFF wakes me gently, reminding me we need to stay together. I bite my lip as I consider the reason but make no comment or complaint.

Sirens who have a hankering to drown me. *Wonderful*.

I find a spot on the stairs leading to the helm with a comfortable vantage of the few working sailors. The pirate with a tattooed face walks by, placing a new bottle of brown liquid into my hand. He retreats wordlessly, a simple smirk on his lips. I hold the bottle as I watch the crew work, all muscles and grime.

The sea rocks the ship smoothly back and forth. The wood creaks. Salty air brushes through my hair. Taming my locks will be next to impossible when the time comes, but that's a problem for another day. I sit like that for hours, watching them work until eventually more of the crew appears on deck, their bodies sluggish.

These are the men who drank too much the night before, I suspect. They begin work, and the others head below. They come back several minutes later carrying wooden crates. They walk right by me without a word, setting the crates down and then coming back with barrels, a cup, and a set of dice. A dark-skinned pirate cracks open one of the crates with his bare hands and pulls out more bottles of brown liquid. Then three of them surround the other, sitting on the crates and begin to roll the dice.

I watch, trying to understand the game.

"Want to play?"

I look up at Bluff beside me.

I smile but shake my head. "I like watching."

"Of course."

I don't ask what that means.

"Drinking much?" he asks.

I look down at the unopened bottle. I pull at the cork, surprised when it makes a popping noise and comes loose in my hand. I take a deep swig of the disgusting liquid. Immediately my head spins. I shake it off and hand it to Bluff to drink the remainder of the rum.

"Not bad, huh?" He smiles after a quick pucker.

I smirk back. "Not bad at all. Is that it, for your work? You're all done?"

"For now. The afternoons leave a little free time for the crew. Since we'll be making port tomorrow, the men will be less intent on rationing supplies. Makes for a happy day."

"So this will be my last day on the ship."

"Thank God."

I wrinkle my nose and pull the bottle from Bluff's fingers, taking another sip of rum. "You're eager to get me off this ship, aren't you?"

His smile fades. "Yes. Yes, I am. But believe me, it's better for all of us that you're off the sea."

I nod, remembering the sirens. Captain Stede. Remembering how much Bluff is still hiding from me.

"Sure you don't want to play?" he asks. "Don't want you to regret missing an opportunity you'll regret later."

I smile. "I'm sure it's fun. But it's not an experience I'll regret missing."

He nods. "So what is?"

I look around, from the mildewed planks over to the door to the cargo deck, and consider asking to see below. But then I look up at the sails. Ropes hang intricately, crisscrossing all across the ship, and the masts shoot up straight into the sky. All the way up, at the top of the tallest mast is a small wooden platform. A pirate stands at the top, looking out over the sea.

"I want to see that." I point up to the crow's nest.

His eyebrows rise. "Not a bad choice." He smiles, the look in his eyes hitting me in the chest again, causing my heart to beat faster. "But the boys will be disappointed you don't want to play with them."

"Be sure to pass along my deepest regrets."

He smirks and nods. "Allow me to make a few arrangements. Get us something to eat and I'll take you up in a few hours."

I bite my lip as I watch him walk away, completely unsure what I am getting myself into.

Bluff

"You must go first."

The look on Whitley's face is determined and feisty. I try to hide that I actually like it. Still, there is a trace of fear in her eyes.

She takes a long look up at the ladder leading to the crow's nest.

"This was your request. I'm not making you go."

She turns back to me. "But why must I go first?"

I smirk, passing over so many wonderful comebacks.

"I still remember what you did as we were climbing from that window," she says.

"While I was saving your life from a pirate crew that would have dismembered you? I was such a scoundrel, I know."

"Yes, you saved me. But you didn't need to look up my skirts while you did it." She puts her hands on her hips. Her face shows no sign of amusement, but her eyes... blue like the sea, and glistening with the truth she's trying so hard to hide.

I lean in closer, "Are you telling me you didn't like it?" I whisper.

She jumps backs in such dramatic shock. So obviously fake.

She may not have liked that I teased her about looking up her skirt, but she did like what came after. My bare hands on her legs, her body pressed against mine...

"I promise not to look, all right? But you need to go first or risk falling to your death."

"You think I can't climb on my own?"

I purse my lips. Perhaps she could have the nerve. She's surprised me in the past. "You don't have the hands or feet for it. Your body is just not used to that kind of climb. Wet wood and rope are not easy for anyone, let alone a girl who has never touched rope in her life."

Her eyes narrow. "I've touched rope," she says, quiet and pouty.

"When?" I pause. "Besides the day I saved you."

She purses her lips. "I still don't trust you."

"Good. You're learning. Now start climbing."

She huffs at me and pauses for another moment before determination clouds her eyes. "Fine." She pulls up the outer layer of her dress and wraps the inside cloth around her thigh, tying it in an awkward knot between her legs.

"Would you like help with that?" I smirk.

"You hush."

I watch as she works to turn her dress into a pair of very strange looking pants, amused all the while.

"Ready yet?" I ask finally.

She doesn't give me a response, just indignantly turns to face the ladder and begins a quick climb.

I'm surprised at how strongly she starts out, making her way half way up the mast in only a few moments. Then she slows, and the tremble in her fingers begins to show.

"Just keep going. Don't stop. We're almost there."

Her movements are slow, but she keeps trudging. One step at a time. The salty water spray makes way to a cold sprinkle of rain.

Whitley's toe slips, and she lets out a small cry. Without thinking, I toss my hand up to her waist to steady her. "You're all right."

Now she stops. Her head bowed, tangled hair in her face.

I take a few steps up, so that my hands are grabbing the rope around her waist, my chest against her back and lips at her ear. "Whitley," I say softly. "You're doing wonderfully. Just a few more steps to go."

Slight fib. She has a dozen pieces of wobbly rope steps to climb before it's over, but she's nearly two thirds of the way. Easier up than down, at this point.

"I just need a second," she says between heavy breaths.

"You're stronger than I ever gave you credit for, Whitley. I think you might be stronger than even you know."

She lifts her head and reaches for the next piece of rope. Her climb is steady and strong now, her feet moving slowly, but firm. Determined.

I follow along, as closely as I can manage without risking tripping her.

She pulls herself up onto the base of the crow's nest with one fluid motion, and in an instant, I've joined her.

On her knees, she presses her forehead onto the damp wooden planks as she heaves in huge breaths.

"You're amazing, Whitley," I say, without considering the words.

She looks up at me, her eyes intense. "What is amazing about that? You all do this daily, in just moments."

I nod. "Yes. But we've been doing it since we were children. And our first time was certainly not with the ship at full speed ahead, at night or while it's raining." The last two are slight exaggerations. The rain is more of a sprinkle, and the sky is just now fading into a deep blue, daylight diminishing with each passing moment. But the point remains—this was not an ideal situation for a first climb and yet she succeeded.

She sits up and leans back on the wooden railing, eyes cast to the sky as her breathing evens out. "I still wish I hadn't needed your help."

"You didn't."

She meets my eye.

"What did I do? Tell you to keep going. That's it. You wouldn't have fallen without me there. You would have done just fine."

Her eyes are soft as she considers this. "You did help me though."

"There's a difference between someone helping, and you needing help. You didn't require me. You did it all on your own. I just reminded you that you could do it."

She takes in one long breath and lets it out slowly. "Thank you," she whispers.

I smile and pull a full bottle of rum from my belt and hold it out to her.

Her eyebrows rise. "Is that really a good idea? Going back down while drunk seems unwise."

"We're not going back down. Not tonight, anyway."

Her eyebrows furrow. "We're staying up here all night?"

I smirk. The sky is already dim. The stars will be out as soon as these nasty clouds dissipate. Luckily the weather has warmed up since our siren friends left, and there are clear skies ahead. Even so, the wind is fierce up here. "We took the night lookout duty."

She just blinks.

"So drink up. It'll keep you warm."

She pulls the bottle from my hand and takes a swig. No, not even a swig. She chugs, for a full few seconds.

Okay, then.

I follow suit, and it's not long until the bottle is empty.

Once our drinking binge is over, Whitley stands to take in the view. The clouds are thinning now, exposing the shining moon lighting the sea around us. I stand beside her and try to take in the view like it's the first time.

She sucks in a breath at the beauty, the magnitude of what's around us. "How is it so big?" she whispers.

I shrug. Waves wash over waves, crashing and pulling and swirling like some intoxicating dance. From up here, you can appreciate how small the ship is compared to the ocean's behemoth size.

"The sea isn't really that big. We're just small."

She doesn't respond to that, just watches the water and the lights as we pass them. She looks up to the sky. As more and more stars are exposed, the darkness of night grows deeper.

"Is that the shore?" Whitley points to a few little lights in the distance to our left.

"Yes, we're only sailing a few miles off the coast."

"And we'll reach New York tomorrow," she says flatly.

"Yes," I whisper for the first time letting the desperation leak into my voice. I'm dreading tomorrow as much as I'm looking forward to it.

Because tomorrow Whitley will be gone. Tomorrow, she'll be with her fiancé. Safe in her ivory tower.

Is she thinking about him now?

Does she love him? Does she long for him?

They're things I shouldn't think, shouldn't care to even consider. But as the liquor warms my veins. I can't control where my mind wonders.

Including wondering what Whitley would look like beneath her dress. Wondering what it would feel like to have *her* hands against *my* body. For her to want me back.

She asked if drinking rum up here was a good idea. The answer, I realize now, should have been no. But not because of safety. But for the sake of self-control.

My stomach twists as I finally think the words: *I want her.*

My arms ache to wrap around her. My fingers long to pull her face to mine. My lips groan to touch hers.

I can't deny it any longer— that there must have been something to the prophecy.

This is the girl I'm supposed to fall in love with.

And it just makes her that much more dangerous, because that's only the start of a very bad, very ugly path for both of us. The prophecy cannot come true.

Whitley turns to me, her eyes blazing. The blue in her eyes dances against the starlight like the waves below. I'm being pulled in.

I turn away, quickly and hide the wince of pain as I do.

I can practically feel her disappointment as her shoulders sag and she turns back to the sea, but I thank the heavens when she doesn't push. She doesn't try to get my attention again.

Because I don't know if I could resist a second time.

I pull out an old woolen blanket and offer it to her. We sit on the floor of the crow's nest, both of our shoulders wrapped in the blanket, but no words pass between us.

Good, because I don't know what I would say to her. Every ounce of my energy is devoted to resisting the urge to kiss her.

She shivers, so I allow my arm to very carefully wrap itself around her waist. She leans her head into the crook of my neck.

The warm feeling stirring in my chest has nothing to do with the rum, I realize.

As she sits safely in my warm embrace, eyes drifting shut, my mind spins in the silence. I want to rouse her, to pull her closer, to tell her how much I want her. Because I can feel how much she wants me too... but she won't act on it.

So I use that to my advantage. I work to control my body and the rum and my heart all at the same time, and my mind manages to hatch a plan. Whitley's one thing she'd regret not experiencing was the crow's nest. Mine is *her*.

But that's dangerous, because one moment, one kiss, letting go just once, could lead to so much more. What if she wants more? What if she wants me the way I want her? Could I let her go then? Would she refuse to marry Jeb?

Part of me hopes that she would. The other won't even consider. Because that would be disastrous.

Perhaps, though, there's a way to do it safely. To feel the kind of desire that leads to love, without allowing myself to actually follow it through.

It's enough to convince that longing, the pull within me, to settle. Just a few more hours and it will be safe to give in to the desire. To kiss her, just once before she leaves the sea, and me, forever.

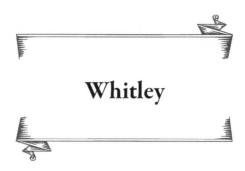

Whitley

Harsh and discomforting sounds rouse me from an awkward sleep: men barking out orders, sea gulls squawking above, and a distant fog horn.

My neck is stiff as I pull my body out of its weird co-cooned position on the hard, wooden floor. My eyes are dry and resist opening to the bright sun beating down on me.

I look around, realizing several things at once. I'm still in the crow's nest. We are in the process of docking, which means we made it to New York. Bluff is not here.

After a moment to collect my thoughts, I begin my climb down the ladder to the main deck to seek out Bluff. I clench my jaw at the thought, because I must say goodbye. It's time for me to go and I'm not certain I want to.

Back on the main deck there are a few pirates rushing around here or there. I notice a new tailored jacket or a fresh shave on a few of the pirates bustling to get us docked. The most marked men—like the one they call Ink with tattoos over every inch, or Lucky Seven who's missing several fingers—have made themselves scarce.

Bluff is also nowhere to be seen, however. I'm at a loss as to where I'd find him. Standing here awkwardly doesn't seem a good plan, so I settle for a trip into the captain's quarters.

Tapping my knuckles on the solid wooden door, my heart throbs. Palms sweating. This should be the easy part. It's not. Preparing to leave this ship, where I am realistically unsafe and unsure, feels very much like losing a piece of myself. A piece of my freedom.

"Come in," a gentle voice calls.

I push the door open and blink back the sight of a very beautiful and put together Rosemera. "Wow," I say. "You look wonderful."

She beams. Her hair is pinned back under a beige bonnet and red satin dress hugs her curves. "Thank you. This port is fairly perilous, so I must play the part. My other option is to dress as a sailor boy, but this is infinitely more fun."

"Where did you get them? The clothes?"

"Oh, I stockpile lovely clothing. The men would simply throw them out, but I steal and save them." She winks.

"You look much better than I do," I tell her with a smile, noting my rat's nest of hair.

"Oh! Here, I have just the thing."

She rummages in a bin in the corner and comes out with another bonnet. "Hide it. No one will know."

"That's wonderful!"

She helps me wrap my hair up beneath the bonnet and tie it on.

"There. Much better." She smiles. "Now perhaps fix the lump under that skirt of yours."

I blink and look down. I laugh as I realize the knot I tied in my chemise pushes the outside layer out in a strange way. Awkwardly, I manage to pull the knot undone and brush the skirt down.

"Very good." She winks again. "I must go and make nice with the port authorities. We were able to send off a message to your fiancé, by the way. We were caught a bit by surprise as we entered the bay with a patrol ship. Bluff aided in smoothing that situation over, and they sent on a message. It shouldn't be long after docking that you'll be taken care of."

I slept through all that? "Thank you," I manage through a dry throat. "Where is he now? Bluff?"

"I'm not sure," she says, her smile fading. "I'll send him to you if I pass him."

I nod but say nothing more. She sweeps from the room with a surprising grace, and I'm left there alone, head spinning.

Jeb will be here soon. Sooner than I thought. I peer out the window, unready to face the next chapter of my journey. It's only a few moments later that the door swings open again.

I spin to meet a familiar boy with large hands, broad shoulders, and dark but well-kept hair.

"Jeb?" I ask. Rosemera just said it wouldn't be long, but this quickly? How? Was he already at the port on some business?

My mind spins.

I should be happy to see him. It's been over a week now, since I was pulled from my cozy future with this boy. He's the safety I've been working towards. And yet, my whole body goes cold at the sight of him.

I don't have time to consider these feelings, because before I can even get another word out, he approaches. I gasp and step away until my back is pressed against the wall, and his chest is a mere breadth from mine.

He stops, heavy breaths pressing on me. The closeness has air escaping my lungs.

I've never kissed Jeb. He's supposed to be my husband, and I knew that would be part of the deal, and I've even thought about it before. But right now, it's not Jeb's lips I want.

"I've missed you," he says breathlessly. Intense expression I've never heard from him. Jeb is not very emotional. He's kind but stiff. This is... different.

Passion. Desire. Desperation. It radiates off of him.

My mind spins so fast I feel dizzy. He doesn't move in to kiss me—yet. There's a sizzle in the air around him. A spark.

And I realize—this isn't Jeb.

I don't know what it means. Why Bluff would come to me as Jeb? Perhaps to save my reputation now that we're in a place where that matters? But in that instant, I do not care. He's here, and I want him. I'm not supposed to, and I'm terrified that even one word would rip the moment from me.

So before that can happen, I close the distance between us, pressing my lips against his fiercely. He groans roughly and opens his mouth to deepen our kiss. His tongue reaches mine, and my hand finds his hair, pulling him in tighter.

I'm so lost in the moment that when he finally pulls away and I open my eyes, I'm shocked that it's Jeb's body in front of me. Not Bluff's.

I don't for a second doubt who it is beneath the lie of the skin and clothing, but it's still a foreign sight.

There is pain in his eyes as he looks into mine before fleeing from the room. "My men will be here to gather your things and take you home," he says, just as he pulls the door closed behind him.

"Wait," I stammer out, rushing after him.

Does he think I don't know? My chest tightens. Does he think that desire, was for Jeb, not him?

Was it some kind of test?

And did I pass or fail?

A sailor in clean blue clothes with golden buttons stands just outside the door as I fling it open. I stop, breathing heavy. I move around him, searching the ship for any sight of him.

Where did you go? I don't dare ask aloud, but my heart screams for him.

"Come, miss. We have a carriage ready for you," the sailor says, motioning towards the dock and street beyond. I blink, spying a clean carriage with a footman standing at the ready to sweep me away from this dirty ship and toward my ivory tower and clean future in downtown, high society Manhattan.

No. No I'm not ready yet. I have to talk to him. *At least let me say a proper goodbye,* I silently beg. "Not yet," I say boldly.

His eyebrows pull down.

I pause. "I... must take a moment to thank my rescuers."

"Of course," he says flatly. "They let you stay in the captain's quarters, did they? That's quite gracious of them. Though fortunate, I suppose— this lot doesn't seem the most above-board crew. For a lady to sail on this ship..." He shakes his head.

"Beggars can't be choosers, sir," I say, keeping my head up. "They did save me."

He nods. "We'd heard about the pirate raid. A shame. For a moment, when this ship docked, we'd thought they were pirates themselves, here to ransom you. Of course, that would have been foolish. No ship would escape this harbor once accused of crimes as heinous as pirating or kidnapping."

I blink, realizing the risk the crew must have taken to get me here. If the New York officers realize they're pirates, it's their necks on the line. Literally.

"A disorderly lot as I've ever seen, but when they offered you up, safe and uninjured, with no request for money at all... well, we didn't look much further into the matter."

There is still no sign of Bluff anywhere. Did he flee the ship? Change into another form so I wouldn't find him? The captain and Rosemera stand at the helm, chatting with a set of sailors and an officer. Captain Taj has conveniently lost a few piercings and is dressed in a tailored jacket with golden buttons. He's still intimidating in appearance, but less so with the lovely Rosemera laughing delightedly beside him.

"You are alright, miss, aren't you?" the sailor leans in to whisper in my ear.

"Yes. Yes, of course. It wasn't the most luxurious trip of my time, but I was treated well enough."

He gives a sharp nod. "Good, good."

Rosemera smiles jovially as I join her at the helm.

"Here comes our welcomed guest now!" she says with a fake British accent. I smile in return.

"Thank you so much, Lady Rose," I say, going along with her ruse. Then I pull her in and whisper in her ear. "Where is Bluff?"

Her face folds into a quick grimace. "Gone. And you should be on your way, miss. We mustn't linger."

There is much beneath her words. Either Bluff doesn't want to see me, or they all realize I shouldn't be seen with him. The gossip would be rampant if I were to be seen with an attractive sailor boy, even just to give him a farewell. I must get on with my new... old... life.

"Will you tell him..."

She raises her eyebrows.

"Goodbye."

Rosemera nods slowly, a sad look crossing her face. "Perhaps we'll see each other again."

My heart throbs, beating faster. "I would be happy to have you at any of my balls. You're welcome any time," I say with a gentle squeeze of her arm. It sounds so vain to say, but it's true.

"Perhaps, one day." She winks at me, a smile spreading across her face that I recognize as sincere.

"Thank you for everything." I give her one small curtsy and then turn back towards my sailor escort.

I continue my search for Bluff as I exit the ship across the shaky plank and onto the entirely too solid and still dock. If he's here, he's not in his own skin. I search for the feeling, the look in his eyes I recognize as him, but see only dull expressions. Only emptiness.

And I know I must let go.

Bluff

I stand in the middle of the ship as we push off, undecided whether I want to be at the bow—watching the sea greet us, focused on the new adventure before me—or watching the city disappear.

I never said goodbye to her.

I'm such an idiot. The way she kissed *him*...

It was me, but she didn't know that. Couldn't have known. No, her fiancé comes to greet her, and she doesn't even hesitate. She kissed him the way I wished she would kiss me. I loved it, and I hated it.

It killed me, but I couldn't stop.

So, so stupid.

I press my eyes together. To think, for even a second, that Whitley cared about me. That's the whole point of the prophecy—I'd fall in love with her, and she'd use me. Control me.

You're letting her go? The wind wisps past my ear. Salty breath in my face.

"Yes," I answer without blinking.

A shimmering female form appears next to me, her webbed hands grasping the ship's rail. I don't turn to face my mother, but I can still tell she's smiling.

"Why are you here?" I ask, arms folded over my chest. Fists clenched.

"I had to be sure it was true. The girl, your girl..." She lets out an animalistic purr.

"She's not *mine*," I say through gritted teeth.

My mother's smile grows wider. "Oh no, she is. You're just too stubborn to realize it. And that will be your downfall."

"Whitley is gone. Away from the sea and away from Stede. Protected by her privilege and rich fiancé."

Glistening green-scaled fingers run down my forearm. "So naive," she whispers, her voice like the rush of the waves.

I pull my arm back to shake off her touch and then slam it into the railing. "Stop!" I shout. "Stop trying to make me doubt. Stop *messing* with me. Just because you lost."

She takes a step back, but doesn't stop smiling, exposing her sharp, inhuman teeth. "What makes you think I've lost?"

"You can't get to her now."

"A siren can no longer reach her, this is true." Her figure begins to fade, until it drifts off into the vapors of the wind and my heart picks up its beat.

"Wait," I say quickly. She gave up too easy. That's what has me shaking in my boots. She wouldn't admit defeat. She'd tell me she has sentries stationed at the docks, waiting for her. At the edge of every river that cocoons this island city. She'd tell me she'd pay someone to throw her into the sea. She'd come up with some far-fetched way to reach her. Instead, she just left.

My stomach is twisting in knots. Something isn't right.

The fact that she doesn't tell me she'll get to Whitley is what makes me think she will.

Another caress of wind blows over my cheek, enough to tell me she's still here. "What aren't you telling me?"

A chuckle drifts through my hair and then out to sea.

Sirens don't change. They're stubborn, not overly clever.

My head whips around, looking for a clue as to what was happening that I haven't yet seen. It would be here, some-where. I have to figure it out.

"Hey, Bluff!" Rosemera's voice calls down to me from above the sails. She'd already changed back into her pirate clothing and climbed up to the crow's nest to watch the city disappear from view.

My breathing grows heavy. "What?" I call.

"Any reason you can think Stede would be docking in New York?"

My whole world shifts, head spinning, don't even know where I am anymore, kind of—sunk.

Rosemera skips down the ropes until she's at my side in a matter of moments. "What?" she asks. "What is it?"

"No, no, no."

Rosemera grabs me by the arm with a tight grip. "Spit it out, Bluff. You're scaring me."

I force my eyes to focus on her face. "They're after Whit-ley."

There's a pause. Her face is blank as she processes. "Why would Stede be after Whitley?" Her voice is soft, but her face slowly morphs into an expression that would shake most men in their boots. "The whole time, we were running from him?"

I knew she'd be angry that I'd lied to her about the risk. "He shouldn't know. He's not supposed to know where she is."

"I thought she was going back to some fiancé? One that was supposed to keep her safe? Why would a pirate crew dock in a city like New York to get some random lass?"

"They wouldn't." I say, turning away, running my hands through my hair. It was less of a risk for *The Freedom* for several reasons. Captain Taj has several forged documents to aid his ability to pass under the radar. Plus, he has me, who can morph into anyone needed to ensure our story is believable. Lastly, we aren't planning anything nefarious. We're actually good guys, at the moment.

Stede has none of those things. How would he plan to get out of the harbor after kidnapping Whitley? I shake my head. This has to be bigger than I thought.

Shit.

Would Stede really risk this? Would this really be worth it? Prophecy or not, it's not enough. So much could go wrong. He could lose his crew, his ship, his life... in a dozen different ways. He would only do this if the bounty was big. Huge. Legendary.

A siren can no longer reach her, that's true.

If the sirens want her, they'll need help. A pirate is the only one they can actually trust. But a normal pirate, under normal circumstances, wouldn't be willing to align themselves with a siren. They wouldn't be that stupid.

What did they promise him?

Rosemera grabs my arm again, pulling me back to face her. "If you don't tell me what's going on, I swear I'll gut you and be done with it."

I take in a long deep breath. "Do you know of the prophecy?"

She tilts her head slightly.

"About me."

She takes in a long breath. "I've heard of one. Didn't think there was any merit to it."

"There is."

She bites her lip, staring out over the water, thinking it through. "Okay. It had something to do with a way to control you, the 'son of the sea.'"

I nod. "A few have come to believe Whitley is the subject of that prophecy. We don't know how or why, but the signs fit." Too many for comfort.

"So she... can control you?"

I shrug. "But if it's true and Stede gets a hold of her..."

"It's over for you."

The crew doesn't seem much bothered by our conversation or seeing Stede at port. A few whispered rumors float by, but the crew is too relieved to have escaped our risky endeavor without losing anything of worth. They continue their work, swigging rum as they go.

"Does it even make sense, though?" Rosemera whispers, looking back at the city skyline, growing smaller in the distance. "That he would risk everything just to control you? No offense, but that doesn't sound like a worthy enough prize."

"It's not." I pause. "There's more to this even I don't know. What I am sure of is that Whitley is the key to that prophecy and they're after her."

Maybe my powers are bigger and more important than I realized. Maybe there's something else I'm missing. Something big.

Rosemera is quiet for a long time, staring out at the sea.

Then, all of a sudden she comes to some silent conclusion and jumps into action. She rushes to the edge of ship, shouting several commands to the crew.

"What are you doing?" I ask, following her.

Without hesitation three of the crew pull over a longboat, ready to drop it into the rocking water below.

She turns to me, her eyes bright and eager. "All those questions, they don't matter. Stede is going after Whitley, you know that much."

I nod, clenching my jaw.

"So you're going after her. That's all there is to it."

I shake my head. "No, there is way more to it."

She turns to the crew and tells them to wait before lowering the boat to the water then she takes a step toward me. "Listen, I could list a hundred reasons why you can't stay here and just wait to find out what happens. The crew won't risk docking here again. It was a close enough call as it is. But you can. Get in this little row boat and go into that city. Make sure she's safe."

I take in a long breath. "I don't want to," I whisper.

Her face falls into something like sympathy. "Does that really matter? I know you care about her, Bluff. Whether you want to admit it or not. And even if you want to deny that all day, you can't let Stede get his hands on her. There is no other choice."

Anger and pain and fear swell in my chest. I don't want to see her again. I don't want to see her happy and in love with her stupid fiancé. But Rosemera is right.

"Wait, just a minute," Rosemera says and then sprints across the ship. Perhaps to update her father of my departure?

I wait patiently, taking the moment to think through what it would be like to just sail away. Forget the paddle boat, and big city. Just accept the sea that wants so badly to control my every move. Just let go.

I must shake my mind free of the gripping fantasy when Rosemera comes back, jogging and carrying a bag over her shoulder. "Come on," is all she says, lifting her leg over the railing as if she were the one climbing into the boat.

"What are you doing?"

"I can't let you go on your own, can I?"

"Um, yes. Yes, you can."

The captain comes walking up slowly, boots clunking over the wooden deck. I blink at everything happening. So fast.

"Bye, Papa," Rosemera says softly over the railing. No tears or even a hug. "I'll see you soon."

He smiles adoringly, then turns to me. "You joining her, lad? Or letting a lady do the hard work for ya?"

A few of the crew chuckle behind him.

I blink. "I can't take care of her. I'm in over my head as it is," I say quickly.

A larger smile spreads across his face. "I'm not hoping you'll take care of her, boy. I'm expecting she'll take care of you. You're gonna need it, from what I hear."

I cough out a breath. "I can't deny that."

"So, off you go."

I sigh, and then without another moment of thought I hop into the boat next to a beaming Rosemera, and we are slowly lowered away from the ship and into the dark harbor.

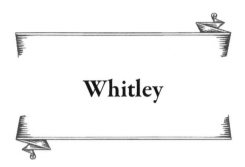

Whitley

I lay my head against Jeb's shoulder, cheek rubbing the stiff fabric of his navy blazer. I wrap my arms around him, sincerely relieved to have someone I trust near me.

But my heart is broken.

My closeness is out of desire to hide my sadness. Inside, my soul is shifting, twisting, and turning, unable to discover just how to be comfortable in a place that was once my sole comfort.

This huge building—cold and stiff but intricately decorated into a juxtaposition of classic and modern fashion—was the one place I imagined my life leading to something resembling happiness.

Now when I close my eyes, I picture the vast openness of the sea.

"Are you all right?" he whispers into my hair.

I know this much closeness makes him uncomfortable, but I refuse to pull away and show him the tears in my eyes. We barely touched for the entire duration of our courtship, and I could never quite figure out if it was due to fear of retribution—his mother was severe in her expectations of modesty and propriety—or if he was sincerely put off by intimacy all together.

That never really mattered though, because the value of our relationship was never in the physical, nor even in the romantic. We were friends. We confided in one another. I was a shield against his parents' harshness—they loved me and my father, though why was difficult to tell—and he was an escape, a way out.

My father's obsession with infiltrating high society led him to extreme measures on occasion, and I knew those measures would include me sooner or later. A pretty daughter was a huge asset. I would be married to someone of high standing. It didn't really matter who.

More than once he'd implied a desire for me to become *friendly* with Mr. Robinson, a man older than my father—and twice as cruel, if the rumors were true. And the expressions on his servants' faces told me they were.

More than once, I'd considered running away. When I turned ten, my father made enough money to buy a flat downtown and hired a maid who told me stories about girls living on the streets of New York, and they were not comforting tales. But even those threats were favorable to the threat of marriage to an awful man.

Then, when he learned my childhood friend, who I spent too much time 'rolling around in the mud' with, was the heir to his parent's old money and well-established estate, my father's focus shifted. And the moment his interest in courting me was established, all that stress fell away like dirt in a warm bath.

My father's countenance changed, for a time. He was... *proud*. He had tea in the Harrison's parlor, schmoozing Jeb's father, bonding over cigars and scotch, while Jeb and I played hide and seek and truth or dare in his massive home.

Just to have a future with someone I cared for, somewhere I felt comfortable—while still pleasing my father—was a dream I had thought lost to me.

That's why I loved Jeb. He was my hope.

But that was until I saw that there was so much more to life. So much more to this world.

And now I can't get it out of my head.

I finally loosen my grasp of Jeb's shoulders and he pulls away.

"Tell me what happened. I was very worried."

I swallow. "Father got in some trouble, I guess. He hastened us away to a town on the coast. But his trouble followed us and—"

"What kind of trouble was so terrible that he had to flee? We could have helped."

Jeb's father appears in the parlor doorway, clearing his throat as he approaches with slow quiet steps, his face flat. "No, we couldn't have."

Jeb whips around to face his father. "What do you mean? You knew?"

"It wasn't the kind of trouble that could be fixed with a good reputation, and we didn't have the money—"

"What do you mean? We have plenty of money."

"We have plenty for what we need, but you have no idea how much it would have taken to free that man from the hole he'd dug for himself. Not nearly enough to be worth—"

"It's all right, Mr. Harrison," I cut him off, knowing the rest of his sentence was not going to be kind to me, and that would only cause Jeb to defend me further, helping no one. I take in a long shaky breath. "It shouldn't have been your responsibility to fix his problems."

He looks down at his feet. "Yes."

"But did you know they were leaving? Or where they went?" Jeb asks with a raised voice.

"No. He'd been planning his contingency plan for a very long while, that much was clear. But he fled too suddenly to know much of anything. And by then, I didn't much care."

I wince, not liking the look on his face. Is he no longer interested in allowing me to marry his son?

Is that even what I want?

No. That was actually an easy answer. But even so, I'm not sure what my other choices are. Bluff and Rosemera are gone. I have no more allies.

If only I'd refused to leave so easily. If only I'd jumped into the sea with the sirens. I shiver at that thought. *All right, maybe nothing that extreme.*

"What does that mean? You didn't care about Whitley?"

"If her father was that much trouble... she wasn't worth crossing the mob."

Jeb clenches his fist, but I place a gentle hand on his forearm. "It's all right."

He turns to me. "How can it be?"

"Because he's right. My father made his bed, and getting involved would have only dragged you down too."

He shakes his head. "We could have come with you, then."

I shrug. "Perhaps. But it doesn't matter now. My father is gone. I don't know nor care where he is. I am here."

Jeb pinches the bridge of his nose.

"I vastly misjudged your father." I look up to see a kind smile on Mr. Harrison's face. "But apparently not so much with you." He was much softer than Mrs. Harrison, and I still worried about what her reaction would be.

"How?" Jeb asks, ignoring his father, looking me in the eye. "How did you get back? I heard something about a pirate ship?"

I smirk. "It's a long story."

"And you'll have a very long time to tell it," his father says, placing his hand firmly on Jeb's shoulder. "Let the girl rest and get cleaned up. She clearly needs it." He wrinkles his nose, and I almost laugh. "There is a ball two nights from now. You should both appear, show nothing is amiss. If you're going to continue your courtship, we'll need a good story about your absence and unconventional return. If indeed *The Spectator* decides to print the story, it will need to be well planned."

"*The Spectator*? Really?" I ask. Was I really that important to have drawn the interest of the upper-class gossip magazine?

Mr. Harrison nods. "So say the rumors."

Jeb takes in one long deep breath then turns to face his father. "Very well," he says quietly. He doesn't seem to have forgiven his father, but accepts his plan. I find it very forgiving, myself.

Now comes my biggest test.

Can I fit back in here? Jump back into high society life like I haven't tasted true freedom and life-changing passion?

My heart aches as I close my eyes, and I am met with the rock of a ship, the crash of the waves, and the gentle kiss of salty air.

Bluff

Rosemera slips through the alleys of the city like an experienced thief, skidding in and out of the shadows. I follow right behind her.

"This place is so big!" she whispers as we reach a busy intersection. The chattering of the crowds fills the air around us. "And crowded."

She lives for moments like this, I realize.

She and I have several things in common. We were born and raised on ships, and though we've each spent some time living on land, most of our lives have been given to the high seas. To her, that makes this a rare adventure. A new place to explore.

To me, it's an annoyance. I have no desire to be part of a place like this. Cities are all the same, full of high society asses who have way more than they need, and the poor, fighting for survival. Both are unpleasant things to witness.

"We should avoid busy places, at least until we get you a change of clothes," I tell her.

She looks down her body—doublet, leather vest and waist belt adorned with several obvious weapons. If only we'd have the forethought to change back into our traditional clothing before leaving the ship. "What's wrong with my clothes?" she asks.

I smile. "You look like a pirate. That's what's wrong. You'll stand out too much."

She crosses her arms. "And you?"

I chuckle and without breaking eye contact change my clothes to a dapper woolen suit and bow tie.

"Show off."

"If we can find a market, I can buy you some clothes."

We pass into another shadowed alley. The brick walls on both sides shoot so far up, I must shield my eyes from the sunlight to see the tops. At least five stories, these are behemoth buildings and the city is full of them. On the corner of one of the buildings, is a red design, nearly a foot in height.

Rosemera flies past the paint without a second glance, so I miss the opportunity to examine it. We simply keep rushing through the shaded alleys, travelling farther into the city.

"How do you think we'll find her fiancé?"

I swallow, ignoring the way my gut wrenches at the word. "We can kill two birds at the market. Get you some high-society clothing and hope for a few rumors. Shouldn't be too hard." She nods, walking slower now. "Any idea where the market is?"

"Nope."

She chuckles.

A figure stands at the edge of the alley and we both come to an abrupt stop.

Rosemera doesn't speak, but her hand drifts to her belt.

The man is large in stature but is too far away to tell much else. When he doesn't speak for several long moments, I decide to break the silence. "Hello there, fellow."

"Fellow?" He tilts his head, giving me an expression that tells me he thinks me a moron.

I shrug. Sounded good at the moment.

"You're in the wrong place, *fellow,*" he says with a curl of his lip as he approaches. I register the pistol in his hand only as he points it right at us.

Rosemera must notice it before I do, because before I can even speak out a warning, she shoves my body into the wall as a shot rings out, missing us both—barely.

Then she acts, running the last few feet to reach the man, and I leap after her. She knocks the gun from his hand, and he hollers, grabbing her by the hair. I grab my own pistol and shoot. He dodges it but loses his grip on Rosemera in the process. She swings out a leg, and I shove his body back, sending him flying to the hard ground. Rose jumps over him, slitting his throat before he utters another word.

She stands there, panting. "What the hell was that?" she asks.

"I suspect we just had our first run-in with the mob," I tell her. "We should leave before we meet more."

Footsteps echo down the alley, and we rush the other direction.

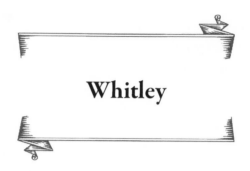

Whitley

My despair only grows as the salt is rinsed from my skin and my hair is untangled, washed and pinned to perfection. The pins pinch my hair, the laces of my corset pull my body into perfect form—because its natural state isn't good enough.

I stare in the mirror, realizing how much I hate everything I see.

I don't want this.

It's the thought I haven't been able to get out of my head the entire day. Every polite conversation I force my way through, I must fight the words from breaking free of the prison I've formed for my true self. Those walls are not near as strong as they once were.

None of this is any different than before. The fashion and snooty looks, the hidden motives and scrutiny. It's just, now, my soul has tasted freedom, and I cannot seem to tame the desire for more.

I'm barely here, as servants dote on me, as decorations are set and the music begins. As guests arrive and the polite questions, full of thinly veiled intentions, bombard me. As Jeb asks me to dance, his hand stiff in mine.

My mind is elsewhere.

"You still seem off."

"A little," I say lightly, looking past him at the intricate fake world they've created.

"Why won't you tell me what it is? What happened while you were gone?"

"It's nothing. Nothing happened, I just..." *am unhappy here.*

I still care for him, he's still the friend he always was. But now, he could never fully understand. If I told him how I continually dream of the sea. Of Bluff...

I shake off the thought.

He leans in, and whispers in my ear with a low serious voice, "If you continue to act strangely, people will talk. Mother says it's already questionable that you made it out of your situation... unscathed."

He leans back for a moment, eyes blank as we continue to move with the music. My mind is frozen, my heart still. My body simply following the motions.

Jeb finally meets my gaze with a soft expression. "You'd tell me, wouldn't you? If something *bad* happened? I wouldn't... It wouldn't change my mind."

I take in a deep breath. *But what if it's changed mine?*

"Jeb, why do you want me?" I blurt out. It wasn't something I ever questioned before. When this just seemed to make so much sense. But I get the feeling Jeb doesn't love me, not the way a husband would love a wife. Is he just being kind? Doing me a favor?

In truth, I find myself hoping for an excuse. I wish to let him go and find something else, anything else, to complete my life. I didn't even care if it led to ruin. Not anymore.

It's a stupid thought, because even suffocating in this world is better than the likely alternatives. I could be happy here, right?

I once would have been.

Still, I search for hope in his eyes. *Let me go*, I beg him.

"What?" he asks, eyes wide at my question. "You, we, I mean... it's always made sense."

I nod lightly. "It did. But—"

"Is it not what you want?" he asks suddenly, stopping even though the music doesn't and we're still in the middle of the dance floor.

I pull him back into motion, and he follows. "I don't know, it is. But—"

It isn't.

"You don't know."

I shake my head. "I don't know what I want, anymore."

He closes his eyes and clenches his jaw. Finally, the song fades to a close, and Jeb releases me. I follow the rules of conduct I've been trained for and walk politely back to the crowd, away from my suitor. His face is fallen the rest of the evening, and I can't help but feel like the worst human being on the planet.

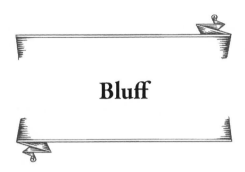

Bluff

My blood rushes cold, hands nearly shaking, as I walk through the massive oak doors and into the hideously decorated hall.

"Wow," Rosemera whispers beside me, blinking at the crystal chandelier which scatters light around the room.

I roll my eyes. The skin I'm wearing is heavier than I'm used to. He's tall, but not so much thin. I figured a little round about the belly was fitting for this lot.

It's an indulgent society, if I ever saw one.

"Remember, stay close, all right? Pretend not to speak English if anyone pries."

She gives me a smirk that tells me she has no intention of doing any such thing. I shake my head. She's only going to be a liability here. I should have insisted she wait outside, but heaven knows she would never have listened.

At least like this, she'll be nearby if I need to sweep her away.

Because Rosemera will never blend in here. Her skin is too dark, her nose too wide, and her speech too rough. No matter how well dressed and put together she is, she might as well have the word "foreigner" written on her forehead.

I hate this close-minded society.

I mentally chide myself for falling in with one of them. *What a fool.*

Rosemera presses into the crowd and I follow. Eyes already glance her way. Too many eyes.

Her dress is red, the light glinting off golden beads embroidered into the fabric. It's a bold choice, but I'm hoping that sells the idea that she's a rich foreigner, here as the guest of some highbrow moron.

A flash of blond hair and blue eyes distracts me just long enough for Rosemera to slip into the dense, well-dressed bodies and disappear.

"Dammit," I spit out from under my breath. A large woman with thinning hair she tries to hide under a black bonnet sneers at me. I smile shyly and turn the other way.

I can't worry about Rosemera or we'll never attain our goal—finding Whitley before Stede does. Even though she's the last person I want to lay eyes on right now.

Especially with her arm wrapped tightly around some large-armed fancy boy like she is right now. I wince the moment the sight registers. His hand is at her waist, and my heart screams a song of wrath and agony. I squeeze my fists until my nails sting my palms.

I hate this feeling.

I hate that I can't force myself to stop caring. I shouldn't. *I was never supposed to care about her.*

And here I am, cracking because her fiancé—who she had all the time we spent together—spins her around in circles beneath that stupid sparkling chandelier.

He has what she desires. He can give her the things she wants.

I can't.

I have nothing to give her. Except more pain. More fear.

Part of me wants to walk away, let her be with her stupid Jeb and fend for herself, but the truth is it doesn't matter whether I walk away or not. My world is coming for her.

It will be my fault that she's miserable. My fault she can't have the life she wants.

At least let me be the one to rip it from her. Perhaps I'll find a quiet joy from that.

I take in a long breath and slip back into the crowd, knowing it's unwise to approach her now. Who knows how her beloved Jeb will react? I certainly don't need a scene.

The next moment she's alone, I'll act.

Now that my target is pinpointed, I'll check back with Rosemera.

I move through the crowd quicker than the man whose skin I'm wearing would ever attempt, but my mind is too distracted to act appropriately.

The room is so large, the crowd so thick, I struggle to track down my lost friend until I hear her impolite laugh ringing through the room. Several heads spin towards her as she snorts in the middle of her belly laugh.

When I'm finally able to reach her, I find two young men entirely too close to her. One is running his finger along the beads of her dress at the waist. I grit my teeth, ready to defend her, but she chuckles again and leans in, whispering something in the boy's ear.

It's easy to forget that Rosemera is anything but typical, especially in this place. She's a pirate. And she doesn't get much opportunity to talk with boys her age, particularly ones she likely finds attractive.

I approach casually. "There you are," I say with a low voice. I hate speaking with a voice other than my own. That is always the strangest part of shifting, and I avoid it when possible.

She blinks as she looks at me, clearly forgetting who I am. I raise my eyebrows, and her face smooths, as recognition settles.

"Yes. Meet my new friends, Thomas and Eddie. They're acquaintances of Jeb."

I grit my teeth. "Wonderful."

"This is my uncle," she tells the two boys. One has sandy blonde hair and light freckles. He's probably only fourteen or fifteen and clearly the shier of the two. He doesn't know quite what to do as his friend gets inappropriately close to Rosemera.

The other boy has long black hair that slips down to his eyes. His lips spread into a mischievous grin. "Nice to meet you, Uncle," he says without taking his eyes off of her.

"I was just telling Thomas here that a trip to the study with him would be rather a bad idea, would it not?"

I almost laugh at her. She's surprisingly good at talking the right way, though by the laugh that brought her to my attention, and the way she leans in too close to her new friend, I realize she's still at risk of being found out, especially if any of Stede's crew shows up. She may be incriminated along with them, just by the evident truth that she does not belong in this world.

"Very much so. We must keep at attention; our friend may be along at any time."

"Right," she says, blinking as if she really had forgotten the real reason we came.

"If I must leave you behind, I will," I say quietly.

"Boo hoo," she says with fake pouty lips. "I'm sure I'll be just fine."

I take in a deep breath. "I hope so."

As the song ends, I turn back to the dance floor to ensure I don't lose Whitley, but I realize I'm too late. Jeb is walking through the crowd towards me, and Whitley is nowhere to be seen.

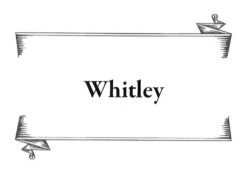

Whitley

I stare at a hand drawn map of Manhattan on the wall of Mr. Peter's study. According to it, I am nearly a mile from the harbor, 5,000 feet or so from the closest drop of salt water.

Waves dance in my mind. Sails billow. Grey-blue eyes watch me.

"What are you doing in here?"

I turn to face a man in a tailored suit and bow tie with grey hair and spectacles. It takes my mind a moment to register his face as the man I've most dreaded for what feels like my whole life.

I swallow and resist the urge to look down at my feet. "Hello, Mr. Robinson," I say politely, but already I'm considering my exit routes.

This man has never hurt me, not physically. His words have always had an edge to them, though—a sense of control. His eyes hold a hint of cruelty that terrifies me, even now.

Sometimes I wondered if it was my imagination, if it was just the rumors that had me jumping to conclusions. But not now.

Now I trust my intuition.

My skin tingles with anticipation of flight. *I do not want to be alone with this man.*

"Well?" His voice is low and commanding, yet holds a hint of wicked enjoyment.

I raise my eyebrows, trying to show anything but the fear pulsing through my veins.

"You didn't answer my question."

"Didn't I?" I say sweetly, keeping eye contact. I won't be an easy victim.

His lips turn up into a sadistic smile. "Avoiding Jeb, are we? I heard about your little tiff. Too bad, when young promising couples fall apart before they even begin." He steps forward casually, as if the motion means nothing, but my pounding heart does not like the dissipating distance between us.

His fingers glide along a cedar shelf as he takes slow steps towards me, his eyes on the photos and books that crowd the borders of the room.

My eyes flit to the open door. A gentle waltz hums faintly from down the hall. He's moving closer, and my heart picks up speed. Every step he takes towards me, I could step away towards the door. But I don't move—that would tip him off to my exit strategy.

I don't know what he has planned for this moment, but I intend to assume the worst and listen to my pounding heart that screams for me to run.

So, I will allow him to believe he is in control. I want him to continue moving towards me. The closer he gets, the clearer my exit route—so long as I move quickly when the time comes.

I settle my feet and clench my fists.

"You always were a quiet one."

Around you, yes.

"Well, anyway, I suppose your disagreement with Jeb is in my favor." Now he looks up to meet my eye. There is one small chair between us, and only a few feet.

My heart throbs, pounding in my ears. I force my eyes not to move towards the door.

"How is that?" I ask, and the sweetness of my tone disappears. Which I suppose is okay, because he may suspect something isn't right if I'm not at a least a little unsure. He wants me to be scared.

"Those pirates were a bit of a wrench in the plan, but, well..." his voice drifts off, like his mind is lost, stuck on something far away. Then his gaze locks on mine fiercely. "You know you have other options, don't you, Whitley?" His voice is quiet as he takes one more step. He's nearly close enough to touch me. My path is wide open, around the other side of the cedar desk.

My heart pauses one beat as I prepare to leap away from him, out of the study and back into the crowded hall—

He pulls a small ring from his pocket, fingering it absently. "Your father will be pleased."

I blink, muscles frozen in place. "What?" I haven't heard a word about my father since the pirate raid. For all I know, he may not even be alive.

He smiles and takes another step. This time I step backwards, away from him, but don't run. I thought his mention of the pirates was strange, but not enough to keep me from fleeing without answers. Now, my eyes move to my mother's ring between his fingers, and my lungs stop working.

"Oh yes, we've been corresponding."

Heat rushes to my face. "He's been *corresponding* with you." My father hasn't spoken to anyone in New York since we left. He broke all ties. Except Mr. Robinson, if I believe him...There's hardly been enough time for a letter to arrive since the raid.

The man's dark eyes shine, and my chest tightens.

"Of course. I was just preparing to make my way down south when I got his message. We both thought that was the end— a pirate raid taking his most valuable commodity." He shakes his head. "Such a shame." He leans against the desk, hand inches from mine. "You'd be ruined, if you managed to survive, and our deal would be off. But you managed to make it out with a solid reputation. I'm very impressed, I must admit."

I press my eyes together. "You made a deal with my father." I don't care about the rest of it. I don't care that my father is alive, or who he's been talking to. The implication here is much worse.

A low chuckle resounds from Mr. Robinson's chest, and he holds out my mother's small and unimpressive emerald ring. When I don't take it, he drops it on the floor.

He knows I don't need to accept it for his deal to stay in place. I have no say in this.

"How much?" I ask, low and firm, then meet his eye, resisting the urge to spit at him. *How much was I worth?* bile rises in my throat.

"Enough."

"My father sold me to you." Chills flow all the way down my body. "You were coming to meet us in our new life, with money to keep us wealthy."

"How else do you think he afforded such an estate, even in Carolina?" He looks over his finger nails, so casual, but obviously loving my panic. "September fourteenth. That was the date of our wedding."

My stomach clenches so hard I pitch forward. How I don't lose my lunch is beyond me. I take the moment to bend down and pick up my mother's ring. I hold it in my clenched fist. No wonder my father wouldn't allow me to wear it during our trip. He ripped it from my fingers and tossed it inside my jewelry box never to be seen again. We were in such a rush, I hadn't had time to argue.

Had he pulled it back out when I wasn't looking and left it as a token their bargain was still on? I swallow, looking at the faded silver.

"Of course, now it must be postponed," Mr. Robinson goes on. "But there are worse problems. I'm simply pleased you gave us a convenient excuse to break off your engagement to Jeb. You've done a mighty fine job at making this work so well for me."

He reaches out and gently brushes a hair behind my ear. I don't remember the last breath I took.

My body finally reacts, and I shoot away from him—not fast enough, though. He grabs my upper arm, pulling me back to face him. I let out a squeal, but I give not one moment of hesitation before I slam my heel down on his toe. He hollers in pain and I pull my arm from his grip with a jerk that sends me to the floor. I hit my head on the corner of the desk on the way down, but I scramble up as he reaches for me again and fly from the room.

"You bitch!" he yells after me.

I run down the corridor and into the crowded hall. Bodies press in around me, but I don't see them. The pounding in my head drowns out the music.

Everything spins.

My father betrayed me. Again. I didn't even known what he was doing. When would he have told me? When Mr. Robinson showed up out of the blue? On the day of my wedding?

I'd rather be with one of those pirates than the cruel man to whom my father bartered me.

I always knew my father would use me. My value was in my beauty. He never kept that a secret. But I thought... I thought I could find a way to please him without destroying everything. Marry someone who could make me happy, and please him at the same time.

He didn't even let me try.

He wouldn't even let me have what little happiness I could gain myself, even if it still fit what he wanted. My happiness wasn't worth enough money. So he sold it.

"Sweetheart," a woman's gravelly voice says behind me, and a soft hand touches my forearm. "Are you alright?"

I don't even look towards her. I don't know if she's sincere or gossip hungry, but it doesn't matter because she can't help.

I push my way through the crowd towards the front door, an incessant need to escape pressing in on me. I run up the stairs to the main exit of Jeb's beautiful home. A home that could have been mine. Would have been. Wondering if this will be the last time that I would set foot here.

"Whitley!" someone calls.

I pause, feeling a soft breeze on my wet cheeks, not even sure when I started crying.

Jeb pushes his way through the crowd towards me.

A shift. A chill. The smell of salt.

Something has changed in the room. I turn to search the crowd, from the edges of the room to the center and back out. I could see it all from my vantage point, high on the marble stairway. The music still plays. People still dance and chat in corners, sipping their drinks.

No one else seems to notice that something is very much not right.

Men from all corners of the room, moving from edge to edge, sweeping the room methodically. They're dressed in something resembling the usual tailored suits of high society gentlemen, but... not quite right.

Like the gold earring in one man's right ear. Or the black scar on one man's lip. The dirt beneath their nails. The stain of blood on one man's bowtie.

"Care to dance?" Jeb says, pulling my attention back to him.

My stomach flips—the first pleasant feeling I've had in days, despite the fear ripping through my chest.

"Not with a bunch of pirates filling the room," I say, looking him in the eye and knowing full well that it is not Jeb I'm talking to.

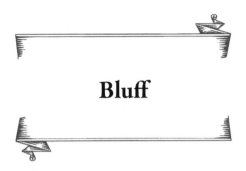

Bluff

I flex my fingers, working to hide my discomfort as she meets my gaze with sea blue eyes full of wonder and an expression I can't quite describe. Her mention of pirates surprises me, not because she's noticed them, but because she'd tell her high-brow fiancé, whose skin I'm still wearing, about them so causally. Does she confide in him that heavily?

"What do we do?" I ask, realizing part of me is testing her. We need to go, get out of here as quickly as possible, but I want to know what she'd do without me. Would she rely on Jeb and his big towering home to save her? Would she run away with him?

Her expression shows a moment of confusion, like my question doesn't belong on my lips. Perhaps Jeb is more controlling than that?

"Run," she says and holds out a gentle hand towards me, eyes seductive— almost like we're not running *from* a dangerous pirate crew, but towards something much more exciting.

Heat rushes to my face at the thought of us doing anything like the last moments we spent together in the captain's quarters. So even though it's not the safest choice to make, I shift back into myself. My clothes stay, prim and proper for the occasion, but my body and face fall back into their natural state.

Her expression stays steady. She shows no surprise whatsoever. While that leaves me a tad confused, I'm even more disappointed that she doesn't react. She's not shocked—or pleased.

Me, Jeb, it doesn't matter to her. Indifference is worse than disappointment I realize, and rage sweeps through me.

But I remember that I wasn't expecting this to be pleasant. This is much more important than feelings.

Her hand is still extended to me, so I give her a moment to retract it, in case her reaction is delayed.

"Are you coming?" she asks.

I blink, then grab her hand, and together we rush from the banquet hall and onto the dark streets of New York City.

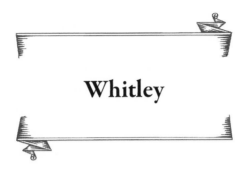

Whitley

A shiver of excitement rushes through my body, enough to overcome the fear of what's happening behind the closed doors of the Harrison's manor. Will the pirate crew kill someone? Will they kill Jeb?

I push the thought from my mind because I don't want to feel those things.

I want to feel Bluff's hand in mine. I want to revel in the moment, in the realization that I haven't lost him, or the freedom I so crave.

The streets are dark, filled with lines of empty carriages. A few lanterns glow along the lane but merely serve to cast shadows, making the in-between appear even more haunting. We pause, each with heavy breaths, as we consider the path in front of us.

One mile. That's how far the harbor is.

That's a one-mile trek through the pitch-black streets of New York city. This city is just as full of slums and criminals as it is of entrepreneurs and high society. When the sun goes down, these streets are anything but safe.

A figure appears from behind a nearby coach. I can't see his face or how he's dressed, but the hunch in his back is enough to make me wary. Bluff steps in front of me.

"Who are you?" Bluff asks as the figure approaches slowly. "Sir?" he says. There's still a possibility it's simply an older man arriving late to the party or a driver awaiting his master.

Then I notice the knife, dripping some liquid I can't quite see but can certainly guess.

I let out a small gasp, and the man charges. In two quick leaps, he is on Bluff, knife glinting in the splotches of candle light.

Bluff grabs his arm just before it contacts his chest and pushes it upward with a massive grunt. At the same instant, he uses a knee to the chest and his other arm to push the man back violently, twisting so he flips onto his back. The smack of his head on the stone pavement reverberates through the streets.

So fast. It's over so fast, and I don't even know if the man is still alive. Can someone die from such a simple move? And yet it's hard to imagine him living after a sound that revolting.

I don't look too closely at his face as Bluff rips the blade from the man's fingers, then pulls me roughly into the darkness, towards the harbor.

Over five thousand feet to our destination. And even then, will there be a ship waiting?

My mind still reels from the quick altercation, the wet crunch replaying over and over. But my feet continue to move as Bluff directs me.

A few moments later, a smear of red against a brick wall catches my attention, and suddenly my whole body is at alert. Ice fills my veins as my mind is pulled back to the present and I recognize the alley we're in.

I shove my feet into the rocky dirt, pulling Bluff to a stop as violently as I can manage.

"What are you doing?" he hisses as he stops and turns back towards me.

The expression on his face is one of pure rage, and it stops me for a moment. Why is he so angry?

"We can't go this way," I say, with a quieter voice than I meant to use. "We have to go back..." I begin to point back the way we came, but he interrupts me.

"What are you talking about?" He rips his hand from mine.

His eyes. That's what strikes me the most. I can't even describe the look there, like storm clouds building within his grey eyes. The worst part is the pain.

He won't meet my gaze.

"What's wrong?" I ask him, suddenly forgetting the panic I'd felt at finding us smack in the middle of mob territory.

"What do you mean what's wrong? Stede is here, and we have to get to the harbor as quickly as possible or we're *dead*." He spits as he finishes his line. "We can't *go back*."

"Yes, I understand that," I say, defensiveness creeping up my chest at his tone. I'm not a moron. "But—"

"Look, I don't want to hear about Jeb or the perfect life I ripped you from. I'm sorry, but I don't care about your happiness. You go back and you're dead. Understand?"

I flinch. "You think I want to go back to Jeb?"

"I mean that you can't go back—ever."

I narrow my eyes, realizing—of course he thinks that's what I want. This was always my destination. New York. Jeb.

It's the only place I'd ever expressed a desire to go—because I didn't know another option.

So he thinks I ran to save my skin for the moment, but plan on seeking out that same life once the coast clears. He doesn't know I was planning to leave with or without him.

"I don't want to go back... ever," I say quietly.

His expression shifts, confusion softening his anger. But before he can respond, the shattering of glass just down the dark alley causes us both to freeze.

"Also," I say in a whisper, "I forgot to mention, we're currently in Five Points. One block from the bar where the mob meets."

Bluff

Well, that's good news.

I curse under my breath. Someone is down the alley, still out of sight in the darkness, and based on the information Whitley just gave me, odds are it's a member of the mob.

Yes, the mob that chased her father out of New York to start with, and who very well may know exactly who she is if they catch a glimpse. And that's if they don't decide to kill us on the spot just for entering their territory.

We stand frozen, waiting to react until we know for sure whoever smashed the glass bottle is coming this way.

We sit in silence.

For that moment I allow my heart to slow, for hope to grow—maybe we can just back our way out of here and go around.

Pounding footsteps stomp down the alley towards us, and the breath flees from my lungs. I can get out of this if the mob catches us—but can Whitley?

Unlikely. If she was married to Jeb they'd simply pay for her freedom. But here, now? They might as well be Stede's crew.

I must do something to ensure they don't look at her closely.

I turn quickly to Whitley, panic searing my every cell, a hasty plan forming in my mind. "Scream," I whisper.

"What?" she asks, eyes darting from my face to the alley in front of us.

"Scream," I hiss, as I begin to shift into a massive figure right in front of her.

A high-pitched squeal escapes her lips, and for a moment, I blink, believing she's really terrified. Whether her fear is true or not, I still need to act.

I grab her by the waist and shove her against the brick wall lining the alley, just as a man comes into view through the darkness ahead. I press my now large body against her slight one. Hips to hips, chest to chest.

She lets out another scream, but it fades to a whimper as I press my lips to her neck, her hair plastering to my face. For one long moment all that exists is Whitley. Her hair in my face, neck on my lips, between my teeth...

She groans and I suppress the urge to do the same.

For this little act to work, the mobster has to believe I'm a criminal attacking an unsuspecting high society victim—which is impossibly disgusting, but given our situation, the ways she's dressed, it's the only thing I thought we could sell to get away with being here and hide Whitley's face in case he recognizes her.

I'm hoping my new form—a muscled and tattooed man in tattered woolen pants and stained cotton shirt—works well enough to make it believable. I had to pull off the first image that popped into my mind. The clothing might be off for this place. The tattoos might be wrong.

I just hope he doesn't look too closely.

And groans bordering on moans of pleasure aren't doing us any favors—as much as I like it.

"Looks like you caught a pretty one," the man says as he approaches, eyeing us.

I run my hand up her thigh, and she lets out another groan that sends shivers through my whole body.

Her smell intoxicates me. She's supposed to be terrified, but all I can feel is anticipation.

I grip her waist, fingers squeezing uncontrollably. *She likes this*, I think, and suddenly my mind is spinning. I must force myself back to the issue at hand, but God is that hard right now, with my hands on her skin, her skirt hiked up...

This girl is like a drug to me.

The man chuckles. "Sounds like she likes it."

God, I want her to want this.

But again, it's not me. It's all a game of pretend, and I can't help but feel like she's just messing with me now.

She's messing with me, and it's working. I clench my jaw, letting anger overcome my desire.

"She won't for long," I snarl and press my body harder into hers. She gasps and cries out.

"Stop! Just let me go, please!"

Again, the man laughs. "She one of the Lockhart sisters?" he asks casually, shaking his head like *this would be just like them.*

I realize now that he doesn't think she's an innocent victim. He thinks this is a planned tryst, and now that we've been caught, she's only pretending to be a victim. I hold back a laugh.

That would be so much like a high brow woman. Blame it on the poor man if they're caught.

Either way, it works for me—so long as the mob doesn't shoot us for being in their territory or recognize Whitley and take her captive.

"Look," he says when I don't respond, "I'm not one for interruptin' a man getting his jollies, but you got to take this elsewhere. You're encroaching on our territory, and anyone else comes along, they won't be so kind."

I look up and around like it was the first time I'd noticed where we were. "Shit. Didn't realize we came this far."

The mobster raises his eyebrows.

"She runs fast." I smirk.

"I'm sure. Take it a block that way. That'll do fine."

Whitley wiggles in my arms like she's trying to break free. I tighten my grip and smile. "Thanks, brother," I say in a low and sinister voice, then pull Whitley down the alley away from the mob territory.

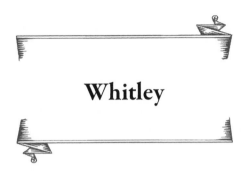

Whitley

Bluff finally releases me once we reach an area so dark that I can't see my own nose.

I'm gasping for breath for so many reasons at once. My mind spins, body tightened like a spring, adrenaline pulsing. Every place where Bluff's body contacted mine sings—and that's a whole lot of my body.

Bluff's rapid breaths nearby are a comfort, the only hint that he's still here. I remain unmoving, allowing us both time to wind down. My mind won't let go of the sensation of his hands on me, his breath on my neck. But we're still in danger, so I try not to dwell on it too much.

It's so strange to want someone that badly, even when they don't look or move like the person you desire. But he still *feels* like Bluff, even in someone else's skin. I was supposed to be scared. I was supposed to be a victim. But I couldn't push the desire down. I couldn't hide it.

Pretty sure that almost got us both killed.

In truth, a part of me wanted him to know how much I want him. The look he gave me, just before the mob member came, had me questioning how he sees me.

"We have to go," he finally says, his voice low and harsh.

"Are you mad about something?" I ask. I can't help it. I was thrilled to be with him again, to just see him again. Yet he seems miserable to be around me.

"You really don't want me to go into how I feel about all of this. And I certainly don't want to hear your feelings either. So just let it go."

I roll my eyes. "Fine. What's the plan?"

"We get to the port, within the hour, before Stede's crew swarms the place."

"You think they're not already?" I stand, wiping dirt from my dress and ensuring nothing is hiked up inappropriately. An image of Bluff's hand gliding up my leg drifts through my thoughts and I swallow. Can't go there now. Clearly, he hates me. "That's exactly how we escaped the last raid, and I highly doubt they'll make the same mistake a second time. We only made it out of the banquet hall because I was already on my way out when they began their sweep. They won't let us make it to the harbor. That might have even been the plan to start with: chase us from the ball and catch us before we reach our escape vessel."

He's quiet for a moment. "Maybe we should go back and find Rosemera."

I jerk my head up, even though I can't see Bluff's face in the darkness. "Where is Rosemera?"

"She was at the ball."

My mouth flies open. I can't believe I didn't see her there! "And you left her there?"

"She'll be fine. She knew we'd leave without her if needed. It was part of the plan."

I shake my head. I don't like that at all.

"She seemed to be enjoying herself last I saw."

I run my hand through my once perfectly restrained hair, pulling a few pins loose and tossing them to the ground. "We can't go to the main port. It's at least three quarters of a mile away still. We have mob territory to go around, and a pirate crew that will be anticipating the path. No way we can make it tonight. But I also can't imagine going back to the manor is good idea. Mr. Robinson will be on the lookout for me. Jeb will ask entirely too many questions..."

"I don't want to hear about Jeb, all right?"

I bite my lip at the harshness of his tone, the pain laced between the words.

"I knew it was you, you know."

Bluff is still. I wish I could see him. Wish I could read his expression. Instead, I just have to take his silence as a clue.

"In the captain's quarters," I clarify.

"I don't know what you're talking about," he says, a rustling followed by a sweeping sound tells me he's up and dusting off his own pants. "We must go."

"Where?" I ask again. We still haven't established a plan.

"The harbor. It's the only place we can go. We have to reach *The Freedom*."

"So they're waiting for us?" If they're already there, then perhaps he's right. But that doesn't seem very safe for them.

"Not exactly. They won't come back to the dock, but they'll be off the coast waiting. We just need a ship to reach them."

Okay. We have to get off shore, but there are many other routes to the ocean than the main harbor.

"Come on," I say, and begin down the alley purposefully.

"Oh, now you're ready to accept my plan?"

"No. I'm not going to the harbor port."

He grips my wrist and pulls me to face him. I've moved far enough for me to get a better look at his current appearance—he's definitely back in his own form, he even has his dapper clothing back on—fine wool suit and silk tie—which causes my stomach to do summersaults despite the way he's acting towards me now.

"What the hell are you talking about? I told you, the harbor is the plan. It's where Rosemera will meet us. "

I shake my head. "That's your plan. Not mine. The harbor port will never work." I don't like that Rosemera will be trying to go there, but I know it's not an option right now. Hopefully she figures that out too. "Besides, you don't know these streets like I do. Just like you didn't know we were smack in the middle of mob territory—still are, by the way, just a quieter part so keep your voice down—I have a plan and you're just going to have to trust me."

"Never," he whispers.

You really hate me that much? I want to ask him, my heart throbbing. But I keep my mouth shut. I'll deal with his pouty tantrums later. Right now, it's my turn to save us.

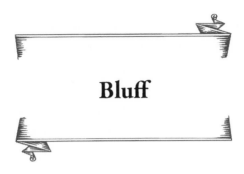

Bluff

My fists are clenched all the while I follow Whitley in and out of alleyways, sprinting down the large open streets until we're safe and secure back in the shadows. We even cross through an open construction site.

I must admit she clearly knows her way here. Knows which places are safe to cross, which shortcuts are worth the risk. But I still hate the fact that I'm following instead of leading. Not because I don't trust her or because I want to be in control all the time—but because, if I were in the lead, I wouldn't need to keep my eyes on her.

I wouldn't see her blond hair flowing behind her as she runs. My eye wouldn't catch on her sleeve hanging loose on her shoulder, exposing more skin than is *ladylike*.

Is that the place I bit? I wonder and immediately chide myself.

I want to focus on the streets, on our survival, not on her.

Eventually, I notice we don't seem to be heading in the direction I would expect. "Where exactly are we going?" We're going west, not south. She mentioned unwillingness to go to the harbor, but we still need to head towards the ocean, I'd assumed...

"The Hudson."

I tap my fingers on my leg. "Is there a dock there?" I ask. The river leads to the ocean, so I understand the potential but I'm unsure of the specifics.

"Not exactly."

I pull her back and settle into another alleyway. Our proximity immediately causes me discomfort. What in the world am I going to do with this girl? I can't be near her, but I can't leave her alone without risking both our lives. She's a risk alone, and she's torture with me.

"Tell me you have a plan more complex than making it to water then find the ocean from there."

She rolls her eyes and pulls her hand from mine. "Yes, I have a plan."

"Care to share it?"

She takes in a long breath. "In Carolina we ran from pirates by finding other pirates. We're doing the same now."

I motion my hand for her to explain further, because that gave me nothing. "Where are you going to find pirates on the Hudson?"

"There's more than one type of pirate in this part of the world. Ever heard of a river pirate?"

I chew the inside of my lip, considering her words. Approaching pirates you don't know is rarely a good idea. It's an interesting concept, however. "Do you know these pirates?"

"Sort of."

"That sounds promising."

"It's a better plan than you have."

I give her that much. "But we'll need to think this through. Whatever type of pirate we interact with, there are rules to follow. They're not the kind of people keen to help others out of the kindness of their hearts. They want something out of it. And if they think they can get more out of betraying you than you're giving, they'll turn you over in a second."

"All right. So, what do you propose?"

I nod and begin to pace, thinking this through. "It's a good plan. But we need to consider what we're going to barter with. We'll need to know their motivation, their greatest desire. Is it money? Power? A place to belong? Do they respect pirates like Stede or do they hate them? Do they admire the elite of New York that you belong to or do they dislike it? All of those things will come into play. Tell me as much as you can about these pirates."

I'm surprised when Whitley tells me all she knows about the pirates she's planning to approach. They're a secretive group, as I'd imagine, that live mostly in the slums and travel through old the canals beneath the city. Their average age is also somewhere around twelve. She said we'd be lucky to find one as old as we are—usually they're recruited by the mob by the time they turn eighteen.

So pretty much they're a ragtag group of orphan thieves who use makeshift weapons and dinghies to commandeer ships on the river in order to survive. She knows where to find them, and that's her most useful bit of information. She's only met one, and she has no idea if he'll be anywhere around—or if he's even still alive.

"Well, I can take a few guesses at what a group like this would want most," I say, "but it's just a guess. We're going to have to think on the fly with this one. Just follow my lead, all right?"

"Want to let me in on your guesses?"

"Well, first, I'm going to assume they are not overly fond of rich people. Yes, that means you." I expect an annoyed expression but get none. She simply nods.

"Very well. Should I change my clothes first?"

I shake my head. "No, we don't have much time, and I'm not sure it'll help. You can only hide the stuck-up rich part of you so much."

At that her mouth hangs open slightly, her eyes suddenly full of pain. A sweep of guilt swings through me but leaves quickly. I don't care if I offend her. It would be better if she hated me anyway.

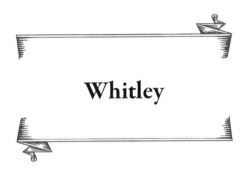

Whitley

I ignore the dagger in my heart as I lead Bluff to the eastern most bank of the Hudson River. Waves shift quietly in the darkness. Everything is still this time of night. There is no sound but the soft rush of the waves pushing against the piles of stone. The only light visible from here is a lighthouse far in the distance, and a few lanterns somewhere over the water.

"Well?" Bluff asks as we stand there with no sign of life anywhere.

I take a few more steps until I'm standing just over a hole in the ground. It leads to an old underground canal. Sudden shuffling below assures me my hunch was right—they're here, just hiding.

I lean down to the hole. It's too dark to see anything, but little noises sound from below: a whisper, followed by a sudden hush, a shift and a grunt, the scattering of pebbles.

"Hello," I say.

Bluff joins me, leaning down over the hole. "Hey, lads, know where we can barter for a ship? We have some business."

"What kind of business?" a little voice calls up at us.

"Hush!" another voice reprimands.

153

"What?" the little voice yelps. "I want to eat today, okay?"

"Yeah, well, you want to be locked up to do it? You see that lady's dress? She ain't here for no business."

"But we are!" I call.

"We're on the run," Bluff jumps in. "We have some bad men after us, and we need to reach our friends in the harbor, but we'll need a ship to do it. We heard you could help."

More scuffling from beneath our feet. I find myself wondering how many kids are down there, and how bad they smell. I wrinkle my nose.

"Yeah, right. I can tell an eloping couple from a true runway, any day."

Bluff jerks his head back, gripping the stone beside the hole like he'll break it. "I wouldn't touch this lass with a ten-foot pole," he spits.

I hold back a scoff at that. If they need to believe there is nothing between us to help, I need to not give away my feelings. Though his words are acid in my veins.

"She's too pretty. No way she's a runaway," an older voice says, eyes peeking up closer than the others.

"Doesn't even have any bruises!" a high-pitched voice calls.

I hold out my arm to them, to show the finger marks Mr. Robinson left. "I've got a nice bump on my head as well," I say.

Bluff's eyes linger on the dark spot in my forearm. Guess he hadn't noticed that.

"That don't prove nothin.'"

"Who told you about us anyway? You bring her here, bloke? Who do you know?"

Bluff's eyes meet mine.

"Charlie," I squeal out.

"There are twelve Charlies down here, miss. Don't mean nothing."

"Don't call her miss, she didn't do nothing to deserve respect."

"Knickerbocker, that's what he went by, once he joined." I'd almost forgotten that part, but he told us all about it one day it was raining too hard to play ball, so we sat around playing truth or dare. That was the day I learned about the child gang on the Hudson.

A hush falls and my heart stops. Is that good or bad?

"Go get Knick," the older sounding boy says to another, then an arm appears from the entrance canal hole, followed by a head and body, hoisting itself out. Several other bodies follow, and I watch in awe as these little bodies unfold themselves into a rag-tag crowd in front of us.

"I'm Tom. Who are you?"

"I'm Bluff and this is Whitley."

"Bluff your real name?"

He shakes his head.

"Well?"

Bluff takes in a deep breath, like it causes him pain to pull out his true identity. "Nalin. My real name is Nalin."

I immediately wonder if it's the truth or if he made up a "real" name.

"What do you want?" Tom asks, seemingly unimpressed with our introduction. He's maybe sixteen. His pants are tight over his thighs and cut off too short. The younger kids around him have the opposite problem—clothes so big they're falling off of their skinny bodies. They're a diverse group, heights ranging from tiny to tall and lanky. There are girls and boys, and skin colors from white as paper with red freckles to as dark as the boy speaking to us now.

"We told you," Bluff says, putting his hands in his pockets casually, "we need a ship to reach the outer harbor."

"The outer harbor? As in all the way to the ocean?"

Bluff nods. The New York harbor follows a thin water way through several other portions of land before reaching actual open water. Apparently, that's where *The Freedom* will be waiting for us, though that's news to me.

"That's not an easy job. You better have some good payment."

I look to Bluff, unsure what his plan is on actual payment. His eyes meet mine before turning back to the leader of the child mob. "I have gold. But I'm guessing it's not going to be enough."

The boy crosses his arm. "If you're guessing, then I'm going to agree with you."

I wince, wondering if we'd have been able to get away with paying what we have without that comment. Too late now.

"I have an emerald ring," I offer and pull the ring out from its hiding place inside my dress's waist belt. "I won't be needing it now."

I can't help but glance at Bluff's expression as I hold it out. His eyebrows are pulled low, confusion written on his face. "Jeb?" he asks.

I shake my head. "Apparently my father made a deal with someone else," I say, my voice only a whisper now.

"Told you she was running from a husband!" a little girl shouts.

"Where's the ring from?" the older boy asks. "Was it given or stolen?"

I bite my lip, considering my answer, but before I can collect my thoughts, whispers begin flowing through the little crowd, and another form crawls out from the canal—a face I barely recognize, but something there is familiar. His face is sallow, and pale, but covered in dirt.

The boy is taller than the rest by at least a foot, even the boy we'd taken as the leader.

"Who is it using my name to make a deal?" the boy says, looking us both over. His eyes linger on mine as recognition dawns. He doesn't look shocked or angry or annoyed or even like he expected it. He just looks tired.

"Whitley," he says quietly. "Hadn't thought I'd ever see you here. Last I heard you were engaged to Jeb."

I nod, almost surprised he was that caught up on the gossip, as it had only become public in the last two days.

His eyes drift to Bluff, looking him up and down.

"You think I'm going to help you flee from an old childhood friend for some other beau?"

"No. That's not what this is."

"Sure looks like it," Tom says.

"I'm not running from Jeb. I'm running from—well a few things actually. My father's schemes and the troubles that came along with them, the mob, Mr. Robinson...."

"That where the emerald came from?" Knick asks.

I nod.

"Isn't that that old guy who beats all his servants?" Tom asks.

"Yeah, that's the household Betsy came from," a boy, maybe seven, says, "all bruised up and starving to death."

"What about Mr. Robinson?" Knick prompts. "Why do you have a ring from him and not Jeb?"

"It was a bribe." I swallow and look to my feet. "My father gave it to him as a symbol for my hand, before we fled the city." My heart is pounding now. "It was my mother's before that."

"You knew this? About the marriage?"

I shake my head. "It was all done behind my back. I only learned of it hours ago now. I don't want that ring anymore. Whether you help us or not, just keep it."

Knick considers this and reaches to take the ring from my fingers.

"I heard you came back from the south on a pirate ship. That true?"

I blink, then nod.

"This one of them?"

I nod again, too tired to consider whether it is something I should lie about.

"If you go back to Jeb, what will happen?" Knick asks.

I think about Jeb's family, his huge home. I think about the pirates and Mr. Robinson, but truth is, even without all that, there is no going back for me.

"I won't. I'll jump into the sea before I go back." These words are so much stronger than the rest. It's true. Even if I could just go back and be with Jeb, I wouldn't. I couldn't.

"And you just need a ship to ferry you out to sea. Nothing more?"

Bluff and I nod in unison. He's been surprisingly quiet through all of this.

"Alright. Let's get this started."

Bluff

The knot in my stomach grows larger and larger as the horizon lightens. I only wish I were as good at these types of knots as I am the sort you tie in ropes. I'm good at knots on a ship. But unraveling the anxiety building in my bones is impossible.

Of all the things you could call me, a carefree pirate I am not.

In fact, I'm probably the worst kind of pirate there is: the kind who hates actual piracy.

And that's one of the many reasons I feel awful at the moment. I step onto the little boat, keeping my chin up as the children row out towards the harbor, towards a ship we'll commandeer—a polite term for *steal*. All the while, I refuse to look back at Whitley shrinking into the distance. At least she didn't insist on coming out with us. That would have been a disaster—in many ways, including that she's reason number two for the knot. I still don't know what to make of her. I know what I want to think, what I want to feel. But I could not stand the sadness in her eyes when she pulled out that ring. When she told me—us—about her father attempting to force her to marry some cruel man.

Perhaps bringing her back to New York, what I thought was giving her the freedom she wanted, was actually just buckling the lock on her prison cell.

Maybe she's as stuck as I am.

"There!" a young boy calls, pointing out towards the silhouette of a ship in the distance. "I bet that's that tobacco ship we've had eyes for!" His Irish accent is actually a bit endearing, if you ignore the meaning behind his words.

"And we keep passing over," Knick begins slowly, "because we don't have the manpower..."

"But what if we do now!" a darker skinned boy hollers, eyes turning to me. "We got a real pirate this time. I bet he could help."

I open my mouth. I probably could help them take a high value ship, but not because of my skill as a pirate, because of my ability to turn into anyone I want. But I don't plan on exposing that skill to this lot, if I can help it.

A larger ship also means higher levels of violence. More lives at risk. Which is exactly what I'd like to avoid.

I don't want to slit anyone's throat or watch one of these youngsters do it.

They've probably done worse. They're doing whatever they must in order to survive. The worse their situation, the worse they'll be willing to do. And their situation is pretty ugly. I look down at the lookout boy's bare feet, covered in black slime.

"No," Knick says after a moment of silence. "That's not what we're here for. They need a ship, any ship, to take them out to sea. We don't need to pick the most protected ship out here in order to do it."

"I know we don't haaave to," the boy whines. "But we could. We gotta take a ship, why not make it most worthwhile for us?"

Knick clenches his jaw. "Because I want this done as quickly as possible. I'm not playing games today, Tim. Now no more arguing. Look for a smaller ship, with sails already set to fly. That's it."

My eyes narrow as I study Knick. It does make sense for them to choose a ship they can gain from, even if not a ship as big as a tobacco freighter. Why does he want this done with so quickly? Is it out of concern for Whitley, a girl he hasn't seen in years? Is it out of guilt for helping her leave Jeb—also a friend he hasn't seen in years and likely never will again? Both options seem unlikely.

And for the first time, I mistrust this pint-sized pirate crew.

Tim crosses his arms and pouts. Knick raises his eyebrows. Tim pulls the spyglass back out, with a grunt, searching the dark waters for traces of a more reasonable target.

"Sorry 'bout him," Knick says without looking at me. "Our crew tends to be a bit eager, and naïve."

"Don't call me big words," Tim sneers and I hold back a laugh.

Knick smiles. "Which word did you dislike?"

"Nave-ie or whatever. If I don't know what it means, I don't like it."

Knick opens his mouth, but the boy shoots him another look. "And I don't want to know what it means!"

I smile and nod, changing the subject. "I've been there, trust me." I remember when overtaking a ship was nothing but a game. An adventure. When all I wanted was to prove myself, so desperate to belong.

That was before I witnessed death. Before I saw what proving myself cost.

I press my lips tightly together and watch as Tim goes back to his search. Knick still refuses to meet my eye.

"There's a teeny thing over that way," Tim says in a flat tone like he's never been more bored in his life. "By the lighthouse on the Jersey coast. Small crew, and they're already hoisting the sails."

"What kind of ship?" Knick asks.

Tim shrugs and looks again. "I see a net. Must be fishermen."

"Head for the lighthouse, boys," Knick calls to his rowing crew. We're pretty piled onto this little thing. We have four rowers, including Knick. Tim is the littlest at the bow, the look out. And one larger boy, with long curly hair sits back quietly, picking at a knife. I'm guessing he's the best fighter.

I'm smack in the middle.

It takes us a half hour before we reach the fisherman's ship. The sun is just peeking up over the horizon now, making our vision clearer than is ideal for this type of piracy. Luckily, the ship is sailing toward us, not away.

As we approach, one of the sailors aboard our target ship spots us. He points and shouts to the rest of the crew. Element of surprise gone.

I wait, heart beating faster, wondering if Knick will call it off and wait for a better time of day—something we can't afford.

No one speaks for several moments, then a few things shift inside our little ship. The larger boy at the back pulls his knife down, hidden next to his thigh. He and Knick both slump down, pulling their heads lower so they're even with the smaller boys.

Then, Tim at the front waves eagerly.

That's when I remember I'm not with a typical pirate crew. To most people, this is just a boat full of children. Not a threat.

There is shouting on the fisherman's ship, and a rope is thrown out to our row boat, which we use to pull ourselves in closer. A ladder is tossed over the side, and the smaller boys climb up first, their weapons hidden inside their pants. The points poke out only slightly— only noticeable if I look closely.

This crew doesn't need darkness to hide their intensions. They don't need to be far out at sea where no one can come to their victim's aid. They don't even need the ability to shift.

Their age is their disguise.

I move to climb up the ladder once Tim, that last small boy, is on his way, but Knick puts his hand on my arm without a word. I stop and wait.

Once Tim is aboard, there is silence for one small moment—then the shouting starts.

Knick and the large curly haired boy jump into action, climbing onto the ship with impressive swiftness. A splatter of blood lands on my hand, and I grit my teeth.

This is the part of piracy I hate.

Destroying someone else's life, in order to help my own.

I know it's necessary. I don't know any pirates who choose this life freely. They choose it because they have no choice. Because their families will starve. Because honorable sailors are stolen from—by the government, by rich men who use their power to control them, by other sailors. They're men who were born deformed and outcast by their own families. Men who were born to the wrong parents.

Many of the pirates I've known were hired to be soldiers on the sea, then when the war was over, they were accused of piracy. England, in particular, was not gracious to men they considered criminals more than soldiers.

Whole crews were hung. Ships stolen.

When they're backed into a corner, and their choice is to kill or die—that's when people choose piracy.

I quickly climb up the rope, feet landing on the slippery deck between two lifeless bodies. Across the small vessel are three other crew members fighting Knick and the large boy. I sprint over to give my aid—to whoever I can.

I jump into the fight, blocking a hammer swinging through the air toward Knick and then throw my shoulder into the sailor's chest, pushing, pushing until he's at the railing. Then I bend over and pull his legs up in one swift motion so that he falls overboard into the water with a scream and a splash.

The next assailant is a younger fisherman, his face only just starting to grow hair.

"I'll take this one," I tell Knick, and the anger in the boy's eyes morphs into fear.

Knick pauses, eyebrows pulled low as he considers me, then he turns to help the other fighter.

The fisherman boy takes a defensive stance, holding a rusty knife out towards me with a shaking hand.

I put my own knife into my belt loop and hold up my palms towards him. "I don't need to hurt you. Just jump overboard."

"No. I'm not just giving the ship to you mongrels!" he spits.

"It's already done. You've lost."

The boy looks around. There is only one person left—a man with grey in his hair, but he fights the remaining pirates valiantly. The smaller boys are already pillaging the cargo holds. I doubt there is much to find. This is a poor lot.

"That's my dad," the boy says. "I can't leave him alone."

"The quicker you leap overboard, the more likely I'll be able to help him too. The way I helped that last one." I nod over the railing where the sailor is splashing through the water, hollering as he does.

The boy looks over at the water, and I take that moment of distraction to my advantage. I push my shoulder into his chest, grab at his sword hand, and push him over the railing.

Even if I don't manage to save his father, I guarantee he'll be happy his son is safe.

I rush over to the last fight, quickly parry the final fisherman's swing, and knock the iron bar out of his hand, I push him up against the sail, forearm digging into his throat.

The large boy rushes at us, knife ready to gouge him.

I put out my foot and trip him. He rolls the ground and leaps back up, knife pointed at me now. "What the hell!" he says.

I turn towards the fisherman. "Surrender," I say.

"No."

I take in a deep breath. *Curse bravery. Always makes this so much more difficult.*

"We have the ship. You die now or you jump overboard with your son and live to fight another day."

"He's alive?" he asks, eyes shifting from anger to desperate hope.

I nod.

"That isn't how this works, Bluff," Knick says between his teeth. "We don't leave survivors."

"I do," I say, looking the fisherman in the eye. "Whenever possible."

"You're a shitty pirate," the large boy shouts.

"Always have been." I don't mind stealing, but I hate killing. My crews never minded that, though. I brought easy sailing and protection against many foes—supernatural or otherwise.

The fisherman looks around, realizing how far he is from the edge of the ship. Right smack in the middle. "I won't make it," he whispers to me.

"You will if I hold them back."

He blinks at me, realizing what I'm saying. I'm going to fight my own crew to give him the chance to escape. What he doesn't know is that it's not actually my crew. Either way, I'm risking my own life for his.

And that's all right with me, other than the thought of leaving Whitley alone. Without me, though, the price on her head will be significantly lower. Stede won't have any need for her. Maybe she'll be okay. I hope she will.

"Go now," I shout as I push him towards to my right side and spin towards Knick and the other boy, knife held out. Knick leaps towards the fisherman, but I grab him by the left wrist.

His right swings towards me, and his fist connects with my temple. Black spots splatter across my vision.

Then the glint of a blade passes my remaining vision, warmth spreads across my head, salty liquid reaches my lips—blood.

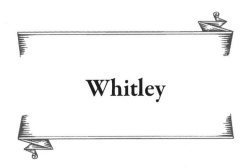

Whitley

I cross my arms to ward off the icy harbor breeze as we row slowly towards the ship Knick and Bluff managed to commandeer.

I try not to think about what it took to obtain our escape vessel. I try not to dwell on what lies behind us, what's still chasing us even now. We're supposed to be moving towards something good, or at least better than what I had, but the pit in my stomach is growing and I don't like it.

The Freedom is waiting for us. My freedom is waiting for me. And I'll see Bluff again in only minutes. So why is my soul screaming at me to leap into the steady waves of the Hudson River?

Escape, something whispers to me.

I look down at the spraying water hitting the side of the boat. I watch as it tosses and turns. Blue and green, fading all the way to black in the depths.

I only look up when the boat bangs against something, jerking me to attention. We're already at the ship, ready to climb aboard. I blink and cast off the hypnotizing fog from my mind.

I climb up the rope ladder shakily, but determined. The feeling of unease does not dissipate at all. I climb over the

169

railing of the ship, realign my skirt to be sure nothing is sticking to me oddly, then look up.

My heart freezes, registering several uncomfortable things, one after the other.

First, it's quiet. Though there are several people aboard, no one speaks.

Second, they're all watching me. Anticipation clouds their expressions.

Third, each one of the ragtag group of child mobsters holds a weapon—a rusty knife, iron bar, rope— gently at his side.

I swallow as I notice they are partially blocking something from my sight. I take a step forward, heart stinging with every difficult beat.

There is a body in a chair, slumped forward. The only reason he's not on the floor are the ropes restraining him. Blood covers half his face.

"Knick!" I holler in anger.

The crowd shifts as Knick steps forward, hands in his pockets.

"What did you do?" I manage to force out through trembling lips.

"You should ask him, not me," Knick says, his voice so full of ease that I nearly leap at him.

"*I can't*," I spit. "He's unconscious." I look at Bluff's limp form, blinking rapidly, then back to Knick, fear lacing my words. "Is he even alive?" I whisper, afraid to hear the answer.

Knick rolls his eyes. "Yes. He's alive and will likely wake soon. Head wounds just bleed a lot. It's not as bad as it looks."

I force a long shaky breath, blowing out slowly.

"We have a seat for you too," Knick says, moving closer to Bluff and patting an empty chair next to him.

I grit my teeth. "Are we prisoners?" I ask. "Are you going to tie me up too?"

"Not if we don't need to."

I walk slowly towards Bluff, bending over to check his wound, and see his chest moving with shallow breaths. I sit in the chair and cross my arms.

"On with it, boys. We have a ship to get to."

"What happened?" I ask, eyebrows still pulled down in anger.

"He broke our rules, fought against us. Made it a whole lot easier to do what needs to be done."

"And what needs to be done?"

Knick looks out at the coast of New York as the sails are hoisted and turned, pulling us slowly out to sea.

"You're worth more than we could resist, Whitley. I am sorry about that." He looks to Bluff, who stirs in the chair.

My stomach sinks.

"Knick?" I say, voice cracking. "Which ship are you taking us to?"

Bluff

My vision is still black, but voices drift into my consciousness. Whitley's voice.

And what needs to be done?

She's scared. I don't like it. I try to force my mind into focus. *What's happening?*

You're worth more than we could resist, Whitley.

I don't know whose voice it is, but it's not a friend's. I groan and attempt to force my muscles to move. I'm not successful.

"Bluff?" her sweet voice sings at me. It makes me dizzy. I don't like the feeling.

Reminds me of unwelcome memories.

"Are you all right?" she asks.

I groan again, but my head is slowly clearing. A rope itches my wrists. There's pressure around my shoulders. I'm tied up pretty good, I realize. A moment later I'm able to hold my head up and blink my vision back.

Soft fingertips graze my cheek so gently I have to resist the urge to move into the touch. *She's dangerous, remember?* I tell myself. *This feeling, it isn't safe.*

Resist. There is so much more at stake.

"What happened?" I manage to force the words from my cracked lips and sore throat.

"I was going to ask you the same thing."

I wince. "Where are we?"

"The fisherman's ship you—they—got for us. Headed out to sea."

"Headed where? To what ship?"

There's a pause, and though my head throbs like I'm a hundred feet below the surface, pressure about ready to explode my brain into little bits, I turn towards her.

She presses something soft against my head, and I wince at the sting. I was cut in the head, I remember now. *Stupid.* Always making stupid choices to save people I don't even know.

It never turns out well for me in the end.

"What are you doing?" I ask in a whisper.

"Trying to clean off some of this blood, see how bad your wound is."

"It's fine. I've had worse. I'm more worried about our current destination, because if it's the wrong ship we won't live long enough for it to become infected." Well, that's not necessarily true. All the signs suggest Stede wants us alive, but his intentions, I have no doubt, will be *worse* than death.

She pulls her hand from my head. "I don't know. I asked, but Knick didn't give me an answer."

"Dammit."

"What?" she whispers.

"He would have answered if it was one we liked. The only reason he'd avoid it..."

Whitley swallows.

"Can you untie me?" I ask her under my breath, unsure who's watching.

"I don't know," she whispers. "They're watching us. They'll notice."

"All right. I should be able to do it myself, it'll just take longer."

"Wait!" Whitley says, her voice suddenly brighter.

"What?" I ask, looking up searching to find what's given her hope.

"It's *The Freedom*, I can see their privateer flag."

I strain to turn my head in the direction she's pointing. She's right, it is *The Freedom*, but the sight doesn't give me quite as much hope as it does her.

I shake my head. "I'm not sure so sure even that's a good thing."

"What do you mean?" she asks. "How could it not be?"

"Knick tied me up, almost tied you up. Said you were worth *a lot*. That line didn't sit well with me."

She looks down at the ground, she agrees.

"Something has changed," I say.

"But that crew, *The Freedom*, they're your friends. Like family, you said."

"They're pirates."

"But..."

"Your father is family too. How much did he sell you for?" My hands curl in fists as I watch her face wince in pain. I don't like her pain, but it's important she gets this. We are not safe on *The Freedom* any longer. "I don't know what their intentions for us are, but they can't be good."

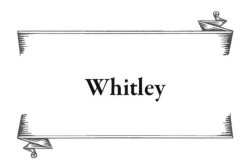

Whitley

The Freedom grows larger and larger, and despite what Bluff said, I can't stop the hope from bubbling up. I believe him— that something isn't right, that climbing aboard that ship won't be like before, but it's still better than the alternative.

For several moments I sit silently, trying not to pay much attention to Bluff's tense shoulders and occasional jerking movements that could expose his attempt to escape his rope bindings.

I'm not even sure what we'd do once he got free. Fight the crews of both ships? This one, I guess he may be able to succeed. Maybe, just maybe, we could defeat the mob of kid pirates, take control, turn the little ship around, and flee.

But that's only if we do it before it's too late, and *The Freedom* is getting closer with each passing second. Bluff's shoulders relax, and I wonder if he's come to the same conclusion.

"It's still better than Stede," I say quietly without taking my eyes off the sails now shadowing over us.

He's quiet for a long moment. "We'll be headed towards Stede, don't get that twisted."

"Perhaps," I say even lower. "But it's a detour. Gives us more time."

Bluff bites the side of his mouth, then nods slowly. "I'd feel better if it wasn't a crew that knew me well."

"Why?"

"They know my tricks. They'll be prepared for them. This crew, for example,"—he nods his head toward a few of the children pirates at the bow—"wouldn't see it coming if I threw Knick overboard, took his skin, and ordered the ship to turn around. But looks like it's too late."

I clench my jaw. I hadn't even considered that.

"We'll figure it out," I whisper, heart pounding, just wanting to say something positive. There has to be a way out of this.

He turns to me, eyes wide yet soft. What is he thinking?

He nods. "Guess we're in this together."

I give him a small smile and try to hide the sadness that suddenly floods me. To me, we've been in it together for a while. But have we really? He was planning to sail away without me. I don't know what changed his mind—was it the kiss? Or because he knew Stede was coming? Or something else? He's always so secretive I can't quite figure him out.

Then there's the words he shot at me, stabbing me in the chest, twisting even still, as we fled Stede's crew back in New York. *I don't care...*

I look back to *The Freedom*. The crews of both ships work quickly to tie the ships together, throwing over a ladder to allow crossing.

After a few shouted conversations between the two ships, Rosemera's father, Captain Taj, climbs aboard the fisherman's ship, his bull-like piercing back in its original place. He doesn't so much glance in our direction before approaching Knick.

"They'll be negotiating for a while, I'd bet."

"So, do we have a chance for escape while they're distracted?"

Bluff shakes his head. "Not a chance. It's the time they'll most expect it."

Before the last words even exit his mouth, three large pirates leap onto our little ship with reverberating thuds, sharp swords in hand. All three sets of eyes turn our direction, then they approach.

The first, I recognize as a pirate called Ink. He's the kind of bloke I wouldn't easily forget—massive, with tattoos covering every inch of exposed skin, even on his face. The next I've seen but don't remember his name. He's covered in black hair—his head, his face, his bare chest. He too is large, but carries as much fat as he does muscle. The third is smaller than the other two, with a kinder face. His skin is darker, his nose wide, and he has an uneven scar all the way down his right arm.

"Timmons," Bluff says casually to the smallest man.

"Got yourself into a good one this time, eh?" Timmons replies.

"Apparently," Bluff says, reclining in his chair like he's comfortable in the ropes. "How much you planning to gain from our lives?"

Timmons raises his eyebrows. "Just her life. You're safe, so far as we know."

"Right," he spits. "You're still going to turn me over."

Not for the first time, I question my trust in Bluff. How much do I even know about him? So very little. Why did he save me to start with? Why did he come back? What's in it for him? I know there is something.

"Remaining alive and being safe are two very different things," Bluff answers.

I blink.

"What's Stede want from you anyway?" The hairy pirate asks the question I'm thinking.

"He wants to control me. Just like everyone else."

The largest pirate, Ink, turns his beady eyes to me, looking me up and down. "Didn't peg you for one to fall in love with a high-class broad."

I let out a sudden cough at this. *What?* Is that what they assume he means by control?

Bluff doesn't look at me, but every muscle on his face tenses, his lips tipped down into an intense frown, his eyes lowered in anger. "Don't oversimplify this, *Marvin*." He spits the name like he's spitting a bug from his mouth.

"Don't call me that."

"Then don't insult me."

As much as I don't think for a second this is somehow all about *love*, I do wonder that he considers it an *insult*.

The pirate leans down to put his face inches from Bluff's, but when he doesn't flinch, he grabs Bluff's neck and squeezes. Bluff writhes in pain instantly, crying out in agony.

"Cut it out," Timmons shouts, and the large pirate releases Bluff with a smile on his face.

"Just a reminder to the lad, that's all."

"He's still an ally," Timmons says.

"A friend," Bluff says through sharp breaths. "And I'll remember that."

I cross my arms and lean back in my chair, uncomfortable. I don't know what to think about all of this, but I don't like the way they look at me or talk about me... even Bluff.

Is it an act? Is it to protect me? I'd like to think so, but my aching gut tells me otherwise.

"Like he's ever getting out of this one. He'll be an ornament on the prow of Stede's ship in a fortnight."

"He wants me alive, not dead," Bluff spits.

"Then she'll be one. Whichever. She'd make a prettier one, anyway. But freedom is one thing you'll never have again."

Bluff rolls his eyes but remains silent.

"I've learned before," Timmons says, his face solemn, "never count this guy out. I'll never bet against you, friend. Even if we're not always on the same side."

Bluff nods, but his eyes are lifeless.

"Will he get out of it once he knows what it'll cost?" the hairy pirate says, his voice deep and slow. "He cares about that lass as much as the captain."

Ink sneers. "Women are always a man's downfall. Might as well be sirens, each and every one of them."

"What are you talking about?" Bluff asks quickly.

It's silent for a long moment. The large pirate turns to Timmons with a subtle smirk still on his face. Timmons, however, looks less than pleased.

"You asked about your price, well, it's not exactly gold."

Bluff blinks rapidly, and I hold in a breath, looking around and remembering that our best ally isn't currently on *The Freedom*...

"Stede has Rosemera. And he's offered an exchange for you two."

Bluff

My whole body sinks into the chair when Timmons finally tells me the terms of our ransom. As much as it doesn't shock me—the idea that this pirate crew I loved like family could betray me—I also knew it would take a lot.

I assumed it was something more than gold—blackmail. A promise of power. Something they couldn't resist.

The life of Rosemera... well that's more than enough.

I don't even blame them, not one little bit. Especially since she's only in this predicament because of me. She wouldn't have been in New York. She wouldn't have been connected to us if I hadn't pulled her in to help.

I hate to think what could have happened to her. She's strong, stronger than most the men on her crew. But that doesn't stop me from wondering. From worrying.

Ink was right. Women are always a man's downfall. Even if you're not in love—or lust—with them, they still have a way of pulling your heart in. Making you feel things. Making you weak.

Rosemera is no different.

I'd die for her. Which is why this just got a whole lot harder. Now I have to worry that if Whitley and I do find a way to escape that it'll cost Rosemera her life. For that, I'd never forgive myself.

I press my eyes closed for a long minute.

"So that it?" Timmons asks after a bit. "You giving up?"

He must have noticed how limp my body went, how my soul seeped away, sinking into the sea.

"As he well should," Ink says with a gravelly voice.

Their footsteps recede but return not long after. They untie us and drag us over to *The Freedom*.

"Good riddance," one of the mob boys shouts at me as I'm prompted to climb aboard. I don't respond. I don't fight. Just move.

One glance behind tells me Whitley follows suit, without a word. She quietly climbs the rickety ladder like a pro. The girl learns quickly at least.

Once aboard the ship, the rest of the crew watches silently. "Tie him to the foremast," the captain says without looking at me. "I want eyes on him all times."

Unsurprising. I've found my way out of a brig on more than one occasion.

Only whispers float through the air as I'm pushed against the foremast, arms pulled behind me and tied in several of their tightest knots, so tight they cut off my circulation. There's little they can do that I can't untie with enough time. It'll just take me all night.

Whitley is guided to the same spot, but there's discussion as to whether she should be tied as well. A few derogatory suggestions are thrown out, and I realize her safety is in jeopardy on this ship for the first time. If I'm not an ally any longer—why not take advantage of the situation?

"Do not touch her," I say with as low and loud of a voice as I can muster.

The captain raises his eyebrows at me. "I have no such plans of making her a plaything, lad."

"I'm not talking to you."

A few chuckles reverberate through the ship. I know better than to think just because the captain doesn't give permission, doesn't mean a few of the crew won't try. They're already thinking it, already whispering about it.

I won't let it happen. Tied up or not. "Touch her—"

"And you'll what?" Ink says, stepping forward boldly. "You're done for, lad. Magic gone in a poof."

"I'll bring the sirens down on you," I hiss the words, low and slow. "I don't need my hands for that. This ship won't ever see the light of another day."

It's silent. No one speaks. Not one snicker leaves one set of lips. Even Ink's eyes are large, mouth parting.

The wind blows eagerly, sails already catching on the strong salty wind of the ocean.

"You heard the boy. Don't touch the girl, yeah?" The captain shouts. "Tie her up beside him, and let's get this bloody business over with."

NEITHER WHITLEY NOR I speak for a long while. Our backs face each other, both pressed against the same pole, hands tied behind us. The only way our hands don't come into contact is through tense, awkward effort.

But I don't want to touch her if she doesn't want me to touch her.

At least an hour passes. The coast fades quickly from view. We don't know where we're headed or how long it'll take to get there. I'm almost surprised we're not just headed back into New York to meet Stede.

Must be he wanted a safer meeting point, one without a hovering military.

Will we be traveling all the way to the Caribbean, then? Bermuda is another possibility that would only take a day or two, but it would sure put the crew on edge.

"Why do they believe you have control over the sirens?" Whitley's voice surprises me, soft but unexpected.

"Long story."

"I think we have a while."

I can see her curling her legs under her body from the corner of my eye. Is she still nervous someone might come for her? That's unlikely now. Sailors tend to be a superstitious bunch, and even those that aren't have seen enough to be unwilling to test my words.

"They don't know if I'm bluffing or not. But they're not willing to risk it. That's really all there is to it. No one knows exactly what kind of powers I have. Not even me if I'm honest."

I'm still avoiding the root of her question. I know it. She knows it. Yet for whatever reason, I don't want her to know that truth. I don't even like speaking the words.

For too long, the wind rushing through the sails is the only sound on board. The sun is already beginning to set. It's been one of the fastest days of my life—and the longest. I suppose it helps that I was unconscious for a few hours of it.

"Did you really give up?" she whispers finally.

"I don't know. I don't want to risk Rosemera's life for mine." Would I risk Rosemera's for Whitley's? That's a question I don't want to answer.

"Do you really think they got her?" Whitley whispers, her sadness obvious.

"I hadn't thought to doubt it. She was right there when the crew came."

"It's possible she got away though, right?"

I nod. "She's a good pirate. Smart. A good fighter. They wouldn't have even known she was there, though, if they hadn't at least come close to capturing her."

I think it through. It makes sense for her to have been caught. But what do we know? What proof did they give? Are they just using the situation to their advantage?

"I almost wonder if she'd be offended that we're assuming she needs to be saved."

I smirk. She's right, Rosemera would be. She'd spend every moment trying to free herself, and she'd hate the idea of me giving up and assuming she'd fail.

"You're kinda smart, you know that?"

"Gee thanks," Whitley says quietly. She's not happy. I mean, why would she be? We are on our way to our worst nightmares, each of us. But I mean something else. She's mad at *me*. I haven't spent much time thinking about her. She's been talking to me, but I haven't given much back. "Are you all right?" I ask, sincerely.

She doesn't respond.

I bite my lip. "I'm sorry."

"For what?"

"Everything." I mean it. I'm the reason she's in entangled in this mess to start. I suppose she doesn't actually know that, though. She thinks this was all about her father, when he was really just a pawn. Just the sign that pointed to her as the target of the prophecy.

Daughter of the scheming land-dweller
A man so bold as to betray a pirate
A beauty of golden hair and secret of low birth
Will control the Son of the Sea, cause him to fall
She alone holds the power to enslave him
Control him, even to his death.

"You never tell me anything, you know that?" Her tone is salty. I don't blame her. I've spent so much time being mad at her for the prophecy, for what I assume she'll do, that I've ignored who she really is. Which is surprisingly amazing.

"What do you want to know?"

"Everything."

I let out a bitter laugh. "Touché." She does deserve more from me, given the circumstances. "Ask me anything, and I'll answer it honestly. I swear."

She's quiet again. I watch as the sky changes color—oranges and pinks, fading into purple at the horizon.

"What's your real name?"

I cough out a laugh. "Really? That's the deep dark secret you want to pull from me?"

"I just want to know it," she whispers.

My heart twists. It sounds like such an intimate thing when she says it like that.

"Nalin." My stomach remains uneasy, imagining the name on her lips. She never says it though. For some reason, I really want her to. Calling a pirate by his real name is usually an insult. We change them for a reason. We don't want to be that person anymore.

Somehow, this feels different. I want her to know me, all of me. Even the parts I hide.

"So you were telling the truth, with the river pirates."

"No real reason to lie."

"Seems like lying comes naturally to you."

I take in a deep breath. "Not lying. Just... withholding the truth. Hiding."

She relaxes her arms for the first time in over an hour of being tied to the ship. Her hands grazes against mine and I have to resist the urge to grip it. Just to touch her skin...

"Did you mean it?" she asks, this time her voice so low I almost can't hear it. I grow dizzy with the sadness laced in the words. I want to turn to her, hold her, but the ropes won't allow it.

"Mean what?"

She clears her throat, forcing the words to have more strength than before. "When we were running from Stede's crew in New York, you told me..." She pauses, "You said you didn't care about my happiness. Is that true?"

I bite my lip, thinking back, not immediately sure what's she's referring to.

I was still upset with her over the way she kissed me as Jeb. I thought for sure she'd be mad at me for ripping her away from her golden life, that she'd want to go back and I... I couldn't bear hearing her say it.

Now, I know more about what her time there was really like. I think about the ring she gave to Knick, about what that ring meant. Her father was going to force her to marry some old man... Is that what she took from my comment? That, like her father, I didn't actually care about her happiness—just whatever I could gain from her.

"No," I say, but I'm not sure how to explain. "I was..." *Honesty,* I remind myself. She deserves that much, even though this is the worst kind. "I was mad at you," I whisper.

"About what?"

I take in a long breath. "I thought—I thought you were going to tell me you wanted to go back to *him*. I... didn't want to hear the words. So, I was unnecessarily harsh. But even then, what I really meant was that I didn't care about what you *wanted*, I just needed to keep you safe." I release the remaining breath through my nose.

"I knew it was you," she says not for the first time. "I told you that once before, but I don't think you believed me."

"I still don't," I say. I did promise to be honest. That kiss wasn't for me. She may have realized it was me after the fact, but during... there's no way she could have known. It happened too fast. No one has ever been able to figure it out that quickly.

"I could... feel it. You. I don't know how to explain it."

I shake my head and don't respond. That doesn't make any sense.

"I'm not the pirate. You can believe me."

I smirk. "You're a woman. I definitely can't."

"I think about it all the time." Her voice sends a shiver down my spine. "I've never been kissed like that before."

My whole body buzzes with excitement over those words. God, do I want to do it again. I hate how much I want her. How much of a pull she has over me.

Stupid prophecy.

"Trust doesn't come easy to me," I tell her, hoping my change of subject takes. My heart is racing, cheeks burning.

"I guess I can understand that. Maybe... maybe I'll find a way to prove it to you."

I am both frustrated and relieved that our bonds make it impossible to touch more than hands.

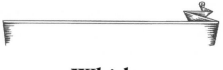

Whitley

The crashing of waves and gentle lull of a rocking ship put my body at ease despite the fact that I'm bound by itchy rope and headed towards a crew that very well may disembowel me.

Or perhaps it's Bluff's hand in mine that keeps my anxiety at bay.

I don't know how long I slept, but when I finally open my eyes the sun is high in the sky, and the crew is bustling about us, sending side-eyes our way as they work. Apparently, no one trusts Bluff, roped or not.

"Bluff?"

"You're finally awake?" he asks, amusement in his voice.

"How long did I sleep?"

"Hard to say. But a while, it seems. You were talking in your sleep. It was endearing."

I groan, not sure I even want to ask what I said.

"Funny because I didn't sleep a wink."

"When's the last time you slept?" It had to have been a while; we've been on the run for far too long.

"Not sure. But—unlike some people— I can't relax enough for sleep in a situation like this."

I smirk. I don't know how I slept either. Just happened.

The crew walk with their backs straighter as they pass, eyes alert and darting around. Tension lines their necks and faces. They seem suspicious of any conversation between us.

"They seem just as uptight," I say, noting a small black man limping past, narrowed eyes pinned to me.

"They should be," Bluff whispers.

I pause for a beat, not wanting to give anything away if he has something in mind. "You have a plan?"

"A plan to make a plan. But that won't surprise these guys. I'm going to need something more."

"Like? Can I help with something?"

"You're my complication, to be honest. I could get out of my binds and hide among the crew. They'd have no way of knowing who I was if I played my cards right... but I can't hide you. And you're worth more than I am."

My eyebrows pull down at that. "Why?" I say after a beat. "What is my value, Bluff?"

He's quiet for several long moments. I'm just some girl whose father swindled a pirate. I can't be worth as much as all this. I can't be worth more than a shapeshifting boy who can potentially call sirens at will... Unless there is something I'm missing. Something big.

"Is our time of honesty already over?"

He lets out a long breath through his nose. "I'm just not sure now is the time. We need to get out of here. And this... is complicated."

I bite my lip and pull my hand farther from his under the guise of stretching. I am rather sore from sitting in this strange position for hours, shoulders bent strangely behind me.

"I'll tell you. I promise. But can you trust me enough to wait?"

I don't know if I trust him. I don't know how much a promise means to him. But he's right about one thing: our top priority is getting free. If we can do that, it won't matter what I mean to Captain Stede. It may not even matter what I mean to Bluff.

"If we can get free, the rest won't matter, I suppose."

He takes in a long breath before responding. "There's a lot I should tell you. Let's just make sure we have enough time left in our lives to do it."

"All right."

"While you were sleeping, I got a little more information," he says under his breath. "We're set to meet Stede on an Island north of the Bahamas, which, with friendly winds, is a five-day sailing from New York."

"Any word about Rosemera?"

"Just that Stede sent a letter with blood on it, a lock of her hair, and the handkerchief she wears."

"That doesn't sound good."

"It sounds wonderful to me." I wish I could see Bluff's face from here, talking back to back makes it so much harder to understand the nuances of the conversation. Is he smirking right now?

"How exactly is that wonderful?"

"It means they don't have her. Probably never did."

I blink. "How do you know?"

"I'm the king of bluffing. I know when I see one." This time I don't need to see the smirk to know it's there.

"You're enjoying this too much."

"You must realize that Stede has developed a reputation. He's cruel. His main tool is fear. He enjoys the hunt as much as he enjoys causing pain. There is no chance he'd send a lock of hair. He'd send in a finger. An ear. A slice of the tattoo on her belly."

I shiver.

"Unless he doesn't really have her. And that handkerchief—do you think she'd wear that into a ball? Not a chance. She left it behind in some alleyway after we stole her dress. She was hesitant to leave it, trust me. But I'm certain it was not on her when Stede came."

My heart leaps to hear all this evidence. Rosemera isn't really in trouble! And Stede doesn't have any real leverage. "Can't you tell the crew all this? If they know Stede doesn't have Rosemera they won't turn us over."

"Unfortunately, I have also developed a reputation. Comes with the name, I suppose."

"They'll assume you're lying."

"Aye. Telling the truth on a pirate ship doesn't get you far. You have to do things on your own. But it does mean one thing: I'll have no issues doing whatever it takes to get us free."

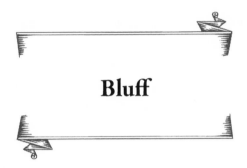

Bluff

As the sun sets, my eyes grow heavy, and I contemplate a nap before I enact the first part of my plan. It wouldn't hurt to wait until after midnight to break free of my confines. The problem is, if I fall asleep, I don't know how long it will be until I wake, and this *must* start tonight.

I blink the sleep from my eyes, but my mind goes dizzy, exhaustion getting the best of me. There's no way I can stay here— awake—for another few hours. My choice is sleep now, or act now. The sky is only just growing darker, the crew is still lively—it's not an ideal time to sneak around.

"Whitley?" I whisper. "Are you awake?"

"Yes," she says so lightly the wind almost masks her voice, even to me.

"Can you stay awake for a few hours?" I pause, watching the few crew members around. This is one conversation I don't want them hearing, "I'm going to need to wake up later in the night."

"Get some sleep," Whitley says louder. A few eyes dart in our direction. I smile. The crew will relax if they think I'm going to sleep through the night.

She never finishes the line, to tell me she'll wake me when the time is right, but I know that is her intention.

I've already prepped Whitley on the basics of the plan. I need to sneak into the captain's quarters to take a peek at our heading. We'll certainly pass several small islands before we reach our rendezvous, and I plan to make one our escape point. If we time it right, we can jump overboard near the island and swim ashore without alerting the crew. By the time they realize we're no longer on the ship, we'll be too far gone for them to find us. It must be a small island, though. It must be at an inconspicuous time. It must be planned right.

I have a particular island in mind, but with any luck we'll have a few options. I just need to see the map with speed markings and our exact direction.

If all goes right, I'll be back in my bindings with our island selected and timed out before they notice I'm missing. If it does not, I'll be forced to toss a crew member overboard and take his skin. I'd like to avoid this option, but then, there are a few crew members I won't mind disposing of, and it very well may be necessary in order to keep my intentions unknown. They can't know my plan.

The only downside to our second option is that it will leave Whitley vulnerable. We're just going to have to hope my threat of *calling the sirens* is enough to keep her safe for a day or two if I'm impersonating a pirate and unable to double down on the bluff.

I let my body relax, but my mind is still whirring. I close my eyes and listen to the waves, but thoughts keep popping into my mind. What ifs. I know I should sleep. Only moments ago, I was hardly able to keep my head up—just that quickly I'm buzzing again.

I shift to find a better sleeping position. My wrists are burning from the tight ropes, my fingers tingling. There is no good place to rest my head.

Whitley must notice my discomfort, because she begins to hum softly. The melody is light and airy, drifting up and down along with the waves and wind. My mind spins with the notes, rising and falling alongside its beauty. Soon my whole body is riding the waves, swirling with them. Darkness drops over my whole self and I am a goner.

A SHARP PAIN TO MY thigh jerks me awake.

"Ow."

"Sorry," Whitley whispers. "You wouldn't wake."

"How did you kick me in this position?" I ask incredulously.

"Talent, I suppose." Her voice is amused, and I smile in return, though I know she can't see it. My mind jumps to what I could do, now that I'm planning to escape my bindings... but I shake them off. I have more important work tonight.

The sky is dark. Even the moon and stars are hidden beneath thick clouds above. Perfect conditions. A few feet away, our guard sits against a barrel, eyes closed, mouth dropped open in a loud snore, an empty bottle of rum beside him. Rum is always a pirate's weakness. That and women.

In only moments, I wiggle my sore wrists from the ropes and slither my way free.

"Wow," Whitley says under her breath. "That was quick."

I turn to face her for the first time in a full day. Strange to spend so much time with someone, but unable to see them. It's refreshing just to lay eyes on the soft lines of her face, even in the darkness. "I have talents too," I say with a wink.

Her eyebrows rise and her lips turn up slightly.

Walking away from her right now is not easy. I must remember who she is. I must remember that I may care about her, but she's only here with me out of circumstance. I don't know what Whitley really wants, but I don't believe for a second that it's me.

She alone will have the power to enslave him

I want her. I owe her. But I will not trust her.

I drag my body away from the woman as beautiful as a siren. That's what they do, what they are. Perhaps Ink was right. All women are sirens. They lure you in, make you believe they love you—then they drag you under and drown you.

It's hard to find a balance between treating Whitley like a human being that is in trouble and in pain—in part, at least, because of me—and remembering that she will be my downfall if I allow it.

I want her to be happy. But I can't let my happiness come from her.

That's why New York was such an ideal plan. Leave her to a life she'd apparently wanted and move on. Too bad Stede had to ruin that.

Or perhaps it was ruined long ago by her father. I don't know.

I shake my mind free of its entanglement with Whitley. I have a plan I must execute. Safety first. I'll figure the rest out later.

I rush through the shadows, quiet as a ghost. I pick the lock of the captain's quarters and slip inside easily but pause as I approach the map, squinting at the darkness.

Captain Taj is slumped over at a desk in the corner, snoring loudly. I can't light a candle or it will wake him. Darkness might be convenient for sneaking out, but less so for map reading.

Instead, I force myself to have patience and get what context clues I can in the darkness.

I draw my finger along the string pinned to the map board, which shows our direction and heading. I'll need two bits of information before I'm able to calculate my escape point: the ship's route and the location of the island on the map. I need light for both.

My navigating instincts are strong enough that I could guess our general direction and speed, but this is a time I'd like to be as exact as possible. There is too much at risk.

So I wait, eyes pinned to the map in front of me, hoping the clouds will clear, exposing the moonlight for even a moment.

The ship rocks and sways, creaking and grinding as it does. Captain Taj snores unevenly, and for one uncomfortable moment, he calls out Rosemera's name. I do feel badly for him. I want Rosemera safe as much as he does. But Whitley was right. She doesn't need us to save her.

I'm confident she'll be just fine. And I hope to God I'm right.

Finally, the sky lightens momentarily, giving me a moment of clearer vision. I find a section of small islands, but there are too many. Too obvious. The sky goes dark again.

This may take a while. The island I'm seeking will be several miles past that horseshoe shaped bunch. I could estimate from there, but I'll need another moment of light before I'll know for sure.

Another twenty minutes pass, and I begin to worry this won't work. The captain could wake at any time. It's unlikely he sleeps for more than a few hours each night, especially in such an uncomfortable spot.

A door slams shut, three loud bangs, and the captain jerks awake.

Shit.

I slip into the shadows as the captain drags himself to the door. I use the squealing sound of the opening door to mask the quick rustling of the clothes I slip behind in the corner of the room.

"He's gone," A pirate says. Timmons, I assume, based on his calm. One of Taj's few truly trusted comrades. He's small but cunning, and always cool in a crisis.

"Damn it." The captain rubs his face with his hands. "But we did expect it. We still have the girl, I assume?"

"Aye."

"Good. We still have a few hours before dawn. See if we can recapture him before the rest of the crew find out."

"CAPTAIN!" another voice calls out. Loud footsteps pound up to the captain's door. "He's escaped! He's—" Timmon's presses his hand over Ink's mouth before he finishes.

"Hush, will you?" the captain barks.

His cry is muffled by Timmon's gag, but I do hear a few "buts" in there. I hold back a laugh at his extreme reaction. Such a tough guy, so afraid when things get rocky. He's a coward hiding behind size and dark marks.

"We need to search for him. Quickly, and quietly," the captain says in a hushed but firm tone.

Ink's eyes remain large, but he stills his body and nods quickly. Timmons removes his hand.

"Let's begin. Wake no one."

All three withdraw from the room and split up communicating in only gestures. I must be caught anywhere but here. They can't know what I was looking at, or my plan won't work. Surprise is key.

So I slip out from hiding place and creep towards the door. It doesn't matter what happens now so long as I get out of this room before they find me.

But just before I reach the door, Ink's huge body blocks the way. He looks more shocked than I am, mouth open and eyes wide.

"Plan B it is."

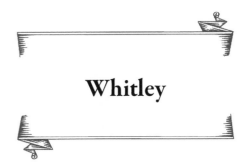

Whitley

The sun is now rising in earnest, and the captain has been searching for Bluff for hours to no avail.

So my unease does not grow to its soul-crushing peak until the crew surrounds me, bodies pressing in closer, their hands clasped over dagger handles. Whispered discussions on what they should do to me suck all the air from my lungs.

I'm their only leverage over Bluff if they can't figure out where he is.

Who he is.

They know. They know he's among them, somewhere. Paranoia is spreading, hooking its claws deeper and deeper with each passing moment. One pirate gasps as he stares into the face of the tallest pirate in the crowd and steps away like he's come to some nefarious conclusion. "It's him! I can smell it! Smells like a siren!!"

A muscled arm wraps around the suspected imposter's neck, and I flinch back as a fight starts— pushing and pulling and punching and yelling. The whole crowd swells with the movement, like a violent storm at sea.

This isn't the first brawl to begin since the crew learned Bluff had disappeared, but it is the nearest to me. Their fists fly near my face and I can feel the rush of air as their bodies

201

tumble to the ground by my feet. It's only a matter of time before they stop pointing fingers at each other and turn their entire attention to me.

"Stop fighting one another, you loonies!" Barns shouts, straw still in his mouth. "We know our enemy." He points a stubby finger straight at my face.

I curl my body in tighter, attempting to hide, but with my arms tied behind my back, it's impossible. I'm exposed, facing a scared pack of dogs—tails under their legs but baring their teeth at their only known target.

"Let's toss her overboard and end it, here and now."

"Slit her throat for good measure!"

"We need her to get Rosey back!"

"Why? What's so important about the little lass?" A man with red hair and one eye permanently shut raises a sharp blade towards me. "Only value is in her pretty face, and I can end that with a flick of my wrist!"

"Her value," the captain's firm voice cuts through the crowd as he steps forward, "is in Bluff's affection. That is her value."

I swallow, assuming his meaning is exactly what I'm dreading—that torturing me is their means to force Bluff to expose himself. But it still doesn't explain why Captain Stede wants me so badly.

I press my eyes together, trying to close out the image before me. Panic presses down on me from all angles—hot breath on every inch of my exposed skin.

"Cut her free!" the captain orders.

I jerk my head up immediately, unsure if this is good or bad.

A man with skin as pale as milk and hair dark as night sends me a sadistic smile, and I know it must be bad. Then the crew cheers, and my stomach roils.

My hands are clammy, my head dizzy as they rip me from the ropes and drag me to my feet.

They press in closer until several bodies are touching me, and I squirm. They laugh.

"I know how we can use the lass to weed out the Bluff-boy," the pale skinned man announces, gently touching my face with the only two fingers remaining on his right hand. I shiver. "Let's have a little fun with her."

More laughter.

I've never been more terrified in all my life, but I know there must be a means of escape. There must be some solution. And I can't rely on Bluff, not this time. If he exposes himself it could be the end of our escape plan, and I won't be any better off.

"Rosemera wouldn't like that," one man says from the back.

"Well Rosemera isn't here, is she?"

I clench my jaw.

"What about the sirens?" the whispered voice cools the crowd instantly.

The pale skinned man grabs me by the upper arm and turns to the crowd. "Boy can't call no sirens. He might be half-a' one but they never listened to him before."

Wait, what?

"But what if!" someone calls.

"Then I'll be the first to drown." The man holding me curls a lip, exposing yellow teeth. "But I'll do it with a smile on my face, knowing I *beat* him."

This was our only chance at convincing the crew not to harm me, even though I didn't understand it. Now I'm beginning to. Just one more truth Bluff withheld.

I blink rapidly as the wall of pirates pressed closer. If the threat of sirens doesn't work, Bluff's lies will be the least of my worries.

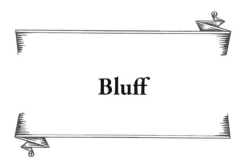

Bluff

My whole body burns with rage. I can't let them touch her. I won't. Already the threat of sirens has dissipated. Forgotten.

But *dammit*, what will exposing myself help? They'll know who I killed once I'm no longer taking his place. And they'll easily discover where he was last. They'll know I was in the captain's quarters. If they know that, they'll easily piece together my entire scheme.

Then it won't be *The Freedom*'s crew ready to destroy Whitley, it'll be Stede's. Same problem, different crew.

But then again, like Whitley said previously, at least it would delay the nightmare. We'd have more time to plan another scheme—more difficult than the last. Every second that passes, every inch we travel closer, every plan foiled, our chance at success diminishes.

If I give in now... I'm unsure we'll make it out of this.

Lucky Seven pushes Whitley back from the crowd toward the railing, and I must act now. That's a pirate's name I will never forget.

"I'll do it with a smile on my face, knowing I beat him."

Acid fills my veins just at the thought. I will *kill* him for those words.

He'll be easy to find, only pirate I know missing three fingers on one hand.

I've only ever killed out of necessity. Never out of rage or vengeance. That trend will end soon. Very soon.

Whitley stumbles to the side of the ship, giving her just a little distance from her pursuers. I can't bring myself to witness the panic on her face. I call out. "Oy!"

A few heads turn in my direction, but not enough. I'm ready to change, ready to expose myself. Ready to fight, if necessary. But just before the magic fills my skin, a feeling of cool mist falls over the ship, followed by a voice, drifting over the waves and hushing the hollers of the crew.

A song. A sinister melody, high and cool—coming from Whitley.

I swallow, even my own hair stands on end at the sound that leaves her soft lips. She stands there, head up, determined. Her eyes are harsh but the sound is so... gentle.

Breath leaves me as I watch. She's... surprisingly convincing. So much so, it makes me sick.

But it's working. The crew steps away from her.

"She's calling them!"

"No. They're already here!" They throw their hands over their ears, eye wide with panic.

"She's *one of them*."

"Told you! Too pretty, that one. Isn't right!"

I fall into the role of terrified pirate, mouth hanging open. "Make her stop!" I yell. It's an easy role, because truth is—I am unnerved right alongside them. I know the song isn't real. It's like someone pretending to know a language they don't. It's pure gibberish. But I'm the only one who would know it. Still, the sound is too close. The feeling is *too right*.

It's beautiful. And I *hate* it.

The worst torture in the world would be to fall in love with a siren. She's not a siren, I remind myself. Yet the sound hovering over the vessel has me doubting what I know.

And the more I refuse to love her, it seems, the closer I get to just that. And even just the image of *her* being one of *them* is a dagger to the heart.

I'd rather the prophecy come true and she somehow have the power, and will, to control my every move for the rest of life, than to love someone and have them become like my *mother*. Cruel and unloving. Unable to care.

Inhuman.

Sirens are not like humans. They have no emotional capacity. They are pure lust and power. The pain in my chest grows deeper at that thought.

The crew panics in earnest now, rushing around to find shelter from the sirens. I stand there, just staring at her, broken heart frozen in place. Then I blink myself back to reality.

I must remember that I am not Bluff. I am a member of the crew and must act like it. I flee alongside the others, trying to force my large body into a small gap below the galley stairs along with three others.

Half my body is sticking out, but we all go still, hoping it's enough. It's quiet, we realize. She's no longer singing and there is no evidence of a siren attack—yet.

"Are they here?" I whisper, a tremor in my voice.

"Don't think so. Maybe she called them off?" Jimmy, who grips my bicep like a doll, says.

I won't be the first to move, first to check if the coast is clear, though I'd like to be. It wouldn't be characteristic of the pirate I'm wearing, so I'll need to act as terrified as possible.

So I wait.

"What was that, lassy?" The captain's cool voice floats over the deck.

No response.

"You one of them, eh?"

I peak through the gaps between stairs. If I bend my head just so I can kind of catch a glimpse. Whitley shakes her head, but this angle is anything but comfortable.

"He teach you to call them?"

My muscles cramp, but I force my body to stay in this painful position. Whitley shrugs. As the shooting pain crescendos, I shake my head, releasing the tension in my neck, only to hit my temple into the bottom corner of a beam. "Ow."

"What'd you see?" Emory asks. He's the youngest of the crew, only a few years my elder, but arguably the bravest.

"Says she's not a siren. Wouldn't answer the rest."

Emory shakes his head. "I don't buy it."

"She'd have eaten us by now, eh? If she were one." I don't want them to think she is a siren, because that would put a different sort of target on her back. Best for them to be afraid but not too afraid.

"Maybe she were just waiting."

"Well, now would be the time, wouldn't it? Before we take her to Stede. She's free of the bindings...if we live out the night."

"Yeah, if."

"Come on out, lads!" The captain calls, and we all scramble to get out of our awkward hiding place before we're seen by the rest of the crew. Once out though, I hang back, not wanting to be the first to approach.

He turns his back to Whitley, facing the crew as we gather around. "Head's up, lads. We need the girl *and* Bluff in order to make the deal for Rosemera. We don't know what either of 'em are capable of, so we won't risk it. Girl isn't touched, hear me?"

I let out a breath. The men around me groan.

"But we don't have Bluff," someone calls.

"We do. We all know he's here somewhere."

"But where? Could be any one of us!" Barn's red hair wiggles as he looks around. "I mean, it's not me! But..."

"Exactly. So, each and every one a' you will be locked below." Now the groans are sincere along with a few shouted complaints of unfairness. It won't be a pleasant trip, all locked below, but I'm actually impressed with the solution. "It's only a day's sailing. Sails are fixed well enough to make it with minimal crew, so the rest of you'll spend the next day in your quarters, door bolted until we reach our rendezvous."

"How will we find the boy even then?"

"Sirens won't come while were docked, will they? We'll use the girl to weed him out then."

I swallow. The plan is too clever. Too good.

How will I communicate with Whitley about the island if I'm locked below? Even if she could find her way down to the crew's quarters, how could she find me? I won't have the chance to signal to her which crew member I am without someone else finding out.

Breaking out from below will be tricky business, to say the least. And I can't be caught trying or we're back to where we were.

This isn't looking good.

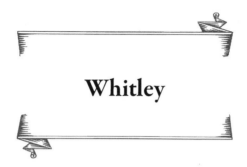

Whitley

My relief is heavy as I'm tied back into my original position on the main mast. My entire body feels weighted, my skin thick. Every breath takes effort.

I wish Bluff were here with me, but I'm simply relieved I made it through the hour unscathed. I don't know where our escape plan lays, though. Did Bluff get what he needed before he was discovered? Is him being locked below going to be a huge deterrent? We only have one day left before we reach Stede. It's midday, and I have to assume tonight will be our last chance at a successful escape attempt. I don't know where this island is, or how to find it. Even if I could make it into the captain's quarters, I wouldn't have any clue how to read the maps.

The deck is tranquil with nearly the entire crew stuck below. I've only seen three pirates out and about in the last hour: the captain, of course, Timmons and a young pirate named Jimmy, who appears only a few years older than Bluff and me. He has a shark tattoo on his forearm, but otherwise I wouldn't necessarily peg him as a pirate. With a good bath, he'd make a fairly handsome and kind-looking fellow.

I'm not sure why these two are the only allowed to remain free. For whatever reason, the captain must believe wholeheartedly Bluff did not compromise them.

For now, I'm going to assume I need to enact this plan on my own.

One good thing about our current situation, I've realized, is that the captain is much looser with his tongue with so few crew members around. And more importantly, without Bluff around. He doesn't seem to mind discussing the rendezvous point around me. Not much of a risk, I suppose, to let the girl who's never even been to the Caribbean overhear that they're meeting near Freeport.

Surprisingly, I *have* heard of Freeport, mostly from stories of pirates in the past. Times have changed in the last hundred years. Then, it was huge pirate port. These days? Not so much. Just flying a pirate flag nearby could be a massive risk. So my guess is that when they say *near Freeport*, they mean in that *general vicinity*. It's likely some smaller, hidden pirate port on a nearby island.

Either way, since I don't actually know where we are now, or how far south a Caribbean island like Grand Bahama would be... well, they're probably right in not worrying about giving me that information. I couldn't do anything with it even if I knew *exactly* where we were headed.

I do know that the Bahamas have tons and tons of islands, and we just need some small island to pass. So it's still good news, regardless.

They also talk of a cove that's very shallow and will require delicate handling of the ship. They've discussed a few options on how they'll navigate that issue when the times comes. With the entire crew locked up, docking will be tricky even in ideal conditions.

Between my moments of spying, I work on unknotting my bindings, which I expected to be especially tricky, maybe impossible, but apparently my siren song unnerved the crew enough they were rather hasty with tying me back up. The knots are loose and fairly easy to untangle.

Sometime around midafternoon, I spy land in the distance. My heart leaps, but I quickly realize there is no way I could get us both free and onto that island in time, even if we could remain unexposed. I'm going to need to get to Bluff long before we reach our escape point, but not so long that someone notices anything amiss. The timing is going to be tricky.

Still, I use it to my advantage and spy on anything I can manage. Like the captain giving brief instruction to the young Jimmy about how to distinguish shallow water. Keeping this close to the larger islands is the quickest route, but also more dangerous. They'll be passing several reefs he'll need to wary of.

When he is at the helm, which will be much more often given the amount of crew available, he needs to be sure we don't travel too close to any shores or risk running aground.

That information very well may be the key to my escape plan. Hopefully, I'll be able to find those same clues once the sun goes down. That may be the trickier bit.

Bluff

The crew's grumblings are ceaseless. It takes everything in me not to tell them all off as they complain about every little thing.

It's so dark.

I can't feel the spray of the ocean down here.

Lars always stinks up the place and we can't even go get a breath of fresh air.

This is one day of their long lives. In two days' time, everything will be back to normal for them. Me? I very well may be meeting a never-ending nightmare. I'll get to watch Whitley tortured until she consents to help them control me. Then, the rest of my life will be spent enslaved by a mother that hates me and the most notoriously sadistic pirate of our time.

I have something to complain about. They don't.

It's not even like we're locked in the brig. We get our own beds, with our belongings and food and rum. These boys are spoiled, indeed.

I lay on Ink's bunk, thinking through contingency plans. I need to break out of here, but how do I do that with a dozen crew piled on top of each other? How can I do anything without being seen? May have been easier if I'd chosen

214

a natural loner. At least then they wouldn't think much of it if I disappeared for a few hours at a time. Ink and his big mouth—they'd notice.

"Hey, Ink!"

I sit up to find Lucky Seven smiling at me, and I resist the muscles in my face turning into a sneer. Of course it would be him calling me.

"What?" I grumble, playing off that I'm annoyed at the situation as much as the next guy. Which I guess I am. But mostly, I really don't want to talk to *him*.

"How's about a game?"

I raise my eyebrows. "What sort?"

"Liar's dice, with rum." He winks.

I hold back a smirk. No one is better at liar's dice than me. Most crews won't even allow me to play anymore. Unfair, they say. *Except, this time, they don't know it's me.*

I stand, allowing a smile to spread across my face. I work to make it a goofy one, not too telling that I'm eager to beat them.

I pull up a crate and settle in next to the empty whiskey barrel we use as a table.

"Loser drinks," are the only instruction we get. Lucky Seven places a massive rum bottle in the middle of our makeshift table.

Now I have my plan. There are six men crowded around the table, including myself. Two others are in the corner drinking rum all on their own. That's seven men that will be sleeping off drink for the rest of the night. It's not the whole crew, but it's a large enough portion it'll leave me with an easy escape.

We each have cups in which we roll our three dice, then peak at only our own.

"Two fives," Lars says. It's a guess at how many fives there are— total. You only get to know your own, but you bet on all the dice on the table, including the fifteen you can't see. If you bid too many and get caught in the lie, you lose.

I'm next. I don't have any fives. My choices are to make a higher bid or call him a liar. With eighteen dice in play, there's no way I'd call him a liar at so low a number. I can take an easy route and only bid a number I have. Or I could lie and lead someone in the wrong direction.

"Four fives," I say. It's a gamble. Forces the next guy to bid very high—hopefully sticking to fives, assuming Lars and I both have some. Unless he calls me a liar, in which case he very well may win.

They key to liar's dice isn't lying or telling the truth—it's remaining unpredictable. If they know you lie every time, they'll have the upper hand. If they know you tell the truth every time, they'll have an even bigger advantage. So, do both. Never let them know which one you're doing when. That's how you win.

Lucky Seven is after me and narrows his eyes. "Six fives," he says after a long moment.

Stevie belly laughs. "Liar!" he calls.

We all expose our dice. There are four fives total—his six bid was too high.

"Shit!" Lucky Seven yells, tossing his cup. Stevie steals one of his die and hands him the bottle. He chugs.

Great start.

Except that Lucky Seven stares at my exposed dice. His eyes narrow, and I'd bet my last gold coin he's noticed that I didn't have a single five. His eyes travel up to mine, unblinking.

The breath rushes from my lungs, realizing something a bit too late.

They know Bluff is good at this game.

They know Bluff is down here somewhere.

What better way to weed me out than to play a game I can't resist dominating? One round is meaningless. But if I keep winning...

It's a much better tactic than hurting Whitley, I will say. But I still can't let them succeed, which means *I can't win* or this game will end with me tied up in a corner, and that's if I'm lucky. I blink back this reality. I guess that plan of mine wasn't such a good one after all.

I must stay in character, I think, clenching my jaw. Right now, I'm Ink.

Ink would certainly play dice, but Ink would also certainly lose.

I suspect there is going to be a lot of rum in my near future.

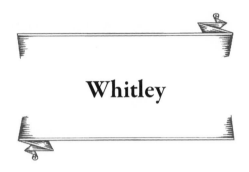

Whitley

A massive moon rises overhead as the sky fades to a deep blue, and I know now is the time. If I don't find a way to reach Bluff and get off this ship without being noticed before the sun rises, I'll be meeting the pirate who has haunted my dreams for weeks.

Despite the rumor's implication that Bluff will be fine after our "trade"—and I won't—I somehow get the feeling the deal poses the greatest risk to Bluff. I don't even know what that would mean. What secrets could he truly be hiding that hold that much danger? The feeling in my body, mind, soul, tells me I must save *him*.

Regardless of my strange instincts, there is one basic truth that's as crystal clear as the Caribbean water we're now sailing through—we must escape from this ship. After that, well, things get a bit murkier. There's a lot that I don't know, and the deeper I go into this mystery, the darker it gets.

But answers must come second.

First, we escape. Then perhaps I can dig and uncover the truths hiding from me.

After spending the whole day loosening the knots, I easily pull my hands of the itchy ropes. I twisted myself back in hours ago, pretending to be bound in case anyone looked too closely. Now that I have an opportune moment, I'm un-restrained in an instant.

Now for the hard part.

I stand and take a good look around. I haven't seen an-other pirate for nearly an hour, since the captain headed to his quarters for the night. There are two others about some-where, which is infinitely better than the dozen there would be otherwise—but there are still two sets of eyes that could ruin everything.

I begin towards the railing, but after just one step I real-ize I have one major issue. The clink of my shoes is entirely too loud. After a smirk reminiscent of the first time I met Bluff, and my "clickity shoes," I sit to rip off the white leather boots. Bare feet are much quieter. The liberty it gives my toes is a happy side-effect.

Then, I resume my mission. At the edge of the railing, I look down at the water. Dark blue waves crash into the side of the ship, white caps fading back to black. Otherwise, there isn't much to see. The sea looks dark as can be, and I can't tell if that's because we're in deep water or simply because it's night time. Will I be able to distinguish the shallower areas without the light of the sun? I'm unsure.

I tiptoe farther back, closer to the helm where I'm guess-ing at least one pirate will be posted through the night. Two quiet voices drift my way. If the captain is truly sleeping, that means the only two I have to worry about are just ahead, making this part fairly easy.

"From here, you just need to keep your southeast head-ing and we'll have a wide berth from the reefs of the Crown."

I creep closer to Timmons' voice; no doubt he's speaking to Jimmy, what with the instructing tone.

"We'll pass that around midnight. Captain will be up an hour or two later to steer us into the Cays."

I peek up at them from my lower vantage point and see Jimmy nod, his face pale in the moonlight.

"You'll be fine, mate. See you in a few hours."

"What about the girl? Won't she be trying to escape tonight?"

Timmons shoots a glance back and forth like he doesn't like those words being uttered aloud. "It would be her best time. But she may not know that. I find it unlikely she'll make it far without Bluff's help."

I roll my eyes, determination filling my chest. Let me prove them wrong.

"I'll check on her before I head in, then just make an hourly check and you'll be fine."

That means I must be back in my bindings right now, before Timmons sees my empty place on the mast. I flee from my spot in the shadows and tiptoe quickly back to the main mast, where I put my arms behind my back and pull the ropes over my wrists, twisting them into some semblance of a knot. Then I pull my knees up to my chest and rest my forehead onto them, pretending to be asleep.

I listen to Timmons' footsteps as he approaches, the pounding of my heart nearly overpowering the sound. He stops in front of me, and I don't trust my face not to expose something, so I don't bother looking up.

He lets out a huff of laugh. "Not a chance," he mumbles, then marches past.

I grit my teeth, but don't lift my head until a few minutes pass, just in case. Once I feel confident that he's gone, I pull my arms back out of the ropes and head straight to the door of the berth-everything beneath the main deck, where, right now, all the crew are stuck until we dock.

There is a rusty padlock on the door.

I purse my lips. It would be fairly easy to break it off. Its half eroded anyway, but that would cause more noise than is ideal. Realistically, I need to find Bluff, tell him what I know, and get off the ship long before we're discovered. We can't be heard. At all.

If any of the crew figure out that we're in the process of escaping before we're long gone, they'll be able to find us too easily. Swimming to shore will take a long time. They'd reach the shore before we do if we're found out.

So any alert at all, would be very bad.

I grip the lock in my hand and shake it slightly, but it's a little firmer than it looks. I tap it with my fingers while I think. My father was a thief with many talents. Though he preferred to be a con-artist, he was also a rather talented lock-pick when I was younger, and though I'd never tried my hand at it, he had told me a thing or two.

I just need something small to insert into the key hole to pry the lever inside into the right position. An old lock like this shouldn't be too difficult.

My mind goes immediately to my hair. It's been days since the ball, and I'm certain nearly all the pins are long gone, but it's such a rat's nest of tangles and so sticky from the salty air that I may get lucky.

I push my fingers through the kinks as the wind whips it around, causing even more of a mess. One hard piece sticks to the knot at the end of one of my curls. It takes more effort to pull the pin from my hair than it did to get my wrists free of the pirates' "expert" knots.

I smirk like Bluff at that thought.

When I finally pull the pin free, I go to work on the lock. It takes longer than I'd like to maneuver the little metal piece to the right position, but I finally hear the click, and the lock falls off into my left hand.

A rush of success fills me. To hell with those pirates who think I can't do anything.

Now, for step two—find Bluff. I still don't know which pirate he's impersonating, and though I am convinced I can tell just based on that feeling, I'm beginning to doubt that ability in these circumstances. What if I can't tell while he's sleeping? What if I pick the wrong pirate? What if I take too long and one of them wakes before I find him?

I sneak below, creeping down the dark hall and realizing I have no idea where I'm headed. This place is much bigger than I anticipated. There is an open space immediately at the bottom of the stairs with several crates and barrels, but I'm unsure where to go next. There are sets of doors at each end and another staircase. My guess is the crew wouldn't sleep too far down on the ship though, so I stick to exploring just this first level.

Through one door, I find the galley where the crew eat. I flinch as the snores of one pirate surprises me. He's spread out on the floor, unmoving. I back out slowly. Back past the crates, I open the next door as slowly as possible. Inside are several beds, filled with snoring pirates. Though they're all breathing deeply in sleep, my heart thuds in my chest. Just hours earlier, these men were determined to hurt me in ways I don't even want to think of. One wrong move and I could wake the whole lot. I do not want to repeat my close call of the last morning.

My breathing quickens. Pressure settles over my head, making it hard to think. I try to force myself to calm, but my mind is spinning, my breathing becomes even more labored, and I realize I'm on the brink of a legitimate panic attack.

Breath, I instruct myself. *Think good thoughts*. The first thing that comes to my mind is Bluff. Salty air, bright morning sun streaming through the window, and the feeling of his hands on my back, and in my hair. His lips on mine.

I told him I'd prove it to him—that I *knew*, that day in the captain's quarters.

I open my eyes and search the room full of sleeping pirates with a new determination. I'll find Bluff here, and I'll make sure he has no more doubts.

I start to the left and sweep past the beds. Large pirates, small pirates, skins dark and light and everything in between. Hair long and stringy, heads so bald they very well may be shaved clean. My heart continues pounding, but otherwise my body is empty of feeling. At least the one I'm hoping to find.

I pass the pale pirate with three missing fingers, and I shudder. I know without a doubt that *he* is not Bluff.

At the end of the last row, my heart falls. I passed every bed and nothing. Is he not here? Or am I just failing?

My eyes shift to a barrel in the corner, with a massive bottle of rum laying on its side. I approach the table and realize the bottle is bone dry. And there is a body lying on the ground next to it.

I raise my eyebrows, and they pull even higher when my fingers begin to tingle. Why would Bluff have drunk this much knowing we needed to escape? Was he pretending for the crew? Had he given up hope? Or is the feeling in my fingers wrong?

I lean down over the body of Ink, the man who was rather nasty to us both just a few days ago, and there's a quick fluttering in my chest. Would Bluff really pick this man to impersonate? I suppose if it required killing the pirate that he picked, Ink wouldn't be a bad choice. I rather wish he'd picked seven fingers over there, though.

Then I think about what I'm about to do, and realize I'm very glad he isn't in that pale pervert's body. Ink is large, his arms thick and muscular and covered in strange and elaborate tattoos that travel all the way up even to his face. He's not exactly my type.

I close my eyes. I don't want to see—I want to feel.

I lean in close to his face and smell rum on his breath. I shudder but keep going with my plan. I breathe in through my mouth, long and deep, and that's when I feel it. Really feel it.

Bluff. His name is like a whisper through my whole body.

Both hands around his head, knee between his legs, I hover my chest against his. My lips press against his. The body beneath me stirs, and for a moment I still I feel the largeness of Ink's lips, and coarseness of his hair-covered cheeks.

Then a hand grabs the back of my head and pulls me in. The lips move, kissing me back. Everything else falls away and I feel only Bluff. It's like flying. Excitement sings over every inch of my skin. Now I press my hips against his and kiss deeper. Longer.

His hands reach my bare legs and run all the way under my skirt, reaching much farther than is at all appropriate for a lady, and I suck in a desperate breath. I grip the front of his shirt. We must be quiet, I remember.

But he tastes so sweet. Feels amazing. It would be too easy to fall. Too easy to forget where we are and the danger waiting just around the corner.

"Whitley?" he whispers as I pull away. He struggles to open his bloodshot eyes. Confusion clouds his expression. I put a finger over his lips and pull my body from his, grabbing his hand, prompting him to rise. He looks around, blinking back more confusion.

Then he follows me out the door.

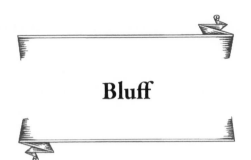

Bluff

My head pounds. Pressure heavy over every inch of my body. I'm so confused. So much of what's happening right now doesn't make sense. It takes a few moments of walking to get the feeling of her off of me enough to think through my rum-hazy mind.

I remember last night. I was locked below with the rest of the crew, with no way to escape without being found out. Lucky Seven successfully conned me into getting drunk playing liar's dice—because I couldn't win without them knowing it was me.

Now the part I can't figure out—Whitley is here. She made her way to *me*. That part is impressive, but how did she know? Even now I'm still wearing Ink's skin. I woke to her lips on mine. Her body so achingly close...

Was that a dream? I shake my head trying to figure it out.

"What are you doing here?" I mumble, once she stops in the middle of a pitch-black hall, facing me.

"Saving your arse."

I smirk, but I run my hand over my face. Oh, how I wish I hadn't played that game.

"How? How did you get here? How did you find me?" I whisper, at least cognizant enough to know we must be quiet.

"Are you drunk?" she asks, hands on her hips, ignoring my question.

I sigh. "Perhaps a little."

"Isn't that a better question? Why? Why would you get drunk tonight?"

"I didn't mean to. It's... a long story." I shake my head. I did manage to win enough rounds to ensure the others got drunk too, and that I wasn't so far gone that I wouldn't wake. Though I did get a little too close for comfort.

"So you didn't... give up?"

I blink. "That's what you think?" But I suppose it makes sense. If I thought all hope was lost, why not get drunk before the worst happens? But then, why did she kiss me like that?

"I don't know what I think," she says, looking down at her bare feet.

"How did you find me? Once you found the bunks, how did you figure out who I was?" I think through how she might have figured it out. What was my flaw? I was sure I hadn't left any gaps in my performance.

"I told you before," she says, the muscles in her face suddenly relaxing, a blush forming on her cheeks. "I can tell. I can... feel you."

I raise my eyebrows. I was the drunk one passed out on the ground. That's the one she picked. I find it hard to believe she'd guess that. Could she really tell? Could she somehow have some ability to feel the power? I suppose it's possible our connection is supernatural. There is a prophecy about it, after all.

It also means that first time we kissed—maybe she was telling the truth. Maybe she knew it wasn't her fiancé. Maybe she was really kissing *me*.

My head spins at that thought, heart aching with such an intense desire. I press my eyes shut. I want her to want me so badly *I can't think straight*. But that's exactly the problem. I have to focus.

"What time is it?" I ask. I know we have bigger issues at hand. I can stress about my conflicting emotions once we're free. But that's if we survive the night. Is it already too late? The sun has long since set. I'd passed out sometime in the late afternoon. How long did I sleep?

"An hour or so after dusk. Around ten, I'd guess?"

I nod. That's good.

"We are set to pass a place called the Crown at midnight."

I raise my eyebrows; the calculations are a little harder than usual with the rum induced haziness, but it's not exactly complex, so I make my way through it. We are around two hours north of Crown Haven, meaning we'll be passing several islands here very soon.

"Any idea which direction we're headed?" I don't actually expect her to know this, but a man can hope. We could be coming in from several, being down here made it impossible for me to tell which route the captain chose. Closer to the open sea, closer to the main land or somewhere in between?

"Southeast."

I blink. "You really knew that?"

She rolls her eyes indignantly. "I'm tired of people thinking I'm worthless."

I smile. "I haven't thought that for a long while. Though, I can't say I never did. You've surprised me on the daily, if I'm honestly."

She smiles, eyes shining in a way that sends a fluttering through my chest. The feeling of her bare skin on my hands, lips on mine, her taste. It all still lingers.

Focus.

Southeast, nearing Crown Haven, means we'll be passing near a set of islands that will work nicely an hour before that. If it's ten, we have maybe an hour.

"They're checking on me hourly. If that matters."

I nod. It does. We have two options: hope they don't notice her gone for a while after we escape or knock out whatever lookout is around and hope he doesn't wake for a long while after we escape. If we do that latter, they'll assume we're off the ship immediately. If we do the former, they'll search the ship first.

"How many are up there? How many are awake?"

"Just Jimmy right now. Timmons and the Captain are sleeping until a few hours after we pass the Crown."

I bite my lip. "Okay, here's what we do. You go back up there, tie yourself back in and wait until the next time they check on you. After they get a good sight of you and leave, come back and get me. I'll be in the hall here, pretending to sleep. We'll take it from there."

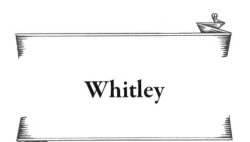

Whitley

"You know you need to get off this ship, right?"

I pry my dry eyes open to see Jimmy standing before me, moonlight shining on half his face, the other half in shadow. I blink back the haze from my mind, realizing I must have dozed off.

"What?"

He squats down in front of me. "We'll be there before dusk tomorrow and they'll trade you off to Stede. This is your last chance at escaping." His voice is calm, but soft as a whisper.

"What time is it?" I ask, wondering if I slept for very long. Did I miss our chance?

"Just after eleven. We'll be passing a few islands that won't be tough swims, but you have to go now."

"Why. Why would you tell me that?" I shake my head. We had a plan to escape, so this conversation is moot, except I can't understand why he'd try to help me.

He stands and looks off into the distance. "Rosemera would have. And she'd want me to too."

I bite my lip. "But don't you want to save her?"

He looks down at me, his eyes heavy. Tired, but not from lack of sleep. "Of course. But I know her better than to think

230

she wants us to sacrifice someone else for her. She'll want to save herself. She's not a damsel and doesn't ever want to be treated like one."

I pull my hands from my pretend knots and rub my raw wrists. Jimmy's eyes grow larger as he watches but otherwise shows no other reaction.

"Bluff doesn't think Stede even has her."

He tilts his head slightly. "Do you have a way to get to Bluff?" he asks, ignoring my comment. He focuses, rather, on my suddenly free hands.

I nod, wondering if it's a mistake to give him this information. This exchange is a strange one. So calm. So matter-of-fact.

"Are you just going to let us go, then?" I ask.

"I'll be back to check on you in an hour and a half. I can't give much more than that." Jimmy's face remains impassive as he turns and walks back to the helm, slowly, as if the whole conversation never happened.

I rub my palm over my face, trying to pull my mind back to the task at hand. My lips tremble as I take in a long breath. Then I rush over to the door to the berth. I knock the lock aside easily and run down the shadowed steps with as light a foot as I can manage.

Just as I reach the bottom, a pair of rough hands grabs me by both upper arms and shoves me up against the wall. The sharp prick of a blade is pushed against my neck. "You bitch," his rough voice says. "You're really so dumb you'd come down here?" His hand is pressed against my mouth in an instant—as if I would scream. Which is better, one pirate or a dozen?

Still, my whole body is screaming for release. My throbbing heart feels louder than any call for help. *Where is Bluff?* I silently beg.

Bluff. The breath of a whisper moves through me. Electricity singes where he grips my arms. Suddenly the fear is gone. I open my eyes.

It isn't Ink's body. The pirate is a taller, but thinner. His skin pale with red freckles all over. He doesn't think I'll know it's him.

I try to speak, but it comes out a mumble against his sweaty hand.

The pirate pulls his hand away slowly and presses a finger to his lips. I nod and swallow.

"I won't tell the rest of the crew... if you don't," he says, his tone suggestive and sinister.

"I said," I begin in a whisper. "*Another test? Really?* "

His eyes narrow. "What?" His tone drops.

"We don't really have time for this, Bluff."

Now he steps back, releasing me from his hold, his face full of confusion. Part of me wants to give him a hard time, drag out my moment of victory. But we really do need to get off the ship. Now.

I rush up the steps, pulling him along with me. He follows without resistance.

He breathes in deep once we reach the fresh sea air of the main deck. Stars cast their light down on him. We both rush to the side of the deck. An island glides past silently, large and close enough that we can see the tops of the palm trees.

"When were you last seen?"

"A few minutes ago. But Jimmy isn't going to be a problem."

He spins his head to face me, then searches the shadowed masts behind us. "Why not?"

I tell him about Jimmy coming to warn us of our chance to escape. I leave out that he had to wake me.

"So he knows we're jumping off now?"

I nod slowly.

The tall pirate in front of me bites his lip, looking around like he's hoping to find some answer among the sails above.

"What's wrong?"

"Two things. One, I don't want him to know which island we're on. And two, if he's trying to help us, that's going to leave him vulnerable."

"You think he'll talk?"

"I think he'll be questioned. And the less he knows, and the less it *looks* like he could have helped us—the better." Bluff takes in a long breath, tapping his hand on his thigh nervously. "Stay here. I'll be back in a just a minute."

I open my mouth to say something, but Bluff is already gone.

I follow him, despite his instruction, and watch from the main deck as he approaches Jimmy, now back in Ink's form. Shock cover's Jimmy's face as the thin pirate grabs him by the collar roughly, whispers something into his ear, and then slams a fist right into his temple.

I hold back a scream and press my hands to my mouth.

Bluff quickly returns. "I told you to stay there."

"Why?" is all I can get out through my heavy breathing.

"Believe me, I did him a favor. If they figure out he attempted to help us, even just by *knowing* we were planning something and not alerting the captain, he'd get much worse than a hit to the head. He's not a good enough liar. Too good of a guy. Now, they won't suspect him. He can give them more information without it hurting us—which is what I told him to do."

My hands shake. I cannot wait to get off this ship.

"You all right?" the body in front of me is Bluff again, and I breathe a sigh of relief.

I look out to the sea and shrug. This whole experience is so much more than I bargained for.

"We'll have to wait for the next set if islands, it'll be a longer swim, but they won't be as likely to discover where we fled to."

I nod and lean against the railing, watching the island drift by. Several moments of silence pass. The open sea spreads out where the island was.

Bluff's fingers lightly trail down my upper arm. "I'm sorry," he whispers.

"For what?" I turn to meet his stare.

"I didn't believe you. I still..." He shakes his head. "I don't understand it. But I trust you."

I study his face quietly, but his gaze turns out to the sea, watching. Waiting. I get the feeling he doesn't want me to see whatever is in his eyes right now.

"You did well," he says with a smile. "Not sure I could have done this on my own. I messed up. You fixed it."

"Are you still drunk?" I ask, just now remembering how I found him only an hour or two ago.

He turns to me now, a smile in his eyes. "I can feel a little. But I slept a lot off. Drank some water. Need for survival will fuel me. I'll be fine."

I nod and say nothing more.

"I think I owe you a proper thank you," he says quietly, so light I almost wonder if he meant for me to hear it.

Another island appears through the darkness ahead. "There she is," he says. "This isn't going to be easy," he warns, his expression much more serious now.

"Long swim?"

He nods. "The waves aren't overly large tonight, but they'll be pulling us. They never seem to like it when I go to shore."

My eyebrows pull down at this, but I don't ask him what he means. I have a lot of questions, but they'll have to wait.

The island grows larger. Another appears farther down.

Bluff puts his foot up on the railing, ready to climb over. He holds out his hand to me. "Ready?"

"I have a request," I say suddenly, a rush pushing through my veins. Head spinning. I'm not ready, but I'll go anyway. "I figure you owe me." I wink, my cheeks warm.

"What's that?"

"Next time you kiss me, I want it to be as *you*. Not some-one else." I pause for one beat to watch the shock cross his face, then pull myself over the railing and throw my body in-to the black waves below.

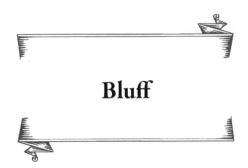

Bluff

A laugh bubbles up in my chest. I shake my head in Whitley's direction, now in the crashing waves, before joining her in the icy black water.

For a moment I am surrounded, every inch of me bombarded by water. By darkness. It swirls and collides, pushes and pulls. *Home*, it whispers in my ear.

My body is heavy in the water as it pulls me below.

I shake my head of its hypnosis and kick myself up to the surface.

I belong to the sea—that will always be true. Which is why I avoid it as much as possible. I suck in a breath of air the second I reach the surface and search for Whitley.

Her blond hair is just visible in the distance, and I begin a brisk swim towards her. It's nearly a quarter mile swim to reach the shore, and I'm hoping she's a good enough swimmer to make it. The longer we stay in the water, the more likely the sirens will find us. I can't save Whitley if they find her in open water. I'd be powerless.

My head spins at the thought. I push it away, because worrying won't help a thing. This is our only option. I reach her moments later, but she doesn't acknowledge me. She's focused on keeping her head above water—it's harder than it should be.

Her dress, I realize, is pulling her own. Heavy and tangling her legs.

"Wait," I tell her.

She stops attempting a forward swim and treads as best she can, her cheeks flushed, eyes bright. God, she's beautiful. *I could kiss her right now.* I clench my jaw. *What a terrible idea.*

Instead, I'm going to undress her. *Wonderful.*

I swallow and swim up until I'm close enough to touch her, removing a knife from my boot in the same motion. The waves rush up and down, splashing in her face, but she keeps steady enough for me to cut the thick fabric of her dress and strings of her corset. She lets out a gasp as I pull several layers of her clothing apart, slipping into the depths, leaving only a thin cotton dress to cover her.

She pulls the dress the rest of the way off, kicking the burden from her feet.

"Better?" I ask, but I can't manage the smirk I'm so used to. All I can think of is her. So close. Her pull is stronger than the waves.

Which is terrifying.

She smiles and nods. I swim past her, hoping to God she can keep up, because right now my self-control is seriously lacking. We must get out of this water.

I swim quickly, focused only on moving my body through the waves and towards the shore. Several minutes later, I look back to make sure I haven't lost her.

She's only a dozen feet behind me, which is actually surprising, since I wasn't slowing down for her, and, well, being the son of a siren means I'm a pretty damn good swimmer. I don't give myself time to dwell on why she too would be an unnaturally quick swimmer. Instead I relish the fact that we'll be reaching safety faster than anticipated.

We keep our quick pace until I can reach the sand with my feet. I let out a breath of relief and once again check to make sure she's not too far behind. She's farther back now, but she's showing no signs of distress, so I walk slowly until I reach the dry sand and flop down.

I'm impressed she was able to do it entirely on her own—besides the whole gown incident. Any of my sailors I'd have expected to pull half the way.

I keep an eye on the water as she comes closer, wondering what these next few days will be like. On a deserted island with Whitley. I don't have a plan for getting off this place. We're hidden from those that want to use and hurt us. Now we'll just have to hope we don't starve to death.

Her shoulders are above the water as she walks slowly to the shore. To me.

More of her body is exposed as she gets closer, and that soaking wet, thin white dress... doesn't conceal much.

I stand as she comes closer. The moonlight casting a soft glow against her skin, every inch of my body buzzing in response. I realize the answer to my question—what will these days on an island with her be like? Because I can't say no. I can't avoid *this*.

Especially now that I know she wants it too.

I'm pulled towards her as she emerges from the water. Her breathing is labored, cheeks flushed, eyes wide, staring straight into mine. I meet her right where the last thin layer of water creeps up to the sand. Where dry meets wet. Rushing gently, then pulling away.

She looks me in the eye but doesn't say anything. Doesn't move. I again look over her body, which is a terrible idea, because I cannot handle how amazing she looks. Water dripping over every inch of her.

I should turn away.

I step forward.

I shouldn't touch her.

Another step.

I should resist.

One more step, and now I'm close enough to reach her. My hands stay put, and instead I lean in close. She sucks in a breath, causing my whole body to shutter as my nose touches hers. I stop.

This is how you fall. This is how you become trapped.

And yet I know it's hopeless to resist. I *need* her.

My hand drifts up to her neck, into the hair behind her head, and I pull her in, pressing her lips to mine. She grabs me and pulls me in tighter, so our hips are pressed together. She groans, this time no mistaking the pleasure behind the sound.

And just like that, I'm a goner.

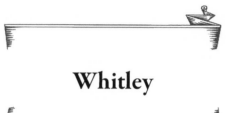

Whitley

Bluff is everywhere. He's everything.

The island is so dark I can't see a thing. I can only feel. And what I feel is Bluff's lips on mine, his tongue. His hands on my back. In my hair.

We fall to the ground, coarse sand scraping against all the exposed skin. He kisses my neck and I feel like I could die at how good it feels. Pleasure streaks down my back and to my legs. How much I *want more.*

"Whitley," he moans in my ear. "I—"

Then suddenly the feeling is gone. He pulls back, his body hovering over me, and breathing heavily. His eyes are wide in panic, and it makes my heart beat even faster—if that's possible.

"Bluff?"

He presses his forehead to mine, closing his fearful eyes. "We should get some rest. It'll be light soon," he says between gasps for breath.

I glance behind him at the horizon, which is still pitch black. No sign of the sun on its way. Is that an excuse? I sit up as he plops down on the sand next to me, working to catch his breath. I want to ask him if I did something wrong. I want to ask him why he stopped. I want to throw myself on-to him and not let him go.

But I don't.

Instead, I lay back down and stare up at the star-scattered sky with unblinking eyes, working to calm my wound-up body and keep my frustration from overflowing. Eventually, I close my tired eyes and allow my stiff muscles to relax as I wonder what tomorrow will bring.

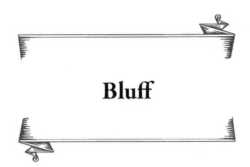

Bluff

My whole body is buzzing as I sit beside her, mind spinning.

I can't believe I did that—the kiss or *stopping* the kiss.

I thought that was it, me giving in. I thought it was over. But then as she kissed me, as she grasped at me, pulled me, like I was water and she was dying of thirst.

She will control the Son of the Sea, cause him to fall.

It was then that I realized I'd almost done it. I'd almost fallen.

Those words sat on the edge of my tongue like an inevitable curse. I knew the moment they were uttered it would be clasping the shackles around my wrist permanently. Whitley would hold the key, and I can't let her have that much power.

Maybe it's already too late.

I press fists to my eyes and suppress a groan of frustration.

I could have her—right now. My whole body aches at that thought. She wouldn't tell me no. I could feel how much she wants me, how desperate she is—

And I was desperate too.

If it was just that, just two bodies that wanted each other, it wouldn't be so hard. It feels stupid. Why not just give in? I've lost already anyway. How long can I really resist for?

And yet, I sit here, not moving. Knowing I disappointed her.

I do care about her. As much as I don't want to, as much as I don't want to admit it. Why must this connection with her be so *heavy*? So burdensome.

Why does it have to mean my own life or death?

I long for a different life. One without bribes and betrayals. One without a mother who doesn't know how to love. One without prophecies or supernatural creatures and powers. One where I was a boy who liked a girl, and that was all there was to it.

I close my eyes and imagine myself in tailcoat and trousers, holding my hand out to Whitley in a pretty gown and pinned up hair. I nearly laugh out loud. Then I shake my head of the image and try again.

Me on a ship, sword at my hip and Whitley with her hair wild and flowing in the wind, loose men's blouse and leather pants. That's more me. And more her, too. I let my mind go farther, thinking of all the things we could do with that much freedom. With no one to tell us no. No one to care. And no destruction waiting on the other side of the door.

It seems such an impossibility. How could we ever defeat all our enemies? They're everywhere. Even fate itself seems against us.

Is there any way we can be together without it destroying us?

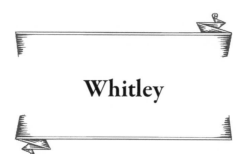

Whitley

It's painful to force my eyes open. They're dry and stiff, the sun so immensely bright.

I groan and roll to hide my face from the light, only to realize that gives me a face full of sand.

I spit and pull my head away from the ground. Sand is everywhere, sticking to every inch of my body. Or at least it feels that way. I blink rapidly to pull my mind back into focus.

Waves rush up to a beautiful sandy beach not far from my feet, beyond which is pure ocean. There's nothing else in view but water and sky. The beach reaches a mile or so in each direction. Behind me is forest.

Last night comes rushing back. We escaped *The Freedom* and our future rendezvous with Stede. Bluff and I swam to shore and then... Heat rushes to my cheeks. It was only a kiss.

An amazing, mind bending—rather long—kiss. But I don't know what any of this means. I don't know what happens now. On the island or with Bluff.

Now I don't even know where he is.

My skirt is bunched on the side, and sand itches my skin, even from the inside my clothes. My hair is plastered to my neck. Sleeping on the beach sounds a lot more luxurious than it is. I adjust the skirt of my chemise—all that's left of my ensemble—and try to brush some of the sand from my chest.

Then, I turn towards the forest behind me, unsure what kinds of creatures, if any, would live in such a place. Twisting brown vines and green leaves, so much brighter than any I've seen before, block the view of anything more. How deep does it go? I step into the shadow of the towering trees, and it gives my skin immediate relief from the hot sun.

There's a rustle of movement inside the brush a few feet in, and my heart stops, like it too is listening for more. I wait, eyes pinned to the spot where I saw something.

The rustling grows louder, closer. I gasp as Bluff immerges from between the vines. He smiles, his eyes shining. "Good, you're awake. I was worried you'd lay in the sun too long."

"Is the sun bad?" I ask. I'd heard it can be, but most of the worry my father had was about how it affects your appearance. Fair is fashionable, apparently. I for one, like the look of tanned skin. Especially on Bluff.

"Too much of it is."

I nod. I suppose that's true about most things. If not all.

I look down and notice Bluff holding onto a cluster of strange brown fruit. Or are they nuts? He notices my gaze and holds them up like a prize he won. "I have breakfast."

"What are they?"

"Coconuts. They'll give us a bit of hydration and energy until we can find fresh water."

No water. That doesn't sound good. Bluff doesn't seem overly concerned about that issue though. Instead he cuts a branch of the tree at the edge of the forest into a sharp point with the same knife that ripped my dress off before our swim to shore. Then he punches the coconut into the point and rips it down, creating a large opening. He chugs from the round object like it's an oddly shaped bottle.

I raise my eyebrows as he hands it to me. "It's good," he tells me.

The coconut is heavy and rough in my hands. The brown substance that covers the outside feels like the coarse hair of an animal. I press it to my lips and slowly tip it back until the liquid flows into my mouth. Somewhere between milk and water, the taste is sweet but odd. I drink more, because I know I should.

"So what now?" I ask.

Bluff gives me an unsure smile. "We make a shelter, fire, and find food. Survive."

"For the rest of our lives? Are we getting off this island?"

Bluff's shoulders sag before he shrugs. "One step at a time. It was a long shot enough to get off the ship. Now let's make sure we don't die of dehydration or whatever other dangers lay here. Then we'll figure out escape plan number two. At least with this one we don't have a strict deadline."

I nod. "All right. Tell me how to help."

Bluff smirks. "The princess wants to get her hands dirty?"

I roll my eyes. "I've never been a princess, as much as my father wanted to make me one."

"You were pretty close," he says, eyes now cast at the ground behind me, like he's afraid to meet my gaze. His voice is gentle, and I almost wonder if that was a compliment rather than an insult.

"Yes, I want to help," I say instead of pushing it.

Bluff shows me where to find palm fronds and instructs me to gather as many of them as possible. Apparently, that's what we'll use to make our sleeping area. He also tells me to keep an eye out for any type of dry wood or kindling. I have only a vague concept of what that means, but I smile and nod anyway.

A few hours later, I drop on to the sand next to a huge pile of palm leaves, face red and hair damp from sweat. Bluff puts his hand on his hip, his expression full of amusement. "Tired?" he asks.

"Haven't slept in days. It's hot as hell here and I just worked for hours straight. Yes, I'm tired."

He takes a seat next to me in the shaded sand and holds out another coconut. "Tomorrow I'll dig a hole to get some water."

I take the coconut and chug.

"And you slept pretty good last night. Stayed asleep well into the morning."

"But what time did we actually go to sleep? It was nearly morning by the time we rested."

He doesn't respond to this. I hope he's thinking about what happened after we arrived at the beach.

I look out to the nearby water. Blue waves crash against the sand. I bet that water is cool, maybe even cold. How incredible would this feel right now—

"Time for a swim?"

He turns to me, eyebrows raised in surprise. I hold out my hand and he reluctantly takes it. Immediately, I pull him up and rush over the sandy beach until we're at the water. Bluff lets go of my hand, pulls off his shirt, then sprints into the water, diving into one of the waves.

I can't help but smile, though the sight of his bare skin makes my cheeks warm. Water laps up over my toes. I close my eyes and feel the moment—the beauty of the scene, the feel of wind blowing through my hair—and as I step deeper into the ocean before me, the water that cools my whole body.

I open my eyes and a few feet away Bluff watches me, entirely still. His expression is hard to read. Watchful. Hopeful, perhaps.

"What?"

He shrugs, his soft eyes never leaving mine. "I like watching you experience things."

My lip curls up on one side. "There are so many things I was never allowed to do. Being a *princess* and all." I roll my eyes at his nickname for me.

"There were also things only people like you could experience."

I nod slowly. "I doubt those things are worth the cost, though."

Bluff rubs his jaw, and I find myself watching his hand. Why is he so standoffish with me still? Like he's afraid. Something seemed to change last night, but then it didn't. He no longer has the excuse of thinking I don't want him back. He knows *I want him*.

How do I break through to him?

I bite my lip, considering. I know what I want. Why must I wait for him to instigate? I step closer. He doesn't move. Closer. Our eyes are still in contact. Soon, our chests are only inches apart.

His breathing grows faster, but he doesn't move.

There are so many things to consider, so many ways to play this. Things I want to ask. Things I'm desperate for him to do. But I'm so tired of waiting. So tired of wondering.

He's taller than me, so when I kiss him, I leap to reach his lips. He catches me around the waist, holding me up to him. Only a moment later, I pull my lips away from his, but his hands don't let me go.

"Can I ask you something?"

His nose touches mine softly and he closes his eyes. "Anything. I'm so tired of secrets."

"Why are you so afraid to want me?"

He clenches his jaw and he gently places me back into the water, where I plant my feet firmly into the sand.

"I'm afraid of losing control."

"Control of what?"

"Everything. I...." He runs his hand though his hair. "Loving someone is dangerous. It leaves you vulnerable. The deeper I get with you, the more I realize I can't control even myself. I was so determined to stay away. So determined to *beat fate*. How stupid is that?"

I want to ask him what he means by 'beat fate,' but I'm more caught up in his mention of love.

"Do you love me?"

He blinks rapidly. "I don't know. What does love even mean?"

I bite my lip. "I don't know."

"Will what I feel for you fade? Or will it grow even stronger? And if it goes away, when will that happen? In a week? A year?" He pauses, closing his eyes. "Never?" he whispers.

I bite the inside of my lip, watching his expression shift like the waves.

"But I'm not supposed to love you. I shouldn't. I..." He slams his hand into the water, I flinch from the splash. "What if loving you destroys me?"

I shake my head. So much more confused now than I was at the start of this conversation.

"Why would it?"

"Because that's what everyone wants. To use you against me. That's what they're all trying to do. Make this—you— be my downfall."

He turns his back to me, looking out into the open water.

"Why would they think that?" They wanted me first for my father. When did it become about my relationship with Bluff? And how did they see it before I did?

"There's a prophecy." His voice is so quiet as he says it.

"About me?" I ask, eyes wide.

He nods. "And me. It's vague, but given the events of the last few weeks it does seem point to whatever is between us being the catalyst."

My mind spins at his words. So confused. What does it mean? What is this prophecy exactly? I step forward and let my fingers drift over his bare back. He shivers but doesn't move as I run my hands over his shoulders and down. I hate his pain.

The rest of it feels pointless. I don't care about a prophecy or whatever anyone else assumes. I only care about this. About him.

"Bluff," I whisper.

He doesn't respond.

"Nalin," I try again.

He turns to me, brokenness shining through his grey eyes.

He steps forward and closes his eyes as his forehead touches mine.

"Can I ask you something?" he says quietly.

"Of course."

"Why do you want *me*?"

I try to meet his eyes, but they're still closed. I pause, wondering how to answer such a question. I shrug. "Because I do. Do you want attributes that I like about you? Do you want me to explain how you make me feel?"

He sighs. "I don't know. I just, I need a reason to trust you."

"Did I ever give you reason not to?"

"No, but..."

"But you're not used to trusting anyone," I say, that truth settling in my chest. He doesn't like to be vulnerable. I can only imagine the pain he's experienced in his past. "I'm not that complicated, Bluff. You showed me a kind of freedom I hadn't dared to hope for. I want that, not money or power or whatever else pirates fight for. I just want happiness. I just want *you*."

His hand grips behind my head tightly, but otherwise doesn't move.

"You said you don't want to lose control," I whisper. "But aren't you letting fear control you now? None of those people, those enemies, are here."

He steps closer so that our bodies are touching. His fingers tremble.

"It's just you and me," I whisper. "We might never make it off this island, so why should the rest of it even matter?"

His lips turn up into a small smile. "I have a better justification," he says. His voice is still quiet, but the slightest bit of amusement leaks into the sound.

I raise my eyebrows, waiting.

"It's too late," he says. "I'm already lost. I'm a fool to think I can resist someone as incredible as you." His face inches nearer, his lips so achingly close to mine.

My smile grows larger, just before his lips collide with mine.

Bluff

I don't pull away this time. I won't. I don't even care about everything else. Whitley is beautiful. Whitley is incredible, and I'm not giving that up for fear of some stupid prophecy.

I let this moment be my everything. Her body, her passion, her hopes. Her desperation for *me*.

This pull, I realize for the first time, is not like the pull of the sea. The sea wants me, so it can use me. So it can toss me in its waves, form me to its desires. Whitley, on the other hand needs me as much as I need her. She doesn't want to use me. She wants me to fill her the way she fills me. We're equals in this.

I *trust* her, and that realization hits me harder than desire ever could.

WHITLEY SITS CROSS-legged in the sand, skirt bunched and pushed off to the side, exposing bits of her legs, as she braids together strips of palm fronds into a sort of rope. I should be doing the same, but instead find myself sitting behind her, playing with her hair, kissing her neck, whispering into her ear.

She laughs lightly and tells me I should be working, but she leans her head to the left, giving me more space to kiss and touch her neck and shoulder.

"I agree. I should be working. You're doing such a good job though." The rope in her hands unravels.

She leans back so her head is resting on my shoulder and sighs. "Perhaps time for another swim?"

My cheeks hurt from smiling but I look up to the sky. The sun is getting discomfortingly close to the horizon. "No," I say too quickly. "It'll be dark before we know it and I really want to have this shelter built before then." There are dark clouds visible in the distance, still far off, and I'm hoping the storm doesn't reach us, but if it does, we'll need some kind of cover. "And you really shouldn't swim alone," I add under my breath. There are no signs of sirens about, and they are unlikely to come into shallow areas where their power is weakened, but without knowing their full intentions it's better to be safe.

"All right." Her words are light, but her eyes betray her disappointment.

"We can swim together later."

I force my body up and into action. The quicker I complete our shelter, the more time I can spend with her.

I've already cut down all the branches we'll need. We have a pile of fronds. It's really only a matter of tying the structure together and then covering it with leaves. I ask Whitley's help to hold the branches that will act as beams while I use the twine to tie it together. Then we do the next side. I'm careful to use the cordage I made on the places that will have the most stress.

"Have you thought much about how we'll get off this island?"

I look up to Whitley, who's wiping her hands on her dress. "Not really. I've been... distracted." My eyes leave her body to meet her eyes.

She smiles at the look I give her. The shelter is only half complete, but I approach her until we're only inches apart. I look her straight in the eye. "I don't know about you," I tell her as I reach up, running light fingers over her collarbone, up to her neck. "But I'm not actually eager to leave this place." I take another step until my lips are just grazing hers. She smiles again and my stomach summersaults. It's a feeling I've become used to since I first laid eyes on her. At first, I hated it. Now I can't get enough.

"Everything is so simple here. Just you and me. Nothing else to get in the way."

"I suppose here isn't so bad," she says, as she wraps her arms around my neck and pulls me into a deep kiss.

I push her up against a palm tree, my chest against hers, and relish the gasp she lets out and kiss her harder. A few moments later, I pull back laughing. "You are such a distraction."

"What?" she asks drowsily.

"We're supposed to be working on the shelter." Right on cue, lightning brightens the sky in the distance followed by a small rumble. I'm not used to witnessing many storms on the sea, as fair weather is a sign of welcome whenever I'm sailing. On land, I don't get the same treatment, and I suppose this tiny island is still *land*, technically. But considering it's surrounded entirely by ocean, no civilization in sight, it hardly feels it. The sea is mere feet from us. I would have thought that would mean most of the same protections I get on a ship.

Apparently not so much, because those black clouds are approaching rather quickly.

Either that, or this is some kind of warning.

"Quickly," I tell Whitley. "Pile the palms onto the top of the structure." The top is tilted down so that water will mostly run off. The bottom is lifted off the ground a few inches so that even if the ground puddles a bit, we'll stay dry. Now I'm just hoping it doesn't rise more than a few inches, because I didn't prepare for that.

While Whitley covers the canopy, I work on finishing the bottom. Then I aid her and make sure as many of the palms are tied down as possible so the wind won't blow too many away. We finish just as the first rain drops fall.

For a moment Whitley tilts her head up towards the sky, letting the water hit her face.

I watch silently. I find it amazing how every simple thing is magical to her. New. So much of her life has been suppressed. It makes me regret how I thought of her when we first met.

The splattering of rain raises to a crescendo, pounding on the leaves above.

We sit in our little shelter, just watching the sky darken into night, listening to the thunder as it rises louder and louder. A few drops of cold water flow through our makeshift ceiling here and there, but so far it's working out well enough. I don't know how comfortable of a night it will be, though. We have a long time until the sun rises.

I consider the beautiful woman next to me and realize I know exactly how to make the most of it. I grab Whitley's waist and pull her onto my lap. She gasps and then giggles as she falls into my kiss.

The storm rages around us, but so long as we survive the night, I would be an idiot to complain for even a second.

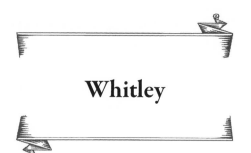

Whitley

The air was chilled the whole night. Water dripping through the canopy grew heavier and *colder* as the night went on. Bluff and I lay together, my head on his chest, arms twisted together, keeping each other warm. Or maybe that was just the excuse.

Either way, I was warmer touching him.

The sun rises early in the morning and I still find myself exhausted, not really wanting to get out of our makeshift bed.

"The sun is out now. We can warm up on the beach," Bluff tells me and pulls me up. We walk out towards the water and sit in the sand. The sun casts its light on our skin, warming us quickly.

"Well, we survived our first storm."

I nod and look down at my tattered dress, now more brown than white. "I wonder what my father would think of me."

"Do you care?"

I shake my head. "Not at all. He'd call me a barbarian. Dirty. Worthless. I don't even know what else."

"*His words* are worthless," Bluff spits out.

I nod. "He'd never realize, or care, how happy I am. He only ever cared how we looked to others. My happiness didn't hold any value."

Bluff grabs for my hand. "My mother never cared either. It's rare in my world to find someone who does, actually."

I pause, thinking of the things the crew implied about Bluff and his *lineage*. Was it true? Could it be?

"You've never talked about your family before."

Bluff goes totally still. Even his expression is icy cold. "I don't like to."

"Right. Sorry," I say, pulling my hand into my lap.

His sad eyes turn towards me. "I didn't mean that I wouldn't tell you."

"I know. I didn't... You don't have to tell me. I won't be mad. I'm not." I put my hand back into his.

"It's complicated."

"Are they human?"

Bluff doesn't react to this. "My father was. He didn't live past my conception. I often wonder what kind of person he was. My mother wouldn't have cared one way or another."

My heart aches. "She's a siren?" It only makes sense, after everything I know and what he just said. It explains his connection to the sirens, why the crew would fear him so much, and think he could be capable of calling them....

He nods, looking out at the sea. "She has no heart. Not like a human does. Dropped me off on some ship as an infant and let me figure it out from there."

"It's surprising you survived at all."

He shrugs. "She probably made sure it was with people who would take care of me. But she never wanted to raise me. She's only tried to use me for her own gains."

"I suppose I can relate to that."

He gives me a sad smile.

"I know we're not eager to get off the island." I give him a side-eye. I understand what he means— it is incredibly liberating to be here alone. No one to judge us or get between us. Nothing to stop us from just being *together*. But I'd also like some actual food. Perhaps a bed with sheets? Some kind of future would be nice. "But what will happen once we do? Where do we go? What do we do?" Another question hangs on the edge of my lips but I'm not sure I want to ask it. Is his future mine? Does he plan to stay with me? Build a life with me? Or does he want to board another pirate ship, and sail off without me?

"You're a dreamer, aren't you?"

My eyebrows pull down. "What does that mean?"

He smiles. "My whole life, I've only ever thought about weeks ahead. I don't have a life plan. I don't even really have goals. I just *live*."

I frown at this. "You don't have dreams? Things you want?"

He shrugs. "I want adventure. I want freedom. I want friendships. But those can come in so many different ways."

I purse my lips. Should I think more like that? Maybe my desire for structure, a specific plan, comes out of fear. This world isn't exactly set for a young girl to do whatever she pleases. I need some place to go, some purpose in order to survive—don't I?

"What do you want?" he asks me. "Some kind of life like the one you last lost? Or something else?"

I shrug. "No. I don't know."

"Do you... want to be a pirate?" he asks, a smirk playing at his lips.

I can't help but smile back. "Do you think I could be?"

"Why not? You're strong enough. Brave enough. That's all it takes, really."

I consider this. "What ship? We couldn't really go back to *The Freedom*, could we?"

"Perhaps we could make our own crew. Together."

My heart flutters at that thought. "Really?"

"Why not? If it's something you think you'd want."

I smile. I don't know if it's the permanent future I'd want, but I love the idea. The power. The fact that Bluff and I would do it, start something new, together.

"Sure."

"It's a plan, then."

We sit there, fingers intertwined for several more minutes. I picture this new dream: tossing my corsets and dresses in the middle of the ocean and sailing away on a ship with Bluff.

"I should head back farther on the island and see if I can get us some fresh water. We'll need more than coconut water soon. Wait here for me?"

He leaves me alone on the beach, off to the jungle to ensure our survival. My heart is full. Stranded on an island in the middle of the nowhere. No food or water. No one even knows where we are. I'm pretty sure this is a worst fear for some people. I've never been happier.

The sun is rising higher now, its rays stronger and hotter than before. Amazing how we can nearly freeze overnight but be boiled alive during the day. I look out at the cool water rushing up to the sandy beach, imagining it over my skin.

Bluff mentioned something about not swimming alone, but perhaps just a quick dip of my feet wouldn't hurt.

I enter the water slowly. Salty miniature waves rush over my toes, and I delight in how it chills my body instantly, even making me shiver. Then I stop, just watching the water ripple in the distance.

I remember once thinking the water in Carolina was incredible, but it was nothing compared to this. The color is somewhere between blue and green but still crystal clear. My mind drifts, peace washing over me until I hardly remember where I am. Who I am.

The crashing of the waves transforms into soft song. Beautiful. Alluring.

I blink back a haze over my mind and realize I'm waist deep in the water. When did I go this far? Just a moment ago I'd simply put my feet in. Why don't I remember stepping forward?

A large shadow shifts through the waves and I shake my head. My heartbeat accelerates, and I struggle to focus. What was that? Had I imagined it?

I look around from the surface but only see the sun glinting off the ripples in purples and pinks and oranges and other colors I can't even name.

A sweet melody floats through the waves, with the waves, pulling me forward. Panic fills my chest for only a moment before every muscle in my body relaxes.

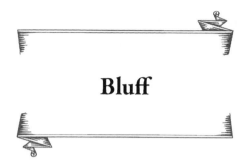

Bluff

Sweat pours from my face as I dig a hole beneath the trees, hoping if I go far enough, I'll find water. I don't actually know how deep that will be. While I also know if I dig too far, I'll likely come to salt-contaminated water. Not drinkable. I've never been stranded on an island like this before, so it's all theory to me. I'm just hoping it works.

The only other time I found myself on a small island, I was much closer to larger land, with an entire crew—our ship had run aground—and was able to get a message to another ship via a siren. I'm not exactly on friendly terms with sirens at the moment, nor do I trust them. I don't know what their role is in all of this, but they've implied they too find value in Whitley, so I don't even want them to know where I am. Which makes getting off this island much trickier. How do I get a message somewhere without also signaling the wrong people?

The dirt turns to mud as I dig, and I can feel victory just on the edge of the thin stone I'm using as a shovel. I just hope it's fresh, not salty.

Wind wisps through my hair gently—a familiar feeling that makes me pause. I listen. Leaves rustle around me. Waves crash in the distance.

Bluff, the wind whispers into my ear.

"What?" I ask harshly. Not in the mood for siren games today.

Tsk tsk. Salty, are we? It's halfway between a wisp and a solid voice now. *I thought you'd be happy to hear from me.*

I swallow and clench my jaw. "You thought wrong. How are you even here? We're in the middle of an island." My mother is very old—hundreds of years, I'd guess. Her siren magic is powerful, her human blood weak. It's impossible for her to take corporal form on land. Even just this is a risk. One I'm surprised she'd take.

"Just small enough for me to reach you." Her form is still mostly transparent, but I can see her hair flowing like it's under water, her coloring like a rainbow glistening in the sun. That's as solid as she can get, I'm sure, this far from the sea. She can't touch us here—that much is a comfort to me.

"Wonderful." I wonder about the storm then. If sirens can reach me this far into the island, why was a storm raging here as well? It means my theory of being close enough to the sea is correct. The other option isn't a good one.

I sit up straighter, my heart pounding harder. I long to run back to the beach to make sure Whitley is safe, but I don't want to expose my fear to my mother. Not yet. Maybe I can still get information from her.

"Are you here to help?" I ask her.

"What kind of help would you like, dear son?"

I roll my eyes. "Don't call me that."

"What? Son? Is it not true?"

"If you cared about me in the slightest, I wouldn't mind. Don't pretend you do."

"*I care for your survival. And it's not looking great at the moment, is it?*"

"You care for my survival so you can continue to gain from my existence. It's not exactly the same thing. And I'm doing just fine."

"*Perhaps. But to answer your question I am indeed sending help. But I am not here for you. I am here for something much more valuable.*"

My stomach sinks.

"*Something you must not cherish as deeply as I thought, leaving her all alone,*"

My hands are shaking. "You can't get to her here," I say more to comfort myself than for her.

"*Sweet naive boy.*"

I close my eyes, icy fear filling my veins.

"*All I need is for her to enter the water alone. Humans are so easy to tempt.*"

My head whips towards the beach as she laughs. *No. No, no, no.*

I don't wait another moment. I sprint towards the beach where I last saw Whitley.

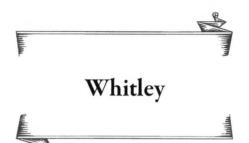

Whitley

The melody is so beautiful. I follow it— deeper. Deeper. Water fills everything. My sight. My soul.

My lungs.

Until there is nothing else. No island. No danger. No memories.

No Bluff. No Whitley.

Water and *the sound*. That's all there is, and all there ever was.

Bluff

The feeling that rushes through my veins when I catch sight of Whitley's limp form in the water is indescribable. Like being dropped into the icy cold ocean with my whole body paralyzed. I just—sink.

There's no one around to save me.

I pause for the longest moment of my life when my feet just barely touch the wet sand, watching her white skirt float through the water.

My heart doesn't beat. My lungs don't expand. My soul is crushed.

Then I push through the panic and run to her, feet splashing in the shallow water. I dive into a wave and swim.

"Whitley," I force out through barely usable vocal cords as I reach her. Her face is up, but her eyes are closed, and her face is so pale, her lips blue.

I grab her shoulders and shake, but there's no response. I call again. "Whitley!" This time so much more forceful. Desperate. *God, please. Wake up.*

There are no signs of sirens. What does that mean? I wonder.

As I pull Whitley's limp body into my arms, pressed against my broken heart, I mostly feel her cold skin, but I also feel something else. A spark. I press my face against her neck. My hand reaches for her wrist, scrambling awkwardly for any way I can feel for a pulse.

Her heart beats. Quickly. It's faint but fast.

That's good but *bad*.

My heart leaps and aches all at once. She's alive. But there's magic beneath her skin that wasn't there before. I've always feared why the sirens would want her. Not to kill her. Not to hand her over the Stede.

They wanted to *turn* her.

Which they'd only be able to do if she had some siren blood in her linage. It explains so much. So much I didn't want to admit to myself.

I don't know which would be worse: Whitley dead, or Whitley as a siren—cold and heartless.

"Please," I whisper in her hair, my voice weak and strangled. "Please wake up," I whisper, tears threatening to fall. My whole body shakes, struggling not to crumble under the weight, the pressure. The darkness.

I squeeze her hair into my hand and let out a scream of frustration. Desperation. The scream turns to a sob, but I can't let my emotions take over. I must keep my mind clear. Can't give up—not yet.

The whisper of a haunting laugh drifts past my ear and I want to scream. She left her here, in the water for me to find. To taunt me. To show me what I'd lost. I'm sure of it.

But maybe I can use her pride as my one last chance.

I dig through every ounce of myself. My mind, my soul. That strange place where my power comes from. Searching for something that may have meaning. The only thing I can feel, the only thing that stands out, are my feelings for her.

I slip through my memories: first seeing her in the prison. When she hid her chuckle at her father tripping out of the carriage—even then I knew she was special. So beautiful. Yet I fought it so hard. When I danced with her, indulging in the safe moment when I wasn't *me* and could touch her. When I helped her escape that house, our bodies so close it made me ache to let go. Still, I fought it. When I asked her if she was worth saving.

I pull back and look at her pale face. So beautiful, even now that death clings to her. I know life still lingers. I run my thumb over her blue lips. "You're worth saving, Whitley," I whisper as the waves rock us. "I was so foolish to fight it for so long."

I press her cold lips to mine, gently. Desperately. The spark pulls towards her. I don't know what it means, but it feels like magic.

I pull back, tears stinging my eyes, running down my cheeks. "I love you," I tell her. I don't even know what that means. Perhaps it's stupid to fall in love after only a few weeks. I don't care. This was an inevitability—not because of some prophecy. Because this girl is incredible.

Suddenly, Whitley's eyes open, and I feel several things at once. Jubilation. Panic. And fear.

Her eyes aren't the same blue they once were. They're... silver. Shifting with colors of green and blue and purple and red.

I blink and release her for just a moment. Her expression is unreadable. Inhuman.

Her body sinks in the water, and I rush to pull her back up, not sure if that even matters. But there's another hand on her now. Scaled and webbed, the siren's hand grasps at Whitley's forearm.

Then, several other forms rise from the water, surrounding me. My heart pounds.

"You can't have her," I tell them with a strained voice. Even I wouldn't believe me.

I keep my hold of Whitley, but so does the siren in front of me. She's smaller than most, with hair black as night, and skin covered in freckles. She hisses.

Then my mother rises, just feet from us. Her body is much more solid now that she's in the water, but there's still a shimmer telling me she's not at her full strength in the shallows.

But there's so many of them. I can't fight nine sirens at once. I can't win this.

"She belongs to us," Mother says so nonchalantly. "You've lost."

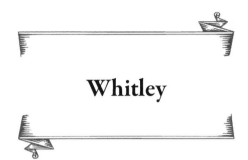

Whitley

I'm so cold.

Water covers my whole world. My soul is drowning. My mind spins, sputters, trying to pull myself to the surface. There's something I need. Someone that needs me. But I can't move. I can't think.

The song is still there, drifting in and out. Soft then harsh. Perfect harmonies and then offkey screeching. It's all I can hear. But then a soft voice whispers in my ear, muting everything else.

I love you.

The shock of those words jerks me forward, and the world around me blinks into focus. I see Bluff, his eyes red, his expression pained but angry.

I try to call to him, but my focus blacks out again. There's a pressure on my chest. Someone holding me down from the inside out, desperate to keep their control over me. The song turns fearful. The shrieks echo around me, the harmony losing form in their panic. *The sirens are scared of losing.*

My body won't react. I can't move. The words I so long to express don't leave my lips.

But at least now I can feel. Bluff is holding onto me. A cold and sharply scaled hand is gripping my arm. Her pull is stronger.

I drift lower. Deeper.

"You can't have her," he tells them, and my heart leaps. *Don't let me go,* I beg inside my head.

"She's belongs to us. You've lost."

Her grip tightens over my soul, crushing me. I writhe in pain but fight back. I must reach him. "Bluff!" I call, and for a moment my sight is opened again.

I can see him. He can see me. His face is so full of fear, and he reaches for me, but I'm pulled away, several bodies ripping us apart, moving between us.

I can still see, but blue ripples cover the bright sun, and this time when everything goes black, I know it's because I'm in the depths of the sea.

Bluff

The sirens screech as they leap at me, several of them all at once, their power and magic overwhelming me. I hold tight to Whitley, but her skin breaks under my nails as she's literally *ripped* from me. A few drops of blood dissipate into the blue water until they too are gone for good.

I keep fighting, even long after she's gone. There's no hope to get her back, but I scream and I kick and claw at everything I can. The sirens hiss as they claw at me, working to avoid my violent thrashes. One by one, they fall back into the deeper water and swim away. I begin to follow, ready to destroy anything in my path, but the deeper I get into the water, the more the darkness overwhelms my soul at the realization that I *lost*.

Whitley is gone. And I can't get her back.

I scream in frustration and slam my fist into the water. Then my mother appears before me, this time, entirely under water. She looks up from her safe place in the sea, only her distorted face visible.

She laughs, her chuckles rising in bubbles.

"I'll kill you if I get the chance," I tell her, my hands in fists.

She smiles. "You won't. Because now I have everything that I need to control you." She winks, and I punch the water where her face is, but by the time the ripples disappear, she's gone.

I lay on the beach, staring up at the blue sky. Soft white clouds float. Everything hurts. My skin stings where the siren's clawed at me. My muscles are heavy and sore. My head throbs. But most of all, my heart is lying in shattered pieces somewhere in my chest.

"This is your fault," I tell the water. The sea pulled her in, the way it's been trying to pull me in my whole life. She just didn't know the risk.

Why didn't I tell her? Why didn't I warn her that the sea isn't our friend? That being alone in the water is *dangerous*. If I had... well, at least she'd have been with me longer. Maybe I was always destined to lose. We were brought together, just to be pulled apart.

Fate won.

I lost.

You don't deserve her, the wind whispers into my ear. I sit up, surprised. I don't recognize the voice. It's not my mother—not this time.

"What?" I ask, wondering if I'm just going insane.

If you give up this easily, then you don't deserve her.

I suck in a breath. "Who are you?"

No answer. I swallow and consider the voice's message. But how do I not give up? I can't exactly go into the Depths. Their power would be so much greater than mine there. I couldn't beat one siren that far below the surface let alone a city of them. That's if I could even reach it. Perhaps if I'd been raised below, I'd have become like them and could fight them. But then I wouldn't have the emotions of a human, and I probably wouldn't want to save her.

My mother left me as a human because she didn't want me. Now, if I go below, I'll either drown—die the good old-fashioned way—or they'll drown me in their magic and make me one of them. Then they'd control my mind the way they now control Whitley's.

My mother doesn't want that, or she'd have done it years ago.

But then again, what does it matter if I don't survive?

I wouldn't win, but neither would they.

I stand and wipe the sand from my pants before stepping into the ocean. But just as the cool water hits me, something gives me pause.

In the distance— usually so empty, only blue as far as the eye can see— now there is the silhouette of sails. There's a ship coming.

I have a feeling I know which one.

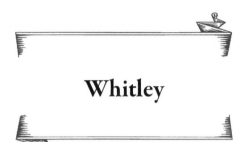

Whitley

A white light shifts, swirling in dark water, glowing brighter, then weaker. Shadows meet the swirling light, twisting together in a strange sort of dance. My body shifts along with their movement.

I blink and I'm balancing on two feet, but only barely. Every shift of the boards beneath me, every rock of the ship, almost pitches me over. I'm certain I'd fall if not for the set of hands clenched tightly over each arm. Hands... scaled and webbed, glistening in the sun.

My limbs are heavy. My vision is fuzzy—everything spins. *Where am I?*

All I can register about my surroundings is that I am on a ship. That, and I really want to lie down and sleep.

A strange feeling throbs through my veins. Like the rush of the ocean waves—the purr of moving water, pulsing through me. That sensation masks the voices around me, making it near impossible to comprehend. *Who is holding me? What is happening?*

Where am I?

Where is *he*?

I can't even think of who *he* is, just that he should be with me.

I can feel him though. A golden drop within the darkness.

"Whitley?" someone says, approaching. His voice is familiar but unwelcome. I wince away from the man's voice.

"Whitley," he whispers, closer now. Soft fingertips glide against my cheek. "Are you all right?" he asks. His concern is believable. I shouldn't believe him though. He never cared about me.

I force my gaze up. He steps back, terror clouding his expression as my eyes meet his.

"Father?" I don't remember why, but the anger simmers within me. *I hate him.*

"Yes!" he says through a gasp. "I... I'm so glad you're okay."

I huff out a bitter laugh, but it takes so much energy. My mind almost succumbs to the darkness. I blink it back, concentrating. Then I look him straight in the eye again and use the anger building to send my hand through the air. It hits his cheek with a resounding *smack*.

This action doesn't take my energy. It fuels me.

Several laughs resound, and a feeling bubbles in my chest. *Power.*

I like it.

"*Yeess,*" a slithering voice whispers in my ear. "*He is a man. He will pay for what he's done.*"

For one moment that feels right. That feels good. But...*Shouldn't you pay, too?* I want to say to the voice. I don't speak.

A conversation commences around me, the voices snapping together in my clouded mind.

"Where is the boy?" a rough and unfamiliar voice echoes. "You brought the girl, but without the boy she is useless."

A tall woman next to me chuckles. "He will come. Don't you worry about that."

"If he doesn't?"

"Then we have everything we need to *force* him here." She places a scaled hand onto my shoulder. I clench my jaw. *I do not like that.*

"Do you even know how this works? Can you make her call him?"

"Trust me. We will not need to. He will come on his own. But if it comes to that, we may choose to experiment. Fear is as much a motivator as pain. One of the two will work."

The bearded man smiles in a way that sends a shiver down my spine. "In that case," – he nods to a red headed pirate next to him— "perhaps we can speed the process up a bit."

The red pirate pulls out a knife that glints in the sunlight.

Bluff

My limbs are shaking, weak. The energy in my chest, though, is fueled by rage as my fingers grip the wet wood of the rocking ship and pull my body up, higher and higher. Thick salt water drips off every inch of me. I will destroy this entire ship if I can manage. I will end every life that dares to conspire against me. Against Whitley.

I revel in the anger and in the power. I do not want to feel. I want to crush everything in my path.

Luckily, there are only enemies in front of me, but if *The Freedom* dares show its face, they'll meet my vengeance as well.

If a single soul survives this, I'll consider it a failure. That includes my own.

I reach the railing of the main deck and find a place to settle. My foot rests on the bottom plank, my arms cling to the railing. I'm exposed enough it's possible I could be seen, but it's unlikely. It's a risk I'll have to take, because I must know what's happening on board before I approach.

"Your thirst for violence will be your destruction, pirate." The voice unmistakably belongs to my mother.

I twist to get a better vantage. Two sirens stand beside a girl with blonde hair and a white dress. Hair hangs over her face. Her head sags like she doesn't have the energy to hold it up. Anger bubbles even higher in my chest.

"Nothing wrong with a little blood lust," Stede's gravelly voice says low and steady. "Besides, it's true, no? Pain will force him here quicker."

A red headed pirate steps forward. A short narrow blade hangs casually in his right hand.

"On second thought..." Stede places a hand on the pirate's shoulder. "Perhaps they are right. There are other ways to punish him without scarring the girl."

Stede steps up, right in front of Whitley. "Everything that happens to you," he tells her in a sinister whisper, "is his fault. Remember that."

Pain like a knife twists in my stomach and I nearly lose my grip and fall back to the sea, but it's nothing compared to the poison that fills my veins when Whitley looks up to Stede with red angry eyes and *hisses.*

A scream explodes inside my head. I'm barely able to hold it in.

I can't stop my mind from spinning through all my worst memories with sirens. A siren laughed the day I broke my arm climbing through the nets of a ship and cried to my mother for help—I was nine. Or the day my mother tried to convince me to plunder an island town I'd lived in for over a year, and had plenty of friends in, just because one man had escaped her attack. Then she "punished" me for this disobedience by murdering a sailor who was like a father to me—looking me in the eye, and *smiling,* as she snapped his neck. Or the one and only time I allowed a young siren to allure me into trusting her. She rewarded that trust by sinking her fangs into my best friend's neck.

It's not only my mother—it's all of them. My mother was simply the one I wanted to care for me, even if in some small way. She never did. Not once.

Those inhuman, harsh, despicable eyes— those eyes are now *her* eyes.

Almost. The cry in my heart almost becomes audible. Whitley is gone. Everything I knew and loved about her has been taken. She's dead and there is no bringing her back.

My heart is in tatters.

I could never love a siren.

Perhaps that's not true. I can love her. The real truth is that *a siren could never love me.* A siren can't love anyone. I've learned that lesson too many times in my lifetime.

Everyone on board laughs at her hiss. They like it. They made her into a monster.

When the laughter dies down, Stede grabs her by the waist, hand pulling at her dress, but the air around the ship instantly turns icy cold as every siren screeches. This time there is no laughter.

Stede freezes, and I relish the fear he can't hide.

Mother rushes forward straight at Stede, back straight, head high, slinking in her unnatural way. Stede releases Whitley, but every muscle is clenched tight. The other sirens pull Whitley behind them—protecting her.

I swallow, unsure how to feel about this.

"No," Mother hisses at Stede.

"What?" Stede grumbles.

"You will not touch her in that way."

"You told me I could have my way. I could cause him as much pain as I can manage."

"You can have all the pain you like, but she is a siren now, and you will not touch her in any way you wouldn't a man."

Stede's shoulders relax. The silence stretches several long moments as he presumably considers this part of the deal. "This is the kind of detail you should make clear before making an agreement." His voice is low and annoyed, but his reverence for the sirens is obvious. At least he's not a complete idiot.

He retreats to his line of pirates, all gripping weapons like they would help them in the slightest. One note from any one siren's lips and they'd go limp as noodles. Stede stands next to the red pirate. "This is allowed, then?" He points to the blade in his hand.

Mother nods and the acidic hate is back.

"Wait!" a shaky voice calls. "That was not part of the deal! You said you wouldn't hurt her if I helped you find her!"

A pirate with dark hair and blue eyes kicks a man not far from me. "Hush, betrayer. You have no leverage here."

The man whimpers.

I inch closer to realize I know this man, though we've never met. It's Whitley's father. My fingers clench the wooden railing hard as I consider ripping his head off here and now. This is his fault.

Or is it?

If he hadn't schemed and betrayed all the wrong people, would the prophecy not have come true? Would it have been someone else fate chose?

It was always Whitley. That's what my heart tells me. He was simply the signal that marked her as the subject of the prophecy. Maybe if he hadn't been such an idiot and made it so obvious, maybe we could have had more of a chance.

I don't know. But his pathetic sobs make it hard for me to hate him. He has received his punishment. Others are so much guiltier and have yet to taste the bitter despair they deserve. I turn and focus on them.

Whitley offers no resistance as pirates shove her into a wooden chair and tie her down. She's like a limp doll. Her life gone.

I watch and realize I don't know how to stop it, what's coming. What power do I have to destroy an entire ship? I can't even kill a single siren this far out to sea.

What is the power they're so desperate for? The ability to change their form? To channel easy winds and kind waves? Sirens themselves have more power than that.

There's something more. I know it.

Perhaps if I could figure out this power they so desire before they're able to use Whitley to control me—but how?

A hand grips her hair and pulls her face up. There is anger in her eyes, but all her muscles are limp. The knife is pressed to her cheek, pushing into her soft skin. Harder. Farther until it gives, splitting, dripping blood down her cheek, and she squeals. The fear in the sound makes my head spin.

Every inch of my body trembles.

The pirate pulls the knife down slowly, ripping her skin apart. Whitley cries out. The sound isn't that of a siren. It's her. It's Whitley. I cannot remain still.

Though I feel so powerless—I don't know how to defeat them—I must try.

I fling my body over the railing, throwing every ounce of power I can find into my limbs. I flicker through several different forms: a massive muscled man, a tall and lanky solider boy, a small one-handed pirate, a siren, Stede, Whitley's father—

I can't even control the forms, they just keep coming, keep moving me without my permission. The sirens hiss and move away, but the pirates jump at me, at least a dozen of them with weapons spinning towards me.

I punch and hit at them indiscriminately. I even manage to grab a sword and plunge it into one man's belly. I don't see his face. I can't see much of anything, but his warm blood splatters onto my face.

"Don't kill him!" a rough voice calls out.

I swing again, but someone grabs my arm with surprising strength. Another set of arms wraps around me from behind. I try to force them off. Every bit of strength, of magic, of anger pulses from me.

But it's not enough.

Their bodies pile on top of me, the weight so heavy that I can't help but succumb. I fall, buried in a tomb built of Stede's pirate crew.

Why did I ever think I could win this stupid game?

Whitley

B *luff.* This whisper shifts through my whole being.

He's broken. I can see it in his eyes and it causes an acid to fill my veins. The sting on my cheek turns to a throb as the attention is pulled away from me and to the boy. Within moments, he's trampled by a mass of pirate bodies and pushed to the floor.

Bluff. I try to push the name from my lips, make it audible. I hardly have control of my own body. I want to go to him. I want him to know I'm here.

They pull him to his feet and his head hangs limp. I wonder if he is unconscious or if he's simply given up.

Bluff. The cry is desperate but silent.

The bearded pirate laughs heartily. "I'm almost disappointed you showed up so quickly, boy. I could have had so much more fun with your little lass."

Bluff doesn't move. The pirate leans in. "Then again, my fun doesn't have to end just because you showed up."

Bluff's muscles jerk like he wants to fight again, but he's restrained by several large pirates.

"I'll kill you." Bluff spits.

The pirate just smirks. "There are worse things than death. I suppose you know that, though. Don't you, lad?"

Bluff goes limp, his fight gone.

Please, I whisper inside. *Don't give up yet.*

"Well, now that this business is taken care of, let's see how this works, shall we?" Everybody on the ship stills as the bearded man approaches me with slow deliberate steps.

He squats next to me. "Hello there, Whitley." He says it like he's speaking to a spooked animal. I'd claw his eyes out if my hands weren't tied.

"You have something I desire," he says coolly.

"Go," I force out with strained voice. "To." I wince at the pain the words cause. "Hell." My chest fills with more power. It's worth the pain, the look on his face as he jerks back from me.

"Do you know what I want?" he asks, his expression calm once again. "Because I think you'd rather like it."

A growl rumbles in my chest.

He takes in a deep breath and smiles. "You have power," he whispers. "And I just want you to use it."

Power? That sounds delicious.

A form slithers up to my side, her face close to my ear as she whispers, "*Tell him to rise.*" Her voice is one-part hiss, one-part melody. My vison blinks in and out of focus, and then my fingers begin to tingle. I can feel it. The power.

It's right here. Waiting for me to use it.

"Rise," I force the word from my lips through my raw throat. Again, pain ripples through my whole body, but this time so does the magic. It escapes my body and strikes the boy. The magic forces his head to rise first, exposing eyes wide with fear. Panic. Pain.

The rest of his body follows suit and stands up straight.

You're worth saving, the memory of his voice drifts through my mind.

As I blink, images come rushing back. A boy in a prison cell. His hands guiding me to the ground after leaping from a window. Bluff standing beside me as we set sail on a pirate ship.

I can make him do anything I want. The power tingles over my skin, seeping into my bones. Filling me.

It's *intoxicating.*

Bluff cries out as he pushes against the magic, fighting against me. He's not strong enough. I'm winning. *He can't stop me.* I want more of this. It feels so good.

But the pain in his eyes— the panic. A despair so great I can't breathe.

I pull back from the magic, but the grip is tight—it doesn't release. And suddenly I'm not sure even I can stop me.

This...isn't what I want.

My heart pounds faster. *Stop*, I whisper inside my mind. *Stop.* The call grows louder, but not loud enough. Panic grips my heart. *No.*

I search his face, so full of desperation that it's all I can feel. My hands shake.

More images: beautiful grey eyes staring at me in the crow's nest. Confusion and desire. Then the kiss, the way his whole being filled me, even wearing another's skin. Another kiss in an alleyway. Another below deck of *The Freedom.* Another on the beach.

"Bluff." Finally. Finally, my call is audible. I know he can hear it, because his expression changes. It's still pained, still fearful, but shock and confusion, even hope, blur into one emotion.

I don't want to hurt him. I don't want to control him.

Stede doesn't seem to notice the change, because he lets out a hearty laugh. So joyful, like this fulfills every desire he's ever had.

"This is how I will destroy you," he tells Bluff.

Anger fills me. A rage so deep it almost scares me. But maybe I need it. Maybe this is what this whole thing is for.

"*Tell him to fall.*" Bluff's mother's whisper is full of vindictive joy. She wants him to hurt. My body trembles as I fight against the order. Because that's what this is—a master commanding her servant. The magic in her voice compels me, it fills my mind until I can't breathe.

I clench my jaw as a tear forms in the corner of Bluff's eye.

A whisper rushes through me. *No.*

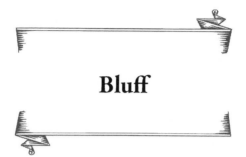

Bluff

A dark future lays before me. I can see it—feel it as it expands.

The pain of shackles bound to me by the woman I love. I'll be living by them for the rest of time. I will cause pain by no desire of my own. I will give power and control to a monster of a mother that never loved me. She will win by using her spawn as if he never had a life or desires or hopes or dreams of his own.

I am a weapon with no control. And it *hurts* in every way possible.

I search the eyes of the girl I fell for despite every logical thought and see nothing beyond the monster on the surface. Red and silver magic swirls in her eyes. No emotion, no consciousness—she's a ghost. She's as much of an empty shell as I'll be when she enslaves me.

For a moment I thought Whitley was still there, but I'd be foolish to believe that. Every bit of evidence tells me it's over. She's gone.

I don't know why she said my name, but it wasn't for the reason I'd immediately hoped.

"Make him fall," my mother says again. Her control seeps through my bones, and yet—nothing happens.

Stede steps forward, his shoulders back in an aggressive stance. "Do it," he tells Whitley. Her eyes don't leave mine. They don't soften. They just... are.

Stede rips a sword from his belt and points it towards her.

"Fool! Put that away," My mother calls.

"She is mine. I was promised the chance to use his power! To control it. Now this bitch won't do it."

"Patience." My mother moves forward. "She's weak and needs time to settle into her new power."

Stede turns to Whitley with rage, pushing the edge of the cutlass against the soft skin at the base of her neck. "You better do as you're told, or I will make your life a living hell."

Whitley's gaze turns to him, eyes narrowed, head titled slightly. "Will you?"

Stede blinks like a child, confused. Then he pushes his shoulders back again and stomps over to me. I wince as he reaches me, just in time to miss his elbow slamming into my cheek with a sickening crack.

A gasp leaves Whitley's body. I open my eyes to watch and for the first time a human emotion crosses her expression. Anger.

Then I feel the magic again, except this time it's coming from me, not her. The buzz begins in my chest, growing and seeping out through my fingertips with a rush like the blowing wind.

It surrounds me. Fills me. This is the power I needed. This is what I could have used to destroy them. I move to take it, use it—but it slips through my grasp.

Instead, it moves to her. Whitley's eyes still hold a violent rage, and it's her that the power bends to. My power is only usable through her.

The rush blows over my body, pushing me up. The hands gripping me release me immediately. The pirate's eyes grow huge as I rise higher, my toes leaving the ship floor. My breathing turns heavy, my heart racing.

"What is happening?" Stede calls.

Mother lets out a sinister chuckle. "She's using her power."

A crackle of thunder resounds through the sky as I float helplessly, unsure of anything at all anymore. The power builds and changes, shifting like the growing storm clouds darkening the sky.

Then the rain unleashes, pouring down on our heads.

I still don't know what's happening, but I do know that this feels different. The pain is gone. The control is here but lesser. I have command over my limbs, just not the power blowing from within my bones.

I try to push my body back down to the ground. For a moment the magic resists, but then allows it and I slowly drift down until my boots hit the deck with a small click.

The pirates around us search for cover from the coming storm as the gusts of wind swirl around us—Whitley and me. The sirens stand still, watching in awe.

Whitley steps towards me, her eyes softer than before but still... inhuman.

I wince as she approaches, closing my eyes, because the hope is too strong. I don't want to see what's really there. I don't want to see the absence of *her*.

"Bluff." I shiver at her voice. I expect her to sound like my mother, but she doesn't. She sounds like Whitley.

And honestly, that's worse.

"Don't," I beg her. She stops moving.

"What do you want?" Her hoarse voice breaks.

"To pay them back for what they took from me. To destroy them."

"Then do it."

I look up quickly, surprised at her response. I blink at the pain in her eyes. Sirens don't feel emotional pain. They don't care enough for it.

Then a power rushes me. Fills me. And for the first time, I have full control.

Whitley

The look in Bluff's eyes is harsh. Angry. It causes a lump in my stomach. But I don't stop him as he uses the power I gave him to send gusts of wind through the ship so hard they knock three pirates over.

They scramble to their feet, then run for cover. Only a few are even above board now. Most were smart enough to hide as soon as the first rain fell.

The sirens shrink from the weather, awkward chuckles simmer through their ranks. They know this comes from me. They believe they have control over me and therefore over Bluff, so they could make this stop at any moment. But they still feel the sting of discomfort. That's the instinct they should be listening to.

Bluff plays with the new power at his fingertips. Lightning strikes into open water at the wave of his hand, at least five hundred feet from the ship. He stops to look at it, curiosity written in his eyes.

Then a laugh rumbles over the distant thunder, and we all turn our heads towards a bearded pirate. The one who tried to force me to use my power. The pirate who tried to hurt me. I tilt my head as I consider him.

"This is POWER!" he hollers through the rain. His laugh is hysterical.

He stomps up to me and my lip curls in disgust as he gently lifts a soaked bundle of blonde hair. "Send a strike of lightening into that man," Stede says, pointing, his expression shining with joy. Sick amusement.

I follow his gaze to the man still cowering against the ship railing. My father. I blink and stand straighter. In many ways I do hate him. And yet, I love him. A strange human emotion. Emotion I could shed if only I'd embrace my new life as a siren.

I look down at my hand, shimmering as I twist it, iridescent webs between each finger.

"No," I tell him, calmly.

His hands clench into fists, muscles tensed to strike.

"Don't touch her," a voice calls. My breath catches as we both turn to face Bluff. His hands are in fists as well, power still flowing off of him.

If I lose my humanity, if I allow it to slip through my webbed fingers, I'd also lose him.

"I will touch her in any way I please." Stede shouts over the pouring rain.

"Have you met your lovely lass since we won? She's prettier this way, I think." Stede wraps an arm around my waist and my whole body goes rigid. I could kill him. Rip his head from his body right now.

Movement catches my attention around Bluff's closed fists. Little droplets of water spin around, gaining speed.

Thunder crashes. Lightning strikes—a warning.

Stede's eyes grow wide.

Bluff's angry eyes turn towards him. "I told you I'd kill you, and now you've given me the means."

Stede takes a step back, unsure. Does Bluff hold this power or do the sirens? Lightning strikes again with just a blink of Bluff's eyes, this time close enough to the ship to send a splash into the air. Several drops land onto the damp boards right in front of Stede's leather boots.

"Tell him to stop," he says with a shaking voice. Bluff steps closer. "Make him STOP!" he yells at me.

"No."

Stede grabs me by the arm, his panic obvious now. "I said make him stop. Now!"

"I am not controlling him."

Lightning strikes the highest mast, sending a violent shake through the whole ship. Stede tumbles to the ground. The sirens hiss and squeal, finally giving in to their instinctual fear and leaping into the safety of the ocean, one by one.

"You wanted to use her to get to me," Bluff says. "Well, you succeeded. I suspect simply not in the way you'd planned."

Stede groans, pushing himself up off the ground. "No. That's not how this works."

Bluff smiles. "Let me show you how this works. As I destroy each and every one of you as repayment for what you stole from me."

Bluff

This time, I put all of my concentration on the evil man in front of me, and when the lightning strikes, it hits the ship right at his feet. The explosion of splintered wood and streaks of water knock everyone remaining on deck to the ground, including myself.

This time, it's me that laughs as I rise to see Stede knocked unconscious and bleeding from a gash along his arm.

The wind picks up speed, rocking the nearly broken ship violently. This thing will be at the bottom of the sea within an hour, and that's even if I don't splinter it further. Hail falls from the sky, pelting me along with everyone else.

I don't care. I don't mind the pain. The bruises that will surely follow are nothing compared to the invisible scarring I'll hold for the rest of my life.

I never wanted this kind of power, never cared to have it. But I'm sure as hell going to use it now that I do. A gust of wind pushes the ship so hard it teeters on its side, inches from capsizing.

Another strike of lightning hits the deck and the flash of blond hair makes my blood go cold. Whitley's body lands hard onto the steps to the helm. I wince as her body crashes, falling limp.

Though I shouldn't, I can't help but run to her. I lean over her broken body and pause, my hand hovering over the inhuman skin of her upper arm, unsure if I want to touch her, knowing that I can't help it. She might be a siren. She might not be the Whitley I so hesitantly fell in love with. But she's still her, in some way.

I run my hand over her cold skin and shiver. "Whitley?"

"Bluff?"

I stop breathing at the sound of my name on her lips, her voice soft and confused. "That's not my name," I tell her, irrationally hoping she'll remember my true name.

She pulls her head up to look me in the eye. My head spins at the contact of her soft gaze. I want so badly to believe she could recognize me. That she still loves me.

But in the next instant, a sharply clawed hand is at my neck, pushing me back. I stumble up, pushed by the siren until my back crashes into a mast with a crack, head hitting hard enough to cause my vision to blink in and out of focus.

"Don't touch her," My mother hisses.

I blink, desperately grasping at this reality. "Why?"

Stede isn't my real enemy, I'm reminded. He only did what I'd expect him to do. He's just a power-thirsty man who will do whatever he can, destroy anyone he must, to gain power. He deserves every bit of pain he gets.

The siren whose hand is squeezing my windpipe closed deserves so much more. My mother—someone who should care for me, at least a little—set me up. And took from me one of the only people I've loved.

She didn't control me when I know she could have. I don't know what this means, but I am in no way ignorant enough to think it's not temporary. Whitley is a siren, and this hesitance will not last. She will destroy my soul. And she'll enjoy doing it.

Whitley lifts her head, her inhuman eyes meeting my desperate gaze. No emotion. My hope crashes around me feet. "Help," I beg, one last desperate plea. Stupid but necessary. If she'd only respond, give me something. Maybe I could hope. Maybe I could believe.

"She belongs to us," Mother hisses when Whitley doesn't move. "We *will* use her, and by extension—you. Even if it means drowning her in magic over and over and over." Her hand squeezes harder over my windpipe, and I struggle, unable to breath. She's too strong for me. If she wants to kill me, she will.

But she won't, I realize. She needs me alive.

"Kill me," I say, testing her.

She smirks. "Never."

I clench my jaw, knowing what my next move is.

There's so much I still don't understand about all of this. How does this power work, and why? But what I suspected from the beginning is clear.

She needs me to achieve her treacherous plans.

I told my mother I'd kill her. But really all I want is revenge—to take away her victory before it's won. "I won't let you win," I gasp out, as she loosens her grip.

She leans in, so close I can feel her unnaturally cold breath on my cheek. "I already did."

My lips curl up into a smile as I throw my knee up. Before she can even blink, the blade is in my hand.

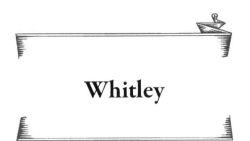

Whitley

My head throbs as I force my body upright.

My breathing is rapid, my stomach uneasy. Across the splintered deck, filling quickly with water, a is siren choking Bluff.

"No," I gasp, surprised when the word is audible.

"I won't let you win," he tells her.

"I already did," she whispers at him.

Bluff moves so quickly I don't realize what's happening until the glint of a blade appears in his hand, soaring towards the Siren Queen—then away. He grips it in a tight fist, his face in an angry wince, as he shoves the blade into his own chest.

"STOP!"

Everything in me freezes. Every muscle. Every drop of blood. The rain even pauses midair. The sound of my own voice reverberates around me. It's only then I realize I'd actually voiced the command.

Because along with my own body, and the rain around me, Bluff's body stills as well. The handle of his dagger, a glint of blade is all that's visible. He doesn't move, but his blood does, slipping past the handle of his dagger, falling over his stomach. His fist still grips it, tightly. His eyes are wide as he meets my panicked gaze.

The Siren Queen takes a stumbling step back and I sprint over, pushing her out of the way and wrapping my arms around Bluff, holding him up.

"I..." the Siren Queen stammers.

"Leave," I growl at her. "Before I kill you."

She blinks, her expression so pathetically confused. "He...he..."

"Now!" I scream, sending reverberations through the sinking ship. "Or he will die and you will lose."

She stumbles backwards one last time before turning and diving into the rocky waters beyond the ship's railing. I turn my attention to Bluff's limp body in my arms.

My hands shake, as I lower him onto the ground. "Bluff," I say, so desperately. "*Please.*"

I press my forehead to his.

"Whitley?" he asks, confused.

"Don't leave me," is all I can get out. I look out at the sea, getting closer and closer as the ship sinks deeper into the waves. The storm clouds have cleared, but the water is still restless. Pushing and pulling, hungry not only for this vessel, but for me too. The only hope of getting Bluff the medical aide he'll need will be at the bottom of the sea in minutes.

So will I.

Fear paralyzes my limbs. I look at my blood-covered hand; the webbing is somehow gone, but it still shines and glistens in the sunlight. Will I forget who I am again once the sea claims us?

"I don't want to be one of them," I whisper.

He reaches up with a shaking hand and grips the side of my face. "Then don't."

My heart pounds. "Without you... I don't know if I can help it."

He presses his eyes shut. "I thought you were gone. I thought..."

Water rushes onto the deck, quickly reaching our feet, and I let out a desperate gasp. I don't want the water to touch me. I don't want it to pull me under again. "I'm scared."

"Me too." He winces in pain. I look down at the blade. There's blood everywhere, and I don't know what it means. Did I act too slowly? Was I too late?

"You stopped it before it reached my heart... but only barely." He gasps and winces as he moves slightly. The blood keeps coming, seeping into my lap.

His face his so pale already.

He swallows and looks around as the water rushes up over our legs. "We can take the longboat. It'll keep you out of the water, and maybe we can row..."

I shake my head, knowing it may save me... for now. But we are too far from civilization to get him medical aid by rowing a tiny wooden boat. I don't know if he has minutes, or hours left but he certainly doesn't have the days or weeks it would take to row to an inhabited island.

But I suppose it's the best we have for now. I let go of my grip on Bluff, grab an abandoned sword just below the surface of the rising water and sever the ties attaching the little wooden boat to the sinking ship. It drops only a few inches. Then I rush back to Bluff. He stands on wobbly legs, and I help him in, then push us out into open water.

We watch as *The Revenge* slips the rest of way below the surface, only the highest masts still visible. I look down at the blood pooling at the bottom of the boat.

It might take hours, but Bluff will bleed out, here in the middle of the ocean.

Bluff

The pain reverberates from my chest, into my back and down to my legs. Every breath is heavy and labored.

I don't know how she's still here, how she could be a siren but still love me. Still remember. But she is, and I don't care if I only have an hour or two with her before my own blade sucks the life out of me, I'll fight for every minute I have.

The little boat rocks in the dark water as I lay between Whitley's legs, her chest against my back and arms wrapped around me. I lay my head back and try not to hate myself. That won't help anything.

"I'm so sorry." I say again, because I don't know what else to say. I don't know what would have happened if I hadn't stabbed myself in the heart. Maybe that was what pulled Whitley's soul back into her body. Perhaps she would have stopped my mother and come to me regardless. I don't know.

Maybe I saved her.

Maybe I ruined everything.

Either way, what's done is done. My blood keeps seeping out of me, slowly now, but that doesn't matter because there is no one around to help.

Whitley

I don't know how long we spend on that tiny boat, floating in the rocky water. I want to fill myself with him. With us. With what we were and what we could have been.

So I talk to him, about nothing, about everything. Even after his eyes flutter shut. His face is relaxed and I don't know if that's good or bad.

I tell him everything good that comes to my mind. I describe the water and the sky, the way he made me feel on that beach.

I tell him that I love him. Because it's true, even if we're both unsure what that means.

"I'll keep fighting for you," I whisper, my whole body shaking as I fight the magic in my limbs, calling me to the waves. *You won't win this one, not right now*, I tell them.

"The sky is so blue," I whisper to Bluff. "White clouds scattered across the horizon."

My heart leaps as I realize one of those white spots is not a cloud.

"Wait," I say, sitting up straighter. "Those are sails."

My heart picks up speed. I don't know what ship it is. I don't know if they're even coming this way, but the small drop of hope is enough to fuel me.

Bluff is still with me, and those sails in the distance are growing larger.

His eyelids shutter closed, then open. "Bluff," I say desperately. "Please." I grip him harder.

"I'm here," he whispers.

The ship grows larger and larger, and it becomes clear they're coming towards us. Looking for the sunken ship, or for us, is unclear. It doesn't matter.

I stand, waving my arms wildly. This ship, whether ally or enemy, is our only chance at getting Bluff the help he needs.

The flag is black, and as it nears, I recognize the skeleton with a knife symbol. It's *The Freedom*. Are they still planning to sell us? Can we trust them?

Then again, where is Stede? At the bottom of the ocean with his ship? Or did the Siren Queen save him? The wreckage of *The Revenge* is scattered in the waves; we've drifted far from it already. There could be survivors in the water that I hadn't seen.

I sit there, my limbs shaking, holding onto Bluff's cold body as the ship takes an eternity to reach us. Shouts are audible as the crew sets to work. A longboat is lowered and a small crew rows out to us.

"He's injured," I tell them and immediately concern covers their faces. Some of them I recognize but their names I can't recall.

Two pirates hop onto our small boat and begin rowing back to their ship. One large pirate carefully and carries him up the rope ladder and onto the ship.

I blink back my shock, unsure what's happening. They don't talk to me. They don't look me in the eye.

I climb the ladder myself, reaching the main deck, gripping my shivering upper arms.

"What happened?" the captain says in a low tone.

His face is blank but his eyes are full of concern. How do I answer that? I suspect they can't know the full truth. What will they do to me if they know I'm...not exactly human now?

"Where is Stede?" he asks, hinting that he knows exactly what happened. "We saw his sails, now this wreckage."

"There was a storm. And a fight. His ship is now at the bottom of the ocean."

Captain Taj nods. This is all he needs to know, apparently.

"Will he survive?" I whisper with a shaky voice.

He sniffs and looks out at the horizon. "Luster is well versed in battle injuries and we have supplies to help him. But I can't say for sure."

"Thank you," I gasp out, holding back a sob, my hands shaking in earnest now.

"You should spend the night in the crow's nest," he says without looking me in the eye. The crew bustles around us, side-eyeing me as they do.

My feet wobble beneath me and my hands shake, but I work to keep upright. The water splashing on the other side of the ship's hull sends a haunting chill through my body. It wants me.

My mind spins. There is a haze over everything. A few images flash through my mind of pirates pushing me back. Threatening. The memories slip away as I try to grasp them. Only pieces, fragments.

All I know for certain is that I can't trust these men.

A tingle in my fingers reminds me of the power beneath the surface.

Kill them, it whispers through me.

The crow's nest is a good idea, I realize. But perhaps not for the reason the captain thinks.

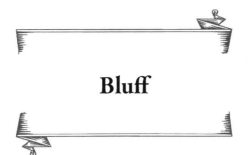

Bluff

I groan and shift uncomfortably in the cotton sheets of the captain's bed. How did I get here?

Someone is standing over me. For a moment I assume it's Luster, the only pirate on this ship able to act as a doctor, but then I notice the tattered dress and tangled blonde hair.

She's still, every muscle tense. I meet her eyes and wince when the silver hue becomes clear. I stop breathing and freeze.

"Ow," I say as I shift, a stabbing pain shooting through my whole body. I press my hand against my chest where red seeps through my bandage.

Forgot about that.

"Hi," she whispers, looking down at my bare dirt-covered feet. Her voice is scratchy and there's a glistening to her skin. Is it obvious enough the crew will notice the change? The magic beneath her skin?

I close my eyes and run through the events before my...injury, and after. Whitley is a siren—that much I remember. But here she is, standing before me, on *The Freedom*.

"Whitley?" I ask.

She pauses. "Yes?" she whispers, finally.

I suck in a breath and rub my face with my open palm. "How?"

She shakes her head. "How did any of this happen?" she says with a weak voice. Now I notice the tremor in her knees. "How are you alive? How did we cause that storm? How do you shift into other forms? How am I a..." She looks down at her hands. A small glistening of web shimmers between her fingers.

I press my eyes closed. "Siren," I spit more harshly than I'd intended. She winces.

"Bluff?"

I look up, noticing the bags beneath her eyes, her sallow cheeks, her trembling fingers. "Are you all right?" I ask. She's fighting the magic, I realize. It's draining her and I don't know how long she can win this battle.

Her knees buckle suddenly, and she nearly falls to the floor. I jerk, needing to reach for her, catch her. Help her. But burning pain shoots through my whole body, and I groan.

She catches herself, but every breath is shaky.

She pants as I wince back the black spots in my vision.

"Don't move," she says. "You'll hurt yourself."

"Come here," I say, acid filling my stomach. Every feeling conflicts with another.

She steps toward me slowly and then crawls under the covers with me, her head resting on my chest, just above my wound.

The bite of her cold skin is a shock at first, but we quickly ease into each other, and I attempt to relax.

"They're going to come after me. After both of us," she tells me.

I nod, my eyes still closed. "All they did was get a taste of the power. They're going to want it more than ever."

"What do we do?"

"There's only one way I know to win. And you stopped me from that harebrained plan." I smile.

"That's not winning. We only win if we're together."

I close my eyes and breath her in. I don't know if we can win this, but we haven't lost yet. So I might as well cherish every small moment of happiness fate will allow.

Find more at

http://www.StaceyTrombley.com

Bluff,

I've received a message from my father and he's informed me of his deeds. I must say, I'm very sorry. Especially because it wasn't even necessary! You didn't really think I'd let Stede get his hands on me, did you?

My new Englishman friend was an aide in my escape, actually. It was quite the adventure and I'll be eager to tell the story next we meet —which I hope to be very soon.

Love, your friend,

Rosemera

P.s. If I get aboard that ship and that girl is barefoot again, you'll have a lashing in your future.

Author Note

Thank you so much for reading my book! It means so much to me that someone would spend time with my characters and (hopefully!) enjoy the experience.

As a new author, reviews can really make a difference in my success so I would love you forever if you'd post a review!

If you'd like to learn more about my books and get updates on my new releases please join my newsletter because I have several things in the works— like Rosemera's story!

Find out more at

http://www.StaceyTrombley.com

And lastly, be my friend!

I'm in Instagram and Twitter @Trombolii

www.Facebook.com/StaceyTrombleyAuthor

The sirens are coming

—both from the sea and from inside Whitley's own mind. Her memories are fading. Her siren instincts are rising. And when she strikes, killing a pirate aboard *The Freedom,* she flees Bluff's harsh reaction—into the sea.
Bluff tracks Whitley all the way back to New York City, in a race to reach her before the sirens. He must convince her to trust him again before she kills half of Manhattan. Which will be challenging, considering she doesn't even remember who he is.

Bound by the Depths, book 2 in the Pirate's Bluff series
Available August 16th

The fight for her heart will decide the battle.

The same power Captain Stede and the Siren Queen so desperately desire is the secret to Whitley and Bluff's survival. But first, they must uncover how to use it without destroying them both. One slip, and Whitley will be back under the control of the Siren Queen for good. So first, they'll track down the Witch that made the prophecy to start with and hope another betrayal isn't right around the corner. The battle is coming, in fact it's already begun—they just don't know it yet.

Treacherous Love, the third book in the Pirate's Bluff series
Available September 6th

Acknowledgements

First, thank you to my husband, Sean. Indie publishing is so much more of a commitment than what we've been used to (because I had to do nearly EVERYTHING myself). Thank you for supporting this dream of mine.

Thank you to my beta readers Kelley York, Stephen Morgan and Michelle Kollar for your suggestions, tough love and encouragement. And Chantal Ostroske for helping to polish the final version. Thank you to Kat Kenyon, for facilitating the Westside Writer's group and Scribblers and Scribes to help keep me motivated and on track!

Thank you, again, to Kelley York for WONDERFUL covers that I adore.

Thank you to my editor Josiah Davis for your calm logic and patience. You helped to smooth out my writing without affecting the voice which is worth more than gold!

Thank you to every person who read Sea of Treason on Wattpad. Especially those who read the book in one night, voting for each chapter as you went. It was a wonderful feeling to know that—right then—my words were keeping someone else up late. When I wrote Sea of Treason I was in a huge writing rut and Wattpad really helped to pull me out of it.

Thank you to all of the amazing indie author Facebook pages and podcasts that helped me learn SO MUCH so quickly.

I'm certain there are more I'm missing and many more to come in future acknowledgements. Til' then!

About the Author

Stacey Trombley is a casino pit boss by night, YA author by day. She lives in Ohio with her husband, son, and GSD Riley. When she's not writing or reading her husband is probably dragging her along on one of his crazy adventures for this travel vlog or competing against him about who can pick the most Survivor winners in the first episode (hint: she's winning). But mostly, she's probably reading.

<u>Www.StaceyTrombley.com</u>[1]

---

1. https://www.staceytrombley.com/

Made in the USA
Middletown, DE
21 July 2019